The RISE and FALL of a 10th-GRADE SOCIAL CLIMBER

Other Graphia Titles

48 Shades of Brown
by Nick Earls

After Summer
by Nick Earls

The Education of Robert Nifkin
by Daniel Pinkwater

The Fattening Hut
by Pat Lowery Collins

I Can't Tell You
by Hillary Frank

Not as Crazy as I Seem
By George Harrar

Owl in Love
by Patrice Kindl

The Road to Damietta
by Scott O'Dell

Zazoo
by Richard Mosher

Check out graphiabooks.com

The RISE and FALL of a 10th-GRADE SOCIAL CLIMBER

Lauren Mechling and
Laura Moser

Houghton Mifflin Company
Boston 2005

All rights reserved. For information about permission
to reproduce selections from this book,
write to Permissions, Houghton Mifflin Company,
215 Park Avenue South, New York, New York 10003.

www.houghtonmifflinbooks.com

The text of this book is set in Apollo.

Library of Congress Cataloging-in-Publication Data

Lauren Mechling and Laura Moser
The rise and fall of a tenth-grade social climber / by Lauren Mechling and Laura Moser
p. cm.
Summary: When her best friend dares her to become part of the popular crowd
and record her experiences in a diary, fifteen-year-old Mimi's world turns upside down
when the diary gets into the wrong hands.

ISBN 0-618-55519-6

[1. High schools—Fiction. 2. Schools—Fiction. 3. Diaries—Fiction.
4. Popularity—Fiction. 5. Best friends—Fiction. 6. Friendship—Fiction.] I. Title.
PZ7.S4529Co 2005
[Fic]—dc22

2004015767

ISBN-13: 978-0618-55519-2

Manufactured in the United States of America
WOZ 10 9 8 7 6 5 4 3 2 1
RRD 10 9 8 7 6 5 4 3 2 1
BVG 10 9 8 7 6 5 4 3 2 1

To Curt and Bert,

our superdads

The RISE
and FALL
of a 10th-
GRADE
SOCIAL
CLIMBER

Dear Diary,

Once upon a time, circa four months ago, I was your regular run-of-the-mill fifteen-year-old smarty-pants. My MO was simple enough: Keep to the back row. Stick to the basic nice-enough, cute-enough, and good-enough-at-school routine, and leave it at that. It sounds pretty straightforward, I know, but in high school, blending in takes as much effort as standing out—more, really, when you're roughly the height of a palm tree.

In Houston I had managed to fit in with the best of them. If you took all the ninth-grade girls at my old prep school and arranged them in a line from the prepubescent white cotton undershirts to the outrageously overpriced all-lace demi-cups, I would have fallen safely in the middle, one of those basic nylon underwire jobs sold in discounted three-packs. I was 100 percent, no-holds-barred normal.

But if achieving that normalcy took fifteen years of hard work, going the reverse direction was far simpler. To become the world's biggest pariah, I needed only a few months, a notebook, and a few evil thoughts.

But wait—I'm getting ahead of myself, as I always do when I open this stupid notebook. Better, I think, to begin at the beginning, with that smoggy afternoon in August when the postcard arrived . . .

Family Trees Need Watering, Too

I WAS HUNCHED OVER THE DINING ROOM TABLE, struggling with the final project for this creative writing course I was taking at the University of Houston. (And no, btw, I'm not some sort of freakazoid fifteen-year-old genius. I'd wanted to spend the summer at Camp Longawanga with my best friend, Rachel, but my all-controlling psychobabbling mother insisted that I stay home and focus on "personal enrichment" instead.) So the assignment—to describe my home in two pages—didn't seem like a big deal at first, but I soon realized it was impossible in my present circumstances. You see, I was about to leave the house where I'd lived for the past six years and move into an apartment in Manhattan that I'd seen only on a digital photo, and a poorly lighted one at that. Which one counted as my real home, and how could I decide in two measly pages?

I soon gave up on the assignment. Instead of working, I slumped on the couch and watched a rerun of a reality show set in Salt Lake City, which chronicled what happens when a bunch of good-looking twenty-somethings from all over America are dumped into a palatial apartment together. The super-uptight New York roommate was flipping out because somebody had moved his jean jacket from the main coat rack to his personal closet, and he was yelling at the Detroit-born marine biologist. I enjoyed the New Yorker's hysteria and even semi-sympathized with the jean jacket crisis. I totally detest when people move my things around without telling me.

Also, I'd be lying if I said I didn't have a soft spot for New Yorkers. Especially my dad, who was working hard to become one again after a six-year absence. He claimed that being a big-city slicker was like riding a bicycle—once you learned, you never lost the hang of it—but I sort of doubted that he had blossomed into an alluring man about town without my guidance. To tell the truth, I couldn't even picture what Dad would look like as an alluring man about town. Would he be wearing a leather jacket? Speaking with a slight foreign accent? Riding a trendy Japanese scooter? I drew a total blank. My notions of cool were skewed after spending the last six years in Houston, where cotton-candy pink is always the new black.

Six years. I no longer knew anything about New York. Apart from taking cabs everywhere, what did New Yorkers even do? The memories I cherished, like ogling oversize toys at FAO Schwarz or tapping on the fish tanks at the Coney Island aquarium, hadn't exactly prepared me for life in the city.

Taking such an enormous plunge was scary, to say the least, but I had no choice. Dad was all alone up there, and I needed to look after him. Though on paper he was a fully developed adult, the man was understandably scarred by Mom's leaving him for Maurice, who was quite possibly the most disgusting creature on the planet.

Saying that my mom "left" my dad is mostly a metaphor, because she never actually went anywhere. That would have been way too normal. What she did was dump her devoted life partner of twenty years, completely out of the blue, describing her bombshell as an "honest life choice." Then, before my poor helpless dad had figured out that his life was over, she announced that she liked the house more, so perhaps *he* should leave it. My sweet daddy, he never even admitted that he had decided to move back to New York to get far away from Mom, to lick his wounds in private—instead he just kept talking about all the "professional connections" he wanted to rekindle. It's beyond lucky that his mother left him a few rental properties along the Jersey shore when she died two summers ago—just enough to guarantee a comfortable income before he hit the big time as an art photographer.

Since returning to New York, my father had called me at least once a day, sometimes two or even five times. He put on a front during our conversations, pretending that he was having the time of his life up there, but I didn't buy his mellow single-guy act for a second. If he was having such a swell time, why was he calling me at eleven o'clock on Saturday night?

Nope, without my mom, Dad was definitely falling apart. He needed protection, a shield from the world's brutalities. He needed somebody to say "good morning" to him, to ask about his day, to eat his (occasionally lumpy) pancakes.

I was the perfect candidate—a daddy's girl to the core. Much to the annoyance of my more discipline-oriented mom and my idiocy-oriented sister, I could do no wrong in my dad's eyes, and vice versa. The two of us looked alike, freckled and gangly. We also had the exact same sense of humor, always a plus.

But, in all honesty, it wasn't just our two-person mutual admiration society that was driving me to Dad's apartment. It was my mom. Over the past few months, she had gone bitchorama on me. She had always been the rule enforcer in the household, but her shit-kicking multiplied by forty after splitting up with Dad. She seemed dead set on proving how different the two of them were, as if to convince us all—me, Dad, my sister, Ariel—that the break was inevitable. She was constantly imposing some new curfew or objecting to how much of *her* (yeah, right) hard-earned money I wasted on bronzing powders or how sloppily I dressed in my gorgeous thrift-store ensembles.

In short, the whole disciplinarian routine was starting to wear on my nerves. But I still had seriously mixed feelings about living in Houston. On the one hand, I loved my life there: my school, my friends, my cat, the amazing eternal-summer weather. On the other, I had just turned fifteen that May and I was ready for some serious freedom. There seemed no better place to break out than downtown Manhattan, with only my out-of-it, omnitrusting father to supervise.

I had just switched off the TV, resolving to tackle my stupid writing assignment, when I heard a rustling sound across the room. I looked up to see my cat, Simon, standing by the door, gazing at me with an incredibly serious expression. His orange ears pointed straight up as if he sensed something important in the air. Right then, lo and behold, a bunch of envelopes poked through our mail slot. They cascaded down in slow motion and plopped on the doormat like no bunch of letters has ever plopped before. I know I have a melodramatic side—at least according to my mom—but I swear this plop signified Something Big. Simon meowed twice. He was a deeply intuitive animal.

I'd received a lot of mail all summer long, mostly from Rachel, who was at sailing camp and secretly dating a sixteen-year-old counselor-in-training named Trevor—or, as Rachel reverentially called him, "my CIT hottie." The more obsessed Rachel became with Trevor, the more letters she wrote me about him. You'd assume the opposite, but Rachel was so devoted a correspondent that she once wrote me an entire eight-pager about entering the dining room to see "my CIT hottie" sitting on a bench and taking the pickles out of a cheese and turkey sandwich. We used to laugh at what we called "Life's Very Entertaining Moments," but now she was becoming very unentertaining.

But right—back to the part about this being a fateful day. True to Simon's premonitions, there it was, stuck between the gas bill and two letters from Rachel: a postcard. Or I should say, *the* postcard. My very first piece of mail from the Baldwin School.

The shiny side of the postcard had a drawing of the Brooklyn Bridge, a close-up crowded with multiethnic foot traffic (my favorite was the dreadlocked man climbing up one of the bridge's cables). A cartoon sun hung in the sky, and the bridge sported wraparound sunglasses.

On the back, next to the sticker with my name and address, was the greeting:

Dear Incoming Sophomores,

We at the Baldwin School hope your summer is full of exciting discoveries and blissful adventures. Take note that our Welcome Home Meeting will take place in room U-3 on Friday, September 7, at 11:30 a.m. We look forward to seeing you there.

Until then, 𝒵𝑜𝓇𝒶

high school headmaster, and the rest of the Baldwin family
P.S. Keep up all that summer reading!

All the words were typewritten with the exception of "Zora," which was scrawled in insanely curly handwriting and took up more space than my address. Zora? I couldn't even begin to imagine a Houston teacher—especially a headmaster—signing a postcard with "Zora," or even being named "Zora," for that matter. Texas was all "Yes, sir" and "No, ma'am" and standing up when elders entered the room—who was Zora? Definitely bizarre. I knew Baldwin was supposed to be the most offbeat school in New York, but there was a difference between offbeat and plain old weird.

And then my eyes fixed on another line on the postcard and my brain emptied of everything but that one date: September 7. September 7 was in exactly a month. Only a month to go before orientation—I couldn't believe it.

Squaring my shoulders, I walked toward my mother's study, where I planned to figure out my life. To get inside the room, I had to hop over the stacks of overdue library books—no easy task, considering that I'm five-eleven, taller and way less graceful than most professional basketball players. (OK, not exactly, but that's how I always felt at school dances, so I might as well have been.)

The Sigmund Freud calendar I gave my mother for her birthday sat in the bottom corner of the desk, still cracked open to February. Coffee rings were splattered all over the page. The only thing she'd written down was in the box for February 5— "Take Simon to vet. Shots!"—with the words "February 6" underneath. That's my mother for you: too absent-minded to put the appointment on the right day. Too absent-minded to notice that her whole family was falling apart, or that her new boyfriend, Maurice, is a hypochondriac headcase. But that's another story.

My mother is a psychology professor at Rice University, a hyperorganized woman who gets everything done on time, but you'd never know it by her study. It's a total pit, with dried-up pens scattered on the shelves and stray rubber bands littering every surface. Month-old Post-it notes reminding her to go to faculty dinners cling to the telephone receiver.

I stared at my mother's catastrophic desk and tried to get a grip. Sometimes, to stop my mind from racing, I write things down. With that goal, I ripped a piece of paper from my mother's old notepad and began to scribble:

Very Important Countdown

30–20 Days to Go

Priorities

1. Pack, shop—new wardrobe (autumny wool sweaters, tights, new flats etc).

2. Rent Woody Allen movies.

3. Send Sam a letter. Other old friends?

4. Eat lots of last-minute enchiladas.

5. Chill. Remember: stress kills complexion.

20–10 Days to Go.........

1. Lose baby fat!

2. Start eating two vegetables a week.

3. Or two spinach enchiladas.

4. Swim three times a week.

5. No more pecan pie. (At least not à la mode.)

10–BLAST OFF...

1. Find new hairstyle.

2. Read book about New York. Edith Wharton? J. D. Salinger? Look for something more up to date.

3. Eat last enchiladas. Twice. (A day.)

4. Learn to eat sushi without wanting to vomit.

The next month flew by, what with my enchilada-pounding expeditions, my abdomen-toning exercises, and my extensive online investigations of life in New York. I crossed most items off my to-do list with little difficulty, saving my raw-fish initiation for my going-away dinner with Rachel. I'm sure my tanned, love-warmed friend would have preferred Rosa's, the cheesy

Mexican joint we both adored, but since I was the one whose life was going topsy-turvy, I was the one who got to choose.

In a recent letter, Sam—my childhood best friend before my parents moved to Texas—had gone on about New Yorkers' passion for raw fish. Ever since, I'd imagined people sitting around fish tanks, scooping up wriggling guppies with their nets. I doubted sushi would ever become my thing because a) it looked nastola and slimy and b) the portion sizes were way too puny.

I took Rachel to the place that my older sister, Ariel, who just graduated from high school, recommended because none of the foreign waiters seemed to realize that in America it's illegal to serve sake to fifteen-year-olds. When Tomiko (at least that's what the nametag said) came to take our order, for some reason I couldn't stop thinking about my old pet goldfish Titan. He used to lodge himself in the crook of the plastic mermaid's elbow and get stuck in there.

In the end, I chickened out and ordered vegetable rolls. They were decent but familiar, and I cleaned my plate (or rather my weird rectangular serving tray). Conversation with Rachel was a less comfortable experience. Since returning from camp, she had been too upset about her long-distance relationship with Trevor to acknowledge that the two of us were about to face a similar challenge. She was, in fact, so absorbed in her romantic anguish that she mentioned our impending 1,500-mile separation only once: "I'm so depressed about Trevor, I can't believe you're abandoning me, too!"

On the bright side, Rachel's obliviousness made saying good-bye a lot less awkward. After dinner, her mom picked us up and dropped me at home as usual, and the whole night seemed far too typical for weepy goodbyes.

The next morning, before I left, I had just one last item to tick off my list. Even scarier than eating raw fish was "letting go" (one of my mom's fave terms) of the hairstyle I'd had since the fourth grade: halfway down my back, with thick bangs covering my forehead. But, after Sam's most recent letter, I knew I needed a new look. "How could I not recognize you?" he had written. "You'll be the only girl at Baldwin with hair down to her butt."

I went to the Beautique to pay my trusty hairdresser Jean-Pascal an *au revoir* visit. "Eye ave been waiting for yew all week!" he exclaimed. "Today is eet. Yew, Mademoiselle Mimi, are my muse. Any eye-dee-uhs?"

I nodded. After wasting a whole week scouring old *Seventeens* for guidance, I had torn out only two pictures, a shoulder-length shag and a chin-length flippy thing. I showed Jean-Pascal his options. "Which one?" I asked, praying he'd pick the longer, safer one.

I should've known better. As indicated by the spiky blond hair on his own head, which he rehighlighted practically every week, Jean-Pascal had a flair for the dramatic. "Eye inseest. Lez make today a very important day." He crumpled both pictures and tossed them into a pile of my predecessor's wispy blue-gray hairs on the floor.

"*Attends, ma chérie, attends,*" Jean-Pascal rasped en route to the shampoo station. I froze when he whispered into the shampoo girl's ear, then sighed in relief when I realized he was only giving instructions for an extended head massage.

When at last he seated me to cut my hair, Jean-Pascal swiveled my chair around to prevent me from looking in the mirror. "Trust *moi*," he assured me.

It took like ten hours. All the other ladies in the salon watched from under their bubble-topped hair dryers as footlong hanks of my hair dropped to the ground. I felt like a circus freak.

"Voilà," Jean-Pascal said finally, and spun me around. *"Magnifique."*

I gasped. My hair fell around my face in dark chunks, exposing cheekbones I'd never known existed. It was amazing, really and truly *magnifique*. I looked, to tell the truth, exactly like an oversize Winona Ryder. I was, dare I say it, almost beautiful.

"You look *exactement comme,* euuhh, euhh, *comment elle s'appelle?"* Jean-Pascal was both genius hairdresser and mind-reader: "Weenonah. Rydaair, *c'est ça? Incroyable."*

"Vrai," I croaked out. *Magnifique, incroyable,* and then some. Maybe it's uncool to base your mental state on your hair, but when Jean-Pascal and I locked eyes under the salon's halogen lights, I *knew* that tenth grade in New York would work out just fine.

Mimi Schulman, Meet Manhattan

AFTER OUR "LAST SUPPER" BREAKFAST OF HERBAL TEA, fruit salad, and a multivitamin smoothie, I was off. Mom and my insane older sister, Ariel, who's dating an aspiring rapper nicknamed the "Vanilla Gorilla," brought me to the airport. Ariel spent the whole ride bitching about having to dump Vanny if she wanted to pledge Kappa at Texas that fall. Apparently, wannabe thugs who work as forklift operators and refuse to speak grammatical English just don't cut it in the upper-crust sorority scene.

"Life's so cruel," Ariel moaned. "I want to follow my heart, but Vanny's getting in the way. I just want to kick his ass, you know?"

Rather than answer Ariel, my mother shook her head in utter bewilderment and mumbled "hormonal distress" and "acting out" every few exits.

I was hugely relieved to board that plane, delighted to ditch my nearest and dearest. Ever since February, when my mom revealed her "existential attraction" to Maurice and gave Dad the boot, I'd been living a TV-movie nightmare. Maurice had two passions: building furniture without using any nails, and detailing his medical problems. He also made strange gurgling noises when chewing. No bigger loser had ever lived. Ever since Maurice's hideous seventeen-year-old daughter, Myrtle, and her hairball collection (she said it was an "art experiment") came into the equation in the spring, I inhabited the most stressful household of all time.

The flight to New York would've been noneventful if the airline hadn't lost my luggage. The two suitcases containing my most treasured possessions had flown the opposite direction and were now making the rounds on a baggage carousel in Phoenix. The airline *promised* to deliver the luggage by the following Monday morning at the latest, but Monday morning wasn't soon enough. The orientation meeting was on Friday.

I might've burst into tears if Dad hadn't been standing there. After a long traumatic summer, I was so happy to see him that I forgot to panic about my orientation outfit. Dad looked a bit pale and puffy, but I expected that, I guess. It was logical that New Yorkers sunbathed and exercised less than Houstonians. And besides, why else was I there but to get him in shape? I gave him another hug and he said, "Miss Mimi, we're going to have a *great* time together!"

I agreed enthusiastically, especially after seeing the place Dad had rented, half of a quaint brownstone in the West Village. It was a total score: The apartment had two floors and was decently roomy, even by Texas standards. To get inside the house you had to walk up a stoop, so the main floor was actually the second floor, and all the bedrooms and Dad's darkroom were on the ground level. My dad had real estate speculation in his blood, it seemed—his mother, the Jewish condo baroness of southern

New Jersey, would've definitely approved. For a helpless, heart-broken bachelor, my dad seemed to be coping pretty well.

He explained that the only other people in the building were a couple of lesbian documentary filmmakers, both named Judy; their daughter, Gilda, whom they had adopted in China a few years earlier; and Willa, their very expensive Labradoodle from the Falkland Islands. No sooner had I stepped into our apartment than our new neighbors appeared at our door bearing a plate of grilled "tempeh fingers."

"We just *love* your dad," Judy #1 told me after insisting I take not one but three fingers off the platter. She was wearing a remarkable pantsuit straight off the set of *Joseph and the Amazing Technicolor Dreamcoat*.

"*Adore*," Judy #2 echoed. Her burgundy chenille tunic swayed in the early-evening breeze. "If we'd met him a few years earlier, who knows what might have happened? We might've persuaded him to, har, donate!"

"Rotten luck," I said, nearly choking on my tempeh finger.

"Could've saved us a few very expensive plane tickets, if you know what I mean!" said Judy #1.

"But seriously," said #2, "we're flipping over with love for Gilda. Her new favorite words are, 'Watch it, buster.' How hilarious is that?"

The Judys started laughing, gruffly and in unison. #2 clapped me heartily on the back, and when #1 said, "Welcome to the family—Barrow Street's been waiting for you," my eyes brimmed with tears.

After the home tour and my tempeh force-feeding session

with the Judys, who showed us clips from the movie they were working on, *Under the Iron Ramp: Problems of Wheelchair Access in the Former Soviet Union*, I could hardly walk for exhaustion. Between faking separation anxiety from my mother and haggling with the airline luggage representative, I had survived an extremely trying day. My dad proposed taking me on a stroll through the neighborhood, but I wanted only to crawl into my brand-new bed and sleep—after, of course, eating a real dinner.

"I consider this my at-home all-you-can-eat buffet," Dad said in the kitchen, rolling out a drawer stuffed full of takeout menus. I chose one near the top of the pile, an Indian restaurant on Carmine Street. The food came within five minutes. Also within five minutes, I efficiently inhaled my weight in saag paneer, tandoori chicken, aloo gobi, four different kinds of naan, and a bunch of other delicacies I was too delirious to remember. Around eight p.m., I passed out in the same clothes I had worn on the flight.

My dad and I spent the following day shopping for new spiral notebooks and enough clothes to tide me over through the weekend, until the arrival of my luggage. With a supply of ballpoint pens, a few simple tops, a pair of black ballet flats, and a pair of prefaded jeans, I felt perfectly equipped for my new life.

With Tenth Grade Comes Great Responsibility

FRIDAY MORNING, AS I WALKED INTO ROOM U-3 of Baldwin wearing an inoffensively preppy outfit, the total, all-consuming fear kicked in. No one had told me that the *U* in U-3 stood for Undercroft, the basement, so I arrived at the orientation meeting nearly fifteen minutes late. I tried to ignore the thirty-six pairs of eyes that landed right on me, and tiptoed toward the back and crouched on the carpet near a bunch of guys who all seemed to have colossal backpacks and pimples of similar proportions. There was a frazzled, gray-haired woman at the front of the room, clutching a coffee mug. She was draped in a dirty V-neck T-shirt that not even my mom's new paramour, Maurice, would've worn beyond the den.

In the whole room, the only person who bothered to smile at me was this gorgeous blonde girl who was sitting half an inch from the teacher at the front of the room. She was probably making fun of me in some obscure way, and I felt a little sick. Where was Sam? Could he have changed schools overnight and forgotten to tell me?

"As I was saying"—the woman by the blackboard cleared her throat in irritation—"middle school's over, and you're no longer the babies of the upper school, either. With the freedom of tenth grade comes great responsibility."

"Beware of her," one of the pimpleheads rumbled in my ear, pointing at the droning woman at the front of the room. "Zora Blanchard. The world's biggest ball buster, unless you're into ceramics. She digs the arty chicks."

"Thanks." I grinned gratefully. So this was Zora, the face behind the loopy signature on that postcard.

"Baldwin sees education as a celebration of sharing and being together," Zora Blanchard continued. She proceeded to launch into this *War and Peace*–length speech about honesty and community and respect and all those other topics that seriously get on my nerves. If there's one thing that bugs me, it's older people thinking that they can train kids to be nice. In my experience, if somebody's a jerk, he's a jerk, period, end of story, and no stupid "welcome home" speech is going to change that.

I felt a burning sensation in my forehead, as sharp as a spitball. I looked up to see it was that same blonde girl, still smiling at me. When she yawned and rolled her eyes sympathetically, I was almost too overwhelmed to roll mine back. She was the most beautiful all-American girl I'd ever seen, a walking Tommy Hilfiger advertisement in her navy blue button-down and a gold-link bracelet. I could practically examine my reflection in her teeth, even from across the room. Thank God I'd gone conservative.

"That was a very important point," Blanchard was saying. "Just to double-check that you all understand it . . ." She scanned the room. "Nona, can you please sum it up?"

"Absolutely" came a slow voice from the center of a cluster of five girls in the corner I hadn't noticed up until that point.

All five of these girls looked unkempt if not dirty, if not homeless then heroin-addicted. And still they possessed an undeniable magnetism: they were by far the most captivating group in the room. I don't know how I overlooked them. They were pretty, actually, but by no means conventionally. I think their appeal had to do more with their energy or their expressions, which simultaneously projected messages of "Help me" and "Fuck off." They didn't make them like this in Houston.

"Any day will do," Blanchard said, shifting her weight from left to right hip.

As we waited, I couldn't help but stare. As a group they were fascinating. A tiny, pixielike girl, perhaps part Asian, with short hair, sky-high cheekbones, and black eyeliner thicker than my index finger, jabbed the girl next to her. This one had broad shoulders and sandy blonde hair and was wearing a thick heather gray–flecked sweatshirt that read NANTUCKET in big block letters. She looked athletic and serious, with open, easy-to-read features. To the left of the Nantucket girl was a flawless, olive-skinned glamour queen decked out in the kind of designer clothing people fly to Milan to scoop up. She had long dark hair and eyelashes and wore an extremely bored expression. She was slumped against a generically glossy preppy blonde—another Texas cheerleader type, but more intriguingly melancholy than the white-toothed blonde across the room. Though carefully dressed in a lavender cardigan and pearls, she appeared not to have slept in a week, with under-eye circles three shades darker than the rest of her face. The more I looked at them, the more entrancing they became. These weren't the kind of girls you'd see in a teen-magazine fashion spread. Still, I had trouble averting my eyes.

"Nona, ahem?" Blanchard shifted position again, thrusting her right clog forward and leaning her weight back into her left hip. She cleared her throat.

The girl Zora kept calling Nona, next to the bedroom-eyed blonde, took her time answering Baldwin's principal, probably because she knew she could. Nona was the most breathtaking of them all, with long dreadlocks pulled into a ponytail and skin the color of a nonfat latte. She was blinking her huge, dilated bottle-green eyes as if she had just been roused from a month-long coma.

"You were saying that we should all, ah, you know, like . . ." Nona scratched her chin. After a long pause the haute couture–clad girl whispered into her ear, allowing Nona to continue: "We should all respect each other and, like, understand? Cultures and stuff?"

"That will do," an indignant Blanchard said, cutting her off. "Anybody else?"

We were all shuffling our feet and coughing, unwilling to risk total geekdom so early in the year. At last a singsong voice broke the silence: "You were saying that we are going to have to challenge ourselves this year. That our fiercest critics come from within."

"Thank you, Amanda." Blanchard gazed, enraptured, at the pretty blonde girl who had smiled at me at the beginning of the meeting.

Blanchard then segued into a spiel about our being the captains of our own ships when it came to signing up for electives. At first I thought she was talking about a politics class.

"If you've already lost your course books," she said, "you'll be thrilled to hear I have plenty of extras in my office. And please take note, Gary in the English department has decided to take the year off to travel through South Asia, so those of you enrolled in his 'Writing About Bollywood' course are going to have to make alternate plans. Better news is that Ruth in the science department has agreed to lead a bread-making seminar. If you'd—"

A curly-headed boy who had been waving his arm in the air for several minutes finally managed to capture Zora's attention.

"Yes, Frank?"

"I just want to make sure before I join: Does a health club membership satisfy the gym requirement?"

"Yes. Until we give our poor neglected gym a face-lift, that policy will remain intact. Yes, Arthur?" She pointed to a guy whose baseball cap was pulled down to obscure the top 90 percent of his face.

"What if we don't belong to a gym?" Arthur asked.

"Then you can take tai chi, modern dance, or any of the stretch classes we offer," she responded. "To name just a few."

"But isn't that, like, discrimination against non–Crunch conformers?" a kid to Arthur's right piped up.

"We'll talk about it in my office whenever you're available, Andrew," Zora answered sternly.

After this endless Q&A segment, Zora called us up one by one to distribute our schedules. I remembered the admissions officer telling me on the phone that no two students at Baldwin had the same exact classes.

"Yes!" shouted one of the jocks. "No classes till after lunch on Thursdays!"

"Lucky bastard!" One of his friends high-fived him.

No such luck for the transfer student: my schedule was jam-packed with courses. Besides all the usual suspects like World Civ, English, French, and math, I was taking puppetry, sculpture, and a "book-binding seminar." On Wednesdays I had a two-hour yoga class.

"I'd switch to squash if I were you!" I heard from behind me.

I spun around and almost collided with that same gorgeous blonde girl. She was pointing at my yoga square.

"It meets at the same time," she explained. "And it's *much* better for your cardiovascular system than yoga. You get a real adrenaline rush—plus, you get a chance to compete with the Manhattan leagues!"

"Thanks," I said, somewhat perplexed.

"I'm Amanda." She extended her French-manicured hand.

"Pleased to meet you. My name's Mi—"

"Mimi Schulman," she finished for me. Glancing down at her penny loafers, she added quickly, "It's not every day there's a new kid at Baldwin. In fact, it's been"—she consulted her watch, a gleaming timepiece pricier than most package holidays to the Bahamas—"six years since we've had someone new who was at least *sort of* normal-looking."

Ouch. I clutched my notebook to my developing chest and stepped back.

"No, no! Not that you're only sort of normal-looking. It's just that the last new kid we had was Ivan Grimalsky, two years ago, and he didn't really count." Amanda pointed down the hallway, where a lanky guy was doing handstands against a row of lockers. He was a freak.

"He's a freak," she said. "It was a bigtime disappointment. We were all so excited about some fresh blood coming in here and . . . Let's just say, we've all been looking forward to meeting you."

"We?"

Amanda gestured with her shoulder, and, like Miss America runners up, four girls fanned out behind her. Their beaming smiles were so identical I wondered if they practiced in the mirror together.

"She's going to switch into squash," Amanda said after introducing me to, from left to right, Courtney, Mary Ann, Ivy, and Sophie. "Aren't you?"

I opened my mouth, but no words came out. I was too stunned. I had been at Baldwin for less than an hour and already the popular girls—blonder and tanner than anyone I had known in Houston—had recruited me. I couldn't wait to tell Rachel, who considered herself more entitled to live in New York than I was, being 100 percent Jewish to my half. She would never believe how un-Jewish and preppy the real Brooklyn was.

"So, what are you up to now?" Courtney asked me on our way

through the lobby, where I must have overheard the word *Hamptons* at least three times.

When we got outside, I noticed a couple of the pimpleheads from the U-Croft huddled on a stoop across the street, smoking hand-rolled cigarettes.

"Wanna grab some TD with us?" Sophie said. "It's our daily tradition."

"Shorthand for Tasti D-Lite," Amanda clarified. "The *best* frozen yogurt in New York City!"

"Or any other city!" Ivy cheered.

As they high-fived one another, I tried to assume an expression of deep regret, which was easy because it was exactly what I was feeling. I had already made plans with Sam Geckman, friend of my youth, who was long-lost and potentially lame. Given that he might be Baldwin's number-one social outcast, I wasn't going to bring his name up in front of these urban goddesses.

"I, ah . . . I can't," I said. "I just flew in yesterday, and I promised my dad I'd come home straight from school so that we can start setting up my new room. He's not used to being a bachelor, and the apartment's a total wreck."

My disappointment was real, and I wished I'd never made that stupid appointment. I'd told Sam I'd meet him at his "spot"—a Yemenite café on Atlantic Avenue. If only I'd put him off a day or two. But then again, when I'd answered that letter, I had no idea that the first day of school would be so . . . Was *easy* the word I was searching for?

The girls exchanged understanding nods, and Amanda proposed that we sit together at lunch that Monday instead. "I promise," I said, and as I rushed off I hoped they wouldn't notice that the Manhattan-bound subway was in the opposite direction. Of course I could always claim that I was lost, and I would have been if I hadn't studied the online street map of Brooklyn Heights so obsessively over the last few weeks.

As I turned onto Atlantic Avenue, I checked over both shoulders as if I were in a spy movie. Why had I lied just now? I couldn't figure it out.

Once I located the Yemenite café he had described in such detail in his last letter, I trudged up the stairs to the entrance and ducked inside. I immediately spotted Sam at a table near the back—his red hair really stood out in that setting. He was sipping from a tall glass and reading the newspaper. I wove through a tangle of men who were all drinking espressos while standing up. It was only after I pulled out a chair and sat down that I noticed Sam's paper was in Arabic.

"Can you pass me the sports section?" I greeted him.

Sam hadn't changed much since the fourth grade—strange that I hadn't seen him in the U-Croft that morning, but perhaps Baldwin's ambient lighting was to blame. Sam had the same carroty hair and freckles, the same gentle green eyes and lopsided smile as in the fourth grade. The only difference was that Sam had gotten very tall over the last few years, but without having gained an ounce. His new physique was a stretched-out version of the one I remembered.

He was assessing me with a funny, startled expression. Was it the waifish hairdo that caught him off-guard, or the effect of my push-up bra beneath my plain white shirt?

"Remember me?" I began when Sam didn't. "My name is Mimi. We used to be best friends. We made ice cream floats together and sometimes even pooped in front of each other." I concluded with the Everything's Cool smile that I'd copied from teenage popstar interviews. I wasn't expecting everything to feel as awkward as everything was feeling. A full five minutes must've passed before Sam pushed out his chair and stood up to hug me.

"Good old Mimi. Whenever I read your letters, I picture you from the end-of-the-year play in fourth grade. When you played—"

"The pig in *Charlotte's Web*?"

"Exactly! My mom took so many pictures, they still pop up sometimes. You in that snout. An outstanding look. Hate to break it to you, but among the Geckman family you're still known as Miss Piglet."

Relaxing a little, I asked Sam about the school meeting—he had been hiding behind the upright piano and was apparently the only member of the entire tenth-grade class not to have logged my late entrance. "I was in the way back," he said. "I was on the lookout for you, but I couldn't see beyond the Afro Scott Rosenfeld sprouted over the summer."

Sam explained that Scott Rosenfeld was a Jewish computer science whiz who decided to become a rap DJ this past summer. I laughed and described Ariel's boyfriend, Vanny, who had no computer skills worth mentioning. Sam then told me that Zora Blanchard used to be so chubby that everybody called her "Custard." Suddenly, before I'd even seen a menu, a waiter appeared and placed a cold drink in front of me.

"But I didn't order anything," I protested.

"That's the charm of this place. Try it."

I took a small sip: cold and sour. "Interesting?" I tried.

"It's an Arabic iced tea. I'm obsessed with them," Sam said.

As I continued to sample my beverage, my former best friend's expression changed. Knitting his brow, he leaned across the small table to look me straight in the eye. "So, Mimi, tell me. What's up?"

"Nothing much," I said. "Just being the new girl on the block."

"You know what I mean. What's going on with your parents?"

I sighed, semi-exasperated. I didn't resent Sam for asking, but I just wasn't in the mood. What are you supposed to say when your mother leaves your father for a roly-poly physicist named Maurice? How do you make small talk out of your father quitting his prestigious job as senior photography professor at Rice University and hightailing it to New York to resume his postponed dream of becoming the most important art photographer of his generation? And oh, what about Maurice's plump, hairball-gathering offspring, Myrtle, and Ariel's contradictory obsessions with the Vanilla Gorilla and Kappa Kappa Gamma? Did I leave out the number of Audrey Hepburn movies I noticed stacked on Dad's TV, or his cheerful admission that he lived on pizza and burrito delivery services?

"Nothing's going on. Except they split up. Not the biggest deal—happens to the best of families."

Sam wasn't going to let me off at that. "Mimi," he insisted, "of *course* it's a big deal. But you don't have to talk about it if you're feeling uncomfortable."

He said the phrase "feeling uncomfortable" very comfortably, as if he said it a lot. I wasn't used to guys my age talking like this—it was so my mom. Could he be seeing a therapist? Rachel had told me that every respectable New Yorker saw one at least three times a week.

"Oh, well, whatever," he said. "Finish up. I'll take you on a tour of Brooklyn Heights, which, despite its yuppie aura, isn't entirely charmless. Although there are no even half-decent record stores. Do you like electronica?"

"Electronica"? In some of his more recent letters, Sam had mentioned musical groups I'd never heard of, but that kind of thing always reminded me of Ariel, so I had naturally tuned them out.

"Well, er, it's not exactly my cup of tea."

"No big whoop. Ready?" Sam stood up and motioned for me to follow. "In forty-five minutes, I can show you everything you'll need to know to survive at Baldwin," he said.

We paid, left the Yemenite café, and started walking up Clinton Street, back in the direction of school. "The hot spots where the Baldwin kids do their drinking, smoking, and gossiping—I'll even throw in a private residential stoop with maximum squatting potential if you want."

"And what about frozen yogurt stores?" I asked. "I hear that's big in Brooklyn."

Sam gave me a strange look. "Frozen yogurt? Is that a new kind of designer drug?"

"Er, never mind. You know, as part of my tour, I think I'm going to have you teach me how to read Arabic." I gestured at his indecipherable newspaper with my chin.

"Sure thing," Sam said as we brushed past a group of kids walking the opposite direction. When one of them murmured "Whassup?" at him, Sam nodded back in a pretty cool I-couldn't-give-a-damn way. "I'll teach you Arabic once I get around to learning myself."

He gave my shoulder a half-punch and for the first time I recognized my old Sam. Our letter writing had become a duty, and I'd forgotten how close we used to be. I was glad to have him around again. Fingers crossed that Amanda and her gorgeous flaxen-haired entourage would approve.

Pad Thai, Interrupted

AFTER LETTING MYSELF INTO THE FRONT door of our brownstone, I flipped through the mail basket that we shared with the Judys. I shuffled through a few bills for my dad and a thick packet for Judy #2 from some organization called "The Friedman Institute for Filmic Insight Without Borders" but found nothing with my name on it. I was disappointed because at the sushi restaurant Rachel had sworn on her virginity that she'd already mailed me a juicy letter. Then again, that was only three nights ago, so it couldn't possibly have arrived yet. Only three nights? I shook my head. I had trouble believing that only three nights ago I was in Houston eating cucumber rolls and chugging hot sake with Rachel.

Two nights, 1,500 miles, a mega-haircut, and a few ounces of Arabic iced tea, and I had aged a lifetime.

I walked into the apartment, which was quiet and deserted. "Hello?" I called out. Getting no response, I went downstairs and stood outside my father's brand-new darkroom. The Do Not Enter sign was up, so I shouted "Dad?" and knocked on the door. "Dad, I'm home!"

"So am I," an unfamiliar voice floated out. "I'll be out in a sec, just gotta put these things on the drying rack. OK?"

"Uh, OK," I answered, slightly mystified. I had no idea who this person was or what he was talking about, but no matter. Coming home to find a complete stranger locked inside my father's darkroom wasn't the weirdest thing that had ever happened to me, not by a long shot.

I went back upstairs to raid the kitchen. I was always starving after school. But then I opened my father's fridge and—ugh—changed my mind. His leftovers would inspire even gluttonous Maurice to go on a diet. You could build a bridge across the East River with all the white cardboard takeout cartons that my dad had crammed in there. There was also a container full of eggs that had expired in August, a can of beer, a jar of discolored pickles, a Tupperware tub full of black-and-white 200-speed film, and some half-and-half that reeked like Maurice after a jog. Holding my breath, I got onto my knees and poked my head inside, an act that I can attribute only to my "self-punishing tendencies" that my brilliant mom had been pointing out since the breakup.

The state of the inside of the fridge was very unlike him. For one thing, in addition to being OCD tidy, my dad was a total health nut. He was an antioxidant addict who did gross stuff like slice fresh ginger into his oatmeal and grill all-birdseed hamburgers. The array of week-old processed food splayed out before me made no sense. Maybe he was trying to make up for all his organic food–eating, Vitamin B complex–downing, wheat germ juice–swilling days? No wonder he'd looked so unsvelte at the airport on Wednesday. I took a bite of a spinach burrito that tasted like body odor, and proceeded to keep searching for something edible.

As I was attempting to dewedge a moldy container of Pad Thai from the bottom rack, the voice I'd heard downstairs made me jump. "You must be the famous Mimi—sorry, didn't mean to scare you!"

Hovering above me was an adorable guy with perfect teeth and rosy cheeks. He was wearing Lennon glasses, a tight-fitting T-shirt, and what appeared to be a lot of styling product. He was about twenty-three or twenty-four, slightly older than the nerdy students my mother persuaded to mow our lawn in exchange for free therapy, but with much, much better pectorals.

"Uh, h-hey," I stuttered, gripping the refrigerator handle like the rail of a building I was about to fall off. "Hi. I . . . live here? At least, I . . . Who are you?"

"Oh, do you really not know?" he raised an eyebrow and decided this news delighted him. "That's so Roger! I'm Quinn, your father's new darkroom assistant. I was the suck-up kid in his color photography class at the New School this summer. Now I pretty much live here."

This total Adonis pretty much lived in Dad's apartment? Make that *my* apartment? I beamed gratitude in Dad's direction, wherever that happened to be.

"Oh, hey. Good to meet you," I said, shaking his hand. He had the same vinegary darkroom smell as my father. It was comforting. "Um, is my dad around?"

With glittering blue eyes, Quinn was ogling me so intensely that I wondered if I had a huge piece of spinach stuck to my front teeth. I was not the type of girl to admire men's bodies— that was more Rachel's specialty—but this Quinn looked like he had just stepped out of a male fragrance ad.

"Oh, you know Roger," he was saying in a low, gravelly voice. "He's been procrastinating in the darkroom all day, then about an hour ago remembered that you'd moved in, so he ran out the door shouting gibberish about sepia-toned reprints and other great domestic necessities."

As if cued, my father barreled through the door right then, huge shopping bags strung on both arms. "Honey, hello," he said, dropping several bags when he saw me. His face broke out in a huge smile, just like at the airport yesterday. It was nice, having that effect on someone. "I see you've met Quinn. I'm so sorry that I wasn't here when you got back—I guess I *completely* lost track of time! But you'll be delighted with what I've gotten you today. I might have gone a little overboard, but this place had absolutely everything! Here, here, have a look," he was rattling on a mile a minute as he overturned several bags onto the grimy kitchen floor. My father—usually so mellow (or, according to my mom, "unmotivated")—was acting off-the-charts hyper just then.

Quinn caressed a beige sequined tank top on top of the pile. "Hey. What's that?" I suspected he was more interested in the kind of woman who might wear that tank top than the tank top itself, but it was nice of him to pretend. "It's *killer*."

"Yeah, cool?" I echoed, liking Quinn for being so nice about my father's off-the-wall vintage clothing obsession. Unfortunately, the rat-eaten garment itself made me shudder. Some times I felt unworthy, being the only fifteen-year-old in America whose dad digs secondhand boutiques more than she does. He's always foraging for old cameras, but he never leaves without sifting through the clothes: the prototype of the modern metrosexual, I guess. He appreciates women's clothing the way some men appreciate beautiful perfume or jewelry. When I was little, I used to accompany my parents to Macy's, where Dad would pick out a handful of designer dresses and make Mom try them all on— never to buy them, just to imagine how she'd look in them. It was too bad that she preferred to dress like an overcommitted career woman, drowning in earth tones and never without a pair of sensible pumps—that is, when she wasn't walking around the house in sweatpants and XXL T-shirts.

Today, with no more Mom to inspire him, Dad seemed to have taken to shopping for me.

"You have quite the father," Quinn told me. "He's the only man I've ever met who knows every thrift shop *and* chic oyster bar in New York."

"I'm a man of varied interests," Dad admitted. "Williamsburg *is* unrecognizable these days, Quinn—I was expecting all factories and Hasids, but was I ever wrong! It was packed with kids your age and incredible boutiques. They had to pry me out of the last one. I was going nuts over an entire section devoted to old Leicas."

The photographers cracked up in unison. It seemed as if they'd both inhaled too much fixer solution.

While still speed-talking about the crate of kaleidoscope scarves he'd unearthed, my dad tossed a red-fringed denim miniskirt at me. "Your bags haven't shown up yet, hon, so I thought, to avoid patronizing another sweatshop, we could spice up your style a bit! And I even found shoes to match—you're still a ten and a half, right?"

Hoping Quinn hadn't heard how obscenely big my feet were, I nodded.

"Consider this your early birthday present!" With a flourish, my father reached into a ratty polka-dotted hatbox. "How's that for making the transition from the Wild West to the West Village?"

Emitting a shriek that the Judys upstairs might confuse with one of their interviews with Eastern European political prisoners, Quinn lunged for the pair of knee-high burgundy leather cowboy boots that my father held before me. "Whoa. These are seriously cool."

I didn't want to hurt my dad's feelings, but I almost threw up when he sprang his next surprise on me: a chartreuse velvet hat with a veil and a hummingbird stapled on top. According to my dad, women's clothing must resemble either a geometry problem or a prewar musical costume. Unfortunately, there was no way I could walk into Baldwin wearing the next dress that Dad pulled out, which seemed to be some sort of hybrid of a tunic and a coffee filter.

Remembering that little horse embroidered into Amanda's shirt, I said very hesitantly, "Do you think maybe tomorrow we could also go to, um, Ralph Lauren? For the, um, essentials?"

"Ralph Lauren?" my dad repeated with a blank look, as if I'd suggested selling my ovaries to science. Before I could explain my reluctance to show up at Baldwin as some gawky, adolescent version of Ginger Rogers, the phone rang. I raced to pick it up and yelped, "Hello?" before the second ring.

"Mimi!" my mother bellowed. "Thank God it's only you! Damn, I've missed you!"

"Oh, hey, Mom," I said in a flat voice. After our chaotic summer, it hadn't occurred to me to miss her yet. If ever. "How's it going?" The cordless was sticky with ketchup.

"Oh, you know, same old, same old. Ariel's still driving me up the wall, begging for a new set of linens for school—can you believe that? That girl has some nerve. New sheets for college—*chambray* sheets? When we have closets full of perfectly good ones right here." She gave a little huff of disapproval before going on: "Now, I'm just calling to check in, see how your reading program's going—if you don't start the semester on track, you know, you'll never catch up. If you need any book suggestions, I just read a really *wonderful* survey about the history of sugar, and I could send it up north if you're interested . . ."

Amazing. She didn't even bother to ask how my brand new upside-down life was treating me. She was too obsessed with her so-called reading program. My mother had allowed me to enroll at Baldwin, where there were no grades, only if I promised to read two books on my own every week. Of course she didn't ask any more sensitive questions. How was your first day of school? Did the kids play nicely? Did you miss your mommy? That was out of her range. No, she just wanted to bitch about bed linens and harass me about extracurricular enrichment. At times, I found my heart going out to her, almost sympathizing with her late-onset life overhaul. The impulse to start over was one I perfectly understood. But then, whenever I was about to forgive her, reality always reared its head. Like now, for instance, when she said: "And that reminds me of another thing we haven't discussed: curfew. Now, Mimi, you *know* . . ."

I had already tuned her out when, miracle of miracles, the call-waiting beep revived me. "Sorry, Mom, hold on—we have another call."

"Call waiting is so rude," she huffed while I clicked over. My mother was jam-packed with policies about answering machines and microwaves and computers, all of which she considered "symptomatic of the decline of civilization."

"Hello?" I said, praying it was Rachel to relieve me. Rachel is known for her amazing timing.

"Hello, may I please speak to Mimi?"

"Yeah," I replied, definitely not to Rachel. "Speaking."

"Oh, phew, hey, Mimi! It's Amanda. You know, from Baldwin? I know you're probably being driven up the wall with stuff to do, but I was just looking through our new directory, and I realized that we live really close to each other! I'm on Bleecker— how great a coincidence is *that*?"

It was great, I agreed, my heart thumping dorkily. "Oh, Amanda, hold on, just one sec—I'm on the other line with my mom in Texas. I'll be *right* back." I clicked back. "I've got to get this call, Mom—it's one of my new Baldwin friends."

"New friends already?" She whistled. I could just see her Proud Look, the same one that had lit her face when I got my period for the first time during her psychology department's open house. Within 2.2 seconds, she had told every single professor there that her little girl had finally become a woman. "Who are these *friends*?" she demanded, all of a sudden interested in my life. "Spill!"

I hated when my mother got chummy, as if I'd magically forget everything that had gone wrong between us. I had no desire to overlook her dumping of my sweet teddy bear of a father for disgusting, doughy Maurice. Our mother-daughter relationship was *not* A-OK. I mean, it's not as if I have anything against adultery on principle, but if you're going to cheat on a guy like dad, you should at least pick a guy whose idea of fun doesn't involve comparison shopping for herbal lozenges.

"Actually," I said, "I'm going to take the call." And just like that, giving her zero chance to rail on about my manners and my father's influence, I clicked back to Amanda.

"Hey there," I said.

"Listen, I was just wondering if you wanted to hang out," she said. "There's this place I go to on Friday nights, and I thought maybe you'd want to check it out."

In Houston the only "places" we ever partied in tended to be people's living rooms or basements. And to think I'd been in town for only forty-eight hours and I was being invited to a nightclub—beyond incredible. A vision of Amanda and myself, in crisp pleated miniskirts, dancing on the tabletop with celebrities springing into my mind, I accepted—"Wow, great! Really?"—with a tad too much enthusiasm.

"Oh, fab! And then maybe the rest of the girls could come

hang out and we could all give you the rundown of life at Baldwin? That is, if you and your dad don't already have a million things to do?"

"No, that's perfect," I said, trying to deflate the eagerness in my voice. "Convenient, I mean—my dad just told me that he has plans tonight, so I'm totally free. Just tell me when and where."

When and Where

W<small>HEN AND WHERE TURNED OUT TO BE EIGHT</small> o'clock at the Gray Dog Café, right around the corner. "It's really cool—you'll love it," Amanda swore. "They have the *best* fat-free muffins."

I'd be lying if I said I wasn't the teeniest bit disappointed by the mention of fat-free muffins. It's not as if I have a problem with weight-watching blondes—my old high school mass-produced them. For instance, on career day, Tara Meriwether, the single most popular girl at my Houston high school, announced her ambition to open a drugstore that carried fat-free aspirin and fat-free toothpaste. Amanda can eat fat-free everything to her heart's content—I just hadn't factored muffins into my night-out equation. It sounded about as sexy as getting together to clip our toenails.

Getting ready was a serious challenge. I mean, if you know you're going to the opera, you put on a ball gown. Or if you're going to the beach, you throw on a bikini and—if you hate your thighs—a sarong. But what are you supposed to wear on a Friday night to eat fat-free muffins, especially when "fat-free muffin" just might be an insider code phrase for a hot new nightclub called La Muffin? I didn't want to look like I was trying too hard, but I also didn't want to look like I didn't care. It was a fine line.

Just that afternoon, watching the gray-haired Judy (that was #1; #2 had a black frizzy mop) tromp onto the street in a pair of banana yellow sweatpants, I swore to devote at least ten minutes to getting dressed every day and another five to hair and lip-gloss. But I had fifteen minutes now and no idea how to fill them.

None of my new clothes seemed right. I settled on a pair of gray pinstripe pants, belted and safety-pinned to hide their bagginess, and a body-hugging wife-beater tank top—the most normal items in my dad's vast wardrobe. As I was yanking the pants over my hips, someone rapped on my bedroom door.

"One sec!" I said, hobbling to zip up my fly. I would die if that Quinn guy walked in searching for a runaway fisheye lens and beheld my purple padded bra instead.

"I'm not looking," my dad said as his arm poked through the door with the cordless. "For you. It's our favorite boy," he practically shouted.

My father was so embarrassing.

"Hello?"

"Mimi? It's Sam."

"What's up?" I fished around under the bed for the black ballet flats I'd kicked there the day before.

"Listen, what are you up to tonight? There's a party going on. Nona Del Nino's dad is going out to L.A. and we're all crashing his pad."

I grabbed one of Dad's shoes. It was a dandyish thing even I could have gone swimming in: a men's size twelve—too big even for my feet.

"Word is, Nona's parents split up this summer and his mother got screwed in the divorce settlement, so she wants as many of us to come over and do as much damage as possible. It should be a totally hot curtain raiser to the school year, and that's coming from me, not the most enthusiastic of guys. So you'll come."

I crawled around the floor and stuck my whole arm under the bed, only to unearth another pair of gigantic two-toned shoes from who knows when. Finally, I fingered a familiar-feeling shoe, the sneakers I'd worn on the plane. I couldn't possibly. Where were the flats? I thought of the burgundy boots with a shiver.

"You there?" Sam said.

"Yeah," I grunted. "Sorry. I just discovered my dad's secret stash of saddle shoes. He is getting *so* weird with age."

"That's nothing," he said, laughing. "My dad's a huge Whitney Houston fan, loud and proud."

"Shut the fuck up." I remembered Mr. Geckman as the kind of guy who ate his Saturday-morning breakfast in a button-down shirt and blazer. I could not imagine him worshiping that past-her-prime chanteuse for the life of me.

"Dead serious. After getting all her other CDs, he even bought a ten most powerful black women singers compilation to get his hands on an obscure techno remix of 'How Will I Know.' He's in deep."

Once again, I couldn't help thinking about how much life changed in six years. When we lived in New York, Mr. Geckman had been my parents' most pretentious friend by far. The last time I saw him was a couple of years ago, when he and Sam's mother had come to Houston for a wedding. The morning after the festivities, he'd forced me to watch, for five straight hours, a videotaped Japanese puppet production of some beyond boring German opera. Some houseguest—Mr. Geckman wouldn't let me eat lunch until the devil appeared and dragged all thirty-six characters to hell. By the twenty-fifth victim, I was wishing the devil would take me, too.

"Anyway," Sam said, "you game?"

"I would, but I already have plans."

"Oh, really?" he said. "So what are you doing?"

"Yes, really—is that surprising? I told Amanda I'd go out with her, er, to this club."

"Oh," Sam said, chuckling, "The Baldwin squash club's holding a meeting tonight? Wow, don't forget your emergency electrolytes. And if you ever get sick of StairMastering, stop by. It's at Forty-Five Reade Street, in Tribeca. Forty-Five Reade Street. Don't forget."

There was a knock on my door. It was my dad again, gazing moon-faced at my giraffe-like body sprawled across the floor.

"I already told you, I don't think I'll be able to make it."

"I'll leave my cell phone on vibrate in case you get lost," Sam was saying. "Or better—I'll text you the directions."

"Whatever. As if I were allowed to have a cell phone." I hung up.

"The boys are chasing you already." Dad wagged a finger at me. "I knew it wouldn't take long."

I just rolled my eyes. Sometimes it's better not to get into it.

The Gray Dog Café was not exactly a breeding ground for the

young and restless. It was a teashop filled with sad music and people with long, tired, and, well, gray faces. Dogs with nothing better to do after dark. Most of the customers were quiet, intense couples who looked as if they were on the brink of either falling asleep or jumping off the George Washington Bridge.

"Mimi!"

Amanda waved at me from a small round table by the window. She was positioned between two older guys with sideburns, both alone, both with chalk complexions, both angrily scribbling into journals.

"Do you think we should introduce these guys to each other?" I said. "Maybe they could work on a collaborative notebook. That way there would be less bad art and one more free table."

Amanda frowned at me as if I'd asked her to flash her armpit hair. After a pause she took a gingerly sip from a crabgrass-colored teacup.

"This place is full of very interesting artistic types," she observed in the tone of my great-aunt describing the crafts fair that comes to her old folks' home in Sarasota every December. "I think there might be a concert here tonight—they have some *really* cool new acts here. Very up-to-the-minute stuff!"

When the waitress came over and took down my order for a Coke and a regular full-fat double-chocolate muffin, Amanda looked shocked. "You should *really* try the low-fat ones. I swear you can't tell the difference."

"But what if I *like* the difference?" I asked.

"Well, they're *also* high protein—I'm not sure how, but it's totally genius. Don't tell anyone, but sometimes," Amanda said, lowering her voice, "I eat one and *a half.*"

There was no way I could respond to such a shocking confession, so I didn't even try. The minutes dragged on: The longer Amanda and I sat there, the less we had in common. With her perfect teeth, shiny blonde hair, and swimming-pool eyes, she was definitely pretty, but she still made me uncomfortable. Even more than the top-ten least attractive people in New York City surrounding us. My Baldwin bliss slowly began to dim.

She wouldn't stop grilling me about Houston—was I on any teams there? Had I ever sung in a choir? Could you really mountain-bike all year round? Because all my answers inevitably disappointed her, the conversation soon fizzled. Finally, rather than describe my dream wedding dress, I turned the tables. "What did you do this summer?"

"Same old, same old." She gave a long sigh. "I stayed out on the Cape with my family—we belong to this great tennis club there . . . And, oh, I also took private voice lessons and learned how to make these really cool lanyard bracelets!" She flung out her skinny bronzed arm to reveal a wristful of creations. "Key chains, too!"

Then, just when things were getting bad, they got worse. One of the sideburned guys rose and approached the muffin display case, where there was a podium I hadn't noticed before.

"Oh, goodie." Amanda clapped as the man, who was approximately six-foot-seven and weighed eighty-five pounds (sideburns included), tapped on the microphone. His face gleamed with sweat, the café buzzed with irritating feedback, and I pretty much wanted to off myself.

"Hello, all you Gray Dogs," he said in a wannabe sultry voice, wiping his forehead with the tip of his polyester shirttail. "Norm the songwriter couldn't make it here tonight, so I'm going to play a double set. A cappella, if no one objects, he he."

I'd never known what *a cappella* meant, but context clues suggested that it involved playing nursery school rhymes on a recorder while slapping your thigh as though it were a horse's butt.

"Isn't he *sooo* gifted?" My companion was breathless with admiration.

Knowing this wasn't a punch line, I nodded in utter disbelief. Rachel had quite a letter in store for her next week.

"Waitress," Amanda chirped between sets, making that little bring-me-the-check-please gesture in the smoke-free air of the Dog. "We're going to need to split fast," she said. "I told the girls we'd meet at Courtney's for our weekly tradition."

My eyes lit up. Maybe our coffee shop date was just a warmup, or some sort of test? It was only a quarter to ten, after all, early for real New York partying. Could my roof-raising, table-dancing fantasies still become realities?

"Every Friday night," Amanda went on, drawing a red leather wallet from her matching red leather purse, "we eat Twizzlers and drink diet root beer and watch *Night News*. But hurry, it starts in fifteen minutes!" Shrieking, she jumped from her seat, left a five-dollar bill on the counter, and bounded athletically to the kennel door.

I nearly choked, staggering after Amanda. Was it possible that the hot blonde girls burned the midnight lamp with cheesy local newscasters? Was this some kind of joke, some reality TV show tryout?

Amanda and I walked down Carmine Street together, but none of the sights and sounds of Friday night in the Village did much to revive our conversation. As I stealthily tried to steer her toward my doorstep, I felt as if I had just scaled Everest rather than endured open-mike night.

Though I'd hoped Amanda had forgotten her earlier invitation, as we turned onto Barrow she looked at me expectantly. "You coming with?" she asked.

"I wish I could," I said, shaking my head. "But I told my dad I'd be home for *Night News*. Isn't that a weird coincidence? It's our tradition, too."

"But I thought your dad was out tonight?"

"Oh, he is—I mean, was. He's coming back especially for the news," I lied, relieved to have reached our brownstone at last. "Well, here I am—thanks *so* much, Amanda, I had a really great time tonight." My other hobbies include taxidermy and hog farming.

"Oh, well." Amanda sighed, her magazine-perfect features crumpling slightly. "Maybe next week we could all watch it together?"

"Yeah, maybe," I agreed brightly. "But you know how dads can be sometimes."

"Do I *ever!* My dad and I always go to boat shows out on Long Island, and if I even *dreamed* of bringing a friend along . . ."

Safe inside our building, I crouched under the hall table and began counting to five hundred to make sure the coast was clear of Amanda. I don't know why I do stuff like that—too many World War II spy movies as a kid?—but it's not a practice I'd recommend. I remained frozen in place for several long minutes, afraid to breathe and paranoid as all hell. I got Gray Dog bored by forty-six. By seventy-two, I was thumbing the September issue of *Vegetarian Snacking,* which had recently hit the Judys' mail basket. I forced myself to read an entire article on foolproof pumpkin tofu niblets and even the recipe for the E-Z microwave version before I felt it was safe to open the door and head back out into the night.

Using my mini-manhattan map—a grudging last-minute gift from my mother—I navigated to Seventh Avenue, where I could catch the 1 train downtown. The night air was warm, redolent of fresh-fallen leaves and urine. When Amanda was around, I had been too distracted by her annoyingness to appreciate the stunning weather. I really did love New York. My heart went out to poor Rachel, wading through the Houston smog to mail me a letter about her counselor-in-training trysts. Life seemed so much bigger all of a sudden.

At the entrance to the station, I could hear the subway pulling in below me. I raced down the stairs, nearly knocking over a short man selling roasted peanuts. I made it onto the train just as the doors were closing.

Unfortunately, it was only when I arrived at 45 Reade Street that I realized I had no idea which apartment the party was in, and the buzzer directory resembled a catalog of European painters. A disgruntled resident stepped off the elevator to find me looking clueless in the lobby. "Just follow the noise pollution," he grumpily advised.

Now, I'd seen plenty of megarich people's mansions in my day.

The prep school I attended in Houston attracted the offspring of many corrupt businessmen and cowboys who'd stumbled upon oil in their backyard. One kid in my class, Tucker Monton, was the heir to a nationwide chain of discount motels. But I had never in my life visited the home of a real movie star—not even close. Nona's place proved that there's a huge difference between an old Texan guy with an oil well and the star of every hit movie made in the 1970s.

The loft apartment—the penthouse, of course—was jammed with people, so I didn't have much time to take in the decorating scheme. But what I did see completely blew me away. It made powder rooms of all those *Architectural Digest* villas my dad used to photograph. It was the size of the first floor of Macy's and contained almost as much merchandise. There were views of the Manhattan skyline, framed pictures of Nona's dad's parties that had attracted just about every celebrity in America, an IMAX-size flat-screen TV, and—weirdest of all—jade Buddhas everywhere, crowning every shelf and counter and crowding the floor. They seemed right out of an art museum, except that someone had outfitted their shiny bald heads with rhinestone tiaras and their fat necks with feather boas.

This was probably an all–high school party, judging by the girls' chests and the guys' goatees. I was feeling rather lost when I saw Sam waving at me from a spiral staircase, where he was sitting with another guy I vaguely recognized from orientation.

I walked past several of the pimply guys from this morning. They were on a black leather sofa, passing around bottles of champagne. Just as in Texas, nobody was using any glasses, but unlike in Texas, where most parties revolve around beer delivery services and bottles of cheap whiskey concealed in brown paper bags, everybody here was drinking champagne or wine, or champagne in one hand and wine in the other. And, for the record, we're not talking about the grape juice that comes in a box, either.

As I reached the middle of the room, a gigantic man with a diamond stud in his left ear barreled into me. "Piggyback express," he said, and with no further ado lifted me and draped me over his enormous shoulder.

"Hey, leave her alone, Aldo," a mature woman's voice commanded. A few feet below me I saw a middle-aged woman decked out like an expensively dressed lap dancer. "I'm Gayle, Nona's mother," she called up to me, then reproached my escort in a flirtatious tone: "Aldo, you are *such* a monster. Let go of the poor girl this instant!

"Welcome to our happy home," she said as Aldo lowered me back to earth. "It's fabulous you could make it. Do let Aldo get you something to drink—we've got champagne, beer—there's a bartender somewhere. Name your poison."

My reluctance to be served by somebody's mom—even one in a fuchsia halter top—trumped my desire for a drink, so I shook my head. "I'm OK for now, thanks."

"Well, here," Gayle said, handing me an unopened bottle of Veuve Clicquot, which I knew for a fact my own parents had only cracked out once a year, on their wedding anniversary. "Take it. It belongs to Nona's father. If you don't feel like drinking it, you can do whatever you want with it. Like this," she reached into a cabinet, pulled another bottle out, and threw it against a wall.

I kind of wished Rachel were there with me. This would definitely fit into her "Very Entertaining Moments" mental folder. Only a handful of people, six at the most, even glanced over to investigate the disturbance; a lone stoner voice observed, "Whoa."

"She must really have it in for the guy," a model-beautiful girl with a cool Afro said.

"Nona's father and I have a very special relationship—very *complicated,* you could say, ha ha! Oh, hello, darling, let me help you with that!" With a maniacal laugh she rushed toward another guest who was attempting to dislodge a massive candelabra from the white baby grand piano without tripping over Buddha.

By the time I reached Sam, open-mike night at the Gray Dog had faded to a dim memory.

"I *told* you," Sam said, practically gloating. "But why didn't you bring your cell phone?"

"And *I* told *you*—because I don't have a cell phone. My dad said he can lend me his if I need it, but that's about it—it's yet another one of my mother's million rules."

"Well, whatever, I tried calling you back at home, but I ended up talking to some guy who was definitely not your dad. I couldn't understand most of what he said because he was blaring Aretha Franklin right into my ear. What's his name—Queen, did he say?"

"No, no, that was *Quinn*," I said. "He's my dad's new assistant." I looked at the guy on the other side of Sam and felt sure I'd seen him at the welcome meeting this morning. Steeled by the half-gallon of Veuve I'd chugged en route, I gave him an awkward little wave. "Hey, I'm Mimi," I said. "I saw you at orientation this morning."

"Huh? Where?" he responded as if I'd mentioned a chance encounter on one of the moons of Jupiter.

"At Baldwin? This morning? I'm the new girl?"

"Oh, really?" He shrugged, then hoisted himself up from the stairs. "I'm gonna get some liquids. Later."

"What'd I do?" I asked Sam as he edged away. "I don't understand."

"No, don't worry," Sam consoled me. "Jebediah's just going through this funny phase where he's pretending to be an out-of-work actor. Mentioning Baldwin cramps his style."

"But doesn't everyone here go to Baldwin? How could he possibly . . . ?"

"But we're not at Baldwin *now*, Mimi." Sam gestured around the loft. "And the only way to survive Baldwin is to behave as if it doesn't exist. Maybe it doesn't work that way in Texas, but it's a total pillar of the Baldwin educational philosophy. There's a time and a place for everything, natch."

What on *earth* was he talking about? Where was gawky Sam, the one who tied his mother's silk scarves into turbans and pretended to be a rug merchant? Who doodled skateboarding dinosaurs in the margins of his letters? What had happened to the iced tea enthusiast of that very afternoon, and why was he talking in that slow, seen-it-all drawl? I gave him a puzzled, somewhat unfriendly glance, as if to say: *Please tell me what's going on.*

"We *all* do it, Mimi," Sam said in a gentler voice. "Everyone has a very specific role to play out there, and I'm just a guy trying to make it in a cruel, cold world, you know?"

I wasn't appeased: Sam was still being super weird. "No need to get all condescending," I said, as haughtily as I could manage. "It's not the world, but Baldwin, that's wack. I swear, what kind of school's popular crowd rocks out by listening to spoken-word poetry in cheesy smoke-free bars?"

"Wait, wait, wait. Back up. What are you talking about?"

After listening to my blow-by-blow description of the fat-free night on the town with Amanda, Sam exploded in raucous laughter. "Amanda? Did you say *popular* crowd?" he repeated. "You're joking, Mims, *please* tell me you're joking. God, you *have* been home—home on the range—for too long!" He clapped me on the back like a rental Santa Claus.

"Let go of me!" I wriggled away. "What's with this whole making-fun-of-every-single-thing-I-say bullshit? You weren't like this in the fourth grade!"

"Yeah, well, a lot has changed since the fourth grade. If you think Amanda and Courtney are the popular crowd at Baldwin, then you need a lot more than a tour of Brooklyn Heights to teach you about New York. Jeez." He shook his head in disbelief. "*This*, my dear Mims, *this* is Baldwin's popular crowd." Sam drew in his breath, and with his index finger designated only the weirdest-looking people in the room—the mesmerizingly aloof girls from that morning.

His finger stopped at the half-Asian pixie I remembered: the black-eyeliner, hole-in-T-shirt, twenty-rings-in-her-earlobes girl. She was drinking pink liquid out of a martini glass. "Like, take her. That's Vivian. She's about as popular as it gets around here."

I sized up this Vivian girl—her weird body, tiny and curvy at the same time—and compared her to a mental picture of Amanda. It was like a pile of biohazardous material next to a beautiful redwood. "Yeah, right. And she's also the star basketball player."

"I'm serious—Viv's sister Mia, who is now a performance artist in Long Island City, was this *legend* at Baldwin, the most popular girl of all time, in the whole history of the school," Sam insisted. "I'd go so far as to say that Mia was the most popular girl in the whole history of *any* school, the most popular girl in all of *history*. There's not a single person at Baldwin who would disagree—her coolness was legendary. Not that Viv doesn't have enough going for her by herself," he went on. "She has fantastic taste in music. She doesn't care about doing well in school and getting into the same colleges everyone else is competing over. She's deeper than that. And actually, when she's not wearing all that makeup, she can be really . . . you know." Sam paused, swallowed, and studied his lap. "Beautiful." He coughed, then added quickly: "Vivian's half Filipino and half Jewish—the best of both worlds, right?"

I looked at her again, my eyes scanning her face. There was something funny about her nose, which was small and round, like a miniature version of her body; the nose ring puncturing it seemed off-scale. She had big lips that would probably be pretty if they weren't smothered in so much dirt-colored lipstick. I saw that Sam had a point: Vivian *was* kind of beautiful, no matter how much crap was smeared onto—or stuck into—her skin.

"Yeah, whatever," I scoffed. "I'll believe it when I see it. What about *her*?" I pointed at a hefty girl in ripped jeans and a bulky sweatshirt reading I VISITED ROCK CITY, the same one who had worn the NANTUCKET sweatshirt this morning. Both items could've come straight from the Winter 1972 collection of the Judys from upstairs. "Is she another supermodel of the sophomore class?"

"Good job, Mims, you're getting it," Sam nodded. "Lily can be a bit, shall we say, headstrong, but she writes these political opinion columns for the newspaper that even my *dad* thinks are smart. She's a total lefty, which everyone thinks is cool. She's also the daughter of the most famous homemaker in America, so people tend to kiss her ass."

"Give me a break, Sam—if her mom's so famous, how come I've never heard of her?"

"You've never heard of Margaret Morton? The hostess of *House and Home*, celebrated television star and affordable linens endorser? Oh, come on, surely they have cable in Texas these days?"

I was flabbergasted. "Margaret Morton? Are you serious? My mom has every single one of her cookbooks, and my mom's never cooked in her life! *That* girl's mom is Margaret Morton? How could the greatest domestic goddess in America have given birth to *that*?"

"Easy now, calm down," Sam hushed me as a ghoul-faced girl in leather pants and a ripped-up tank top stormed up to Lily. Even with her perfect makeup, Miss Leather Pants resembled an early-eighties girl rock star the morning after a bar brawl.

"Who's *that*?"

"Miss Pia Pazzolini," Sam said. "She can be a tad bitchy, but her parents totally neglect her, so who can blame her? They're diplomats from Italy, which explains why Pia has her own chauffeur and goes out of town twenty-five days a month. She's also some kind of math genius, but she'd wear overalls before admitting it—she's much more into her Eurotrash persona. Hmm, who else?" Sam surveyed the room thoughtfully.

"Oh, yeah, Jess Gillespie," he said, his eyes resting on the exhausted-looking blonde, who was wearing the same sweater set as this morning. "She's the toast of every varsity team at Baldwin. She's the prettiest of the coolie crew, traditionally speaking. I guess." Sam shrugged. "She's *extremely* nice, and not at all in an annoying way, but unfortunately she's also a little insecure—spends too much time thinking about sporting events, if you know what I mean."

Sam winked, but I didn't get it. "Well, isn't that precisely what Amanda and *her* friends do? What's wrong with sports?" (Though, to tell the truth, I wasn't a huge fan.)

"No, no, Mimi, I don't mean athletics, but ath*letes*. Jess is a girl who likes a boy in a letter jacket—not that Baldwin has letter jackets, but you know what I mean. Her boyfriend Preston's one of the dumbest jocks around. She's dated practically every athletic dude in the tri-state area. By the time she's twenty, I'd bet fifty bucks that she'll be married to some world-famous Super Bowl quarterback."

He laughed, and I studied the delicate blonde girl, who was wearing the most conservative job-interview outfit I'd ever seen, far preppier than even the racquetball team. Jess seemed the human equivalent of Connecticut: pretty but bland, symmetrical if forgettable. She looked like the kind of girl who wore matching bras and panties every day of her life. The kind of girl who could get any guy she wanted.

"She's on scholarship," Sam was saying, "which probably explains her unfortunate inferiority complex."

"Um, hello, classism?"

Sam was unapologetic. "*You* know. It must be tough, sharing a tiny apartment in Park Slope with your mom when *those* girls are your best friends. Seriously. Vivian's dad, George Steinmann, is on the news like every night, raging about corporate scandals, and meanwhile the guy's buying oil companies in his spare time. And Lily's mom is, well, *Margaret Morton*, and Pia's parents are crazy Eurotrash ambassadors who are so busy partying they probably don't even look at the newspaper. And Jess is . . ." Sam threw up his shoulders. "Well, she may be hot, but wouldn't *you* feel shitty if your dad never paid alimony and your mom worked in a bank? And I don't mean investment bank, either. She's, like, one step above a teller. And, last but not least, there's our hostess—"

"Um, excuse me, but how do you know all these intimate personal details of everyone's lives?"

Sam became grave again. "At Baldwin," he announced, "we all

know *everything*. But, ahem, as I was saying"—he cleared his throat—"there's one more member of the clique—a girl to give royalty an inferiority complex. Our hostess: the lovely Miss Nona Del Nino."

She needed no further introduction. In one synchronized motion, Sam and I turned to watch the dreadlocked girl, who was leaning languidly into the DJ booth. With her creamy skin and overblown lips, she was totally and completely gorgeous in an obvious, uncomplicated way. Why hadn't I seen it this morning? Probably too preoccupied with my own wardrobe difficulties. All of a sudden my throat clenched up. Even without an Academy Award–winning father, this girl would've been special. "And she's the most popular girl at Baldwin?"

Sam's tone was reverential. "Just watch her. *Watch* the way she works it."

For a few minutes neither of us spoke. We just sat there, drinking in Nona's splendor as her hips swayed carelessly to the music and her eyelids continually drooped and raised themselves, like automatic window shades going berserk. Any lesser being gyrating solo to a trashy techno remix would have looked like a total loser, but this girl could pull anything off. She was a goddess in her own living room. I don't know *what* this girl had, but I wanted it.

"She *is* pretty amazing," I sighed. "Do you think I should go and introduce myself? Maybe she'll fall for my new-girl-in-town routine?" (I'm not usually that outgoing—not at all—but by that point I'd polished off a half bottle of bubbly and all I'd eaten for dinner was a chunk of chocolate muffin.)

"Not so fast, Mims. You don't just go up to Nona Del Nino and *talk* to her." As Sam spoke, a tall guy in a hooded sweatshirt approached Nona and pressed something into her palm. Nona was looking at him with an intensity that expressed profound appreciation. He was a normal-looking guy, with baggy jeans, a hooded sweatshirt, and a backwards Yankees cap. I was pretty sure he was giving her drugs. Not pot, either. This was pretty clearly *drugs* drugs.

"Should I go introduce myself to her?"

"Darlin', the rule is pretty simple: you do not talk to Nona unless you're one of the four other popular girls in the grade. Or if you're delivering her illegal goodies—in which case she might acknowledge you for a split second or two," Sam said, pointing at Nona right as she turned her back on the hooded guy.

"How's that possible?" I asked. "Like it's so formal!"

"Yep—for a hyperliberal institution like Baldwin, the politics of popularity couldn't get any more formal. Allow me to fill you in on a little something," Sam said, taking this opportunity to lean toward me again. "Every year, the most popular girls of the sophomore class go on a Christmas break vacation together—the same destination every year, and always top secret."

"Where do they go?"

"How would I know? Am *I* one of the popular girls? It's highly confidential, I said—a tradition that traces back to the beginning of time. Each year the junior girl who led the previous group tells the new chosen ones."

"But who chooses? How does the junior girl know who the popular sophomores are?"

"Mims, what makes the rivers flow to the sea? She just *does*."

"Well," I said, bristling, "I'll have to find out. I'm going to be chosen."

I don't know why I said it, and Sam seemed to think this claim the most hilarious thing he'd ever heard. "Mims, I don't know how to break this to you gently, but it's just not going to happen. You know *I* think you're swell, but convincing the rest of the student body might take a little more work. Not to be crude, but if your dad were some big-deal photographer, you might have a chance attracting friends—you could bring them to cool parties at modeling agents' houses or other equally thrilling events. But as things stand, what can you *do* for these people? You're not rich or powerful or—no offense—a dead-ringer for Grace Kelly." Sam used his chin to gesture at the crowd, which was quite elegant considering that it consisted of drunk sixteen-year-olds and one very angry middle-aged mom. "Invite them to your dad's dark-room?"

"How dare you!"

"Apart from me, you don't know anyone in the city. You don't have any friends at other private schools who might invite you to parties. You don't have any cool ex-boyfriends who can get you into clubs. Your dad doesn't have a country house, or even a townhouse. Your southern girl thing could be somewhat unique, but I wouldn't bank on it." Sam considered. "It's too bad you weren't *born* down in Texas—that might've been more of a selling point. Authenticity goes a long way before hollow eyes."

"Just so you know, Sam, a lot has changed since the fourth

grade! I wasn't exactly a total social reject at my last school." Granted, Rachel and my older sister's party-girl reputations had always come in handy bigtime, but still, I had been popular in Texas, extremely. Or popular enough. Popular with potential.

Sam encircled my shoulder again. "Look, I'm not trying to be a hard-ass, but there's a difference between lording over a bunch of prepubescent Texan debutantes and getting in with, well— with *these* people."

I shoved him off again. "I can wear dark eyeliner with the best of them! You really think I'm not cool enough for this stupid wacked-out school?"

"Nothing personal, Mims. It's just that . . . no, I don't."

I had never been more insulted in my life. "This is unbeliev-able! You have no idea how cool I've become! You don't know what you're talking about. I'll bet some of the biggest dorks at Baldwin come from powerful families with more country houses and tennis club memberships than you can count. But none of that automatically gets them past the velvet ropes. You can't think I'm so stupid I'd believe that."

"Wanna bet?" Sam asked, an obnoxious grin spreading from ear to oversize ear.

I leaped off the stairs and, thrusting out my arm at him, exclaimed, "As a matter of fact, I do."

"It was just a figure of speech," Sam said, "but all-righty then, if you insist. You really think you'll score an invitation to spend Christmas break with the cool girls—or, as everyone at Baldwin calls them, the Coolies? No offense, but no way in *hell*.

Nope, I bet that Amanda ends up becoming your best friend and that you'll never be able to give her the old heave-ho. You'll spend Christmas locked up in a squash court!"

"As *if.*" I never remembered hating him like this in the fourth grade.

"But wait, what are we betting here, by the way?" Sam pulled his hand away abruptly. "What are the stakes?"

While I was trying to think up a wager, Amanda and the rest of the squash team blazed into focus. Five blonde ponytails wagged in synchronized horror at Gayle Del Nino's ritual champagne offering. I felt drunk, headachy, humiliated, confused. "Amanda," I groaned. "*Shit.*"

"You didn't see her? She and her posse rolled in about fifteen minutes ago."

"Oh, *no* . . . Sam, I totally lied to her about tonight!" The old heave-ho, I was thinking, and then, suddenly, I no longer cared. Amanda might as well know, sooner rather than later, how much I disliked organized sports. An evil idea possessed me, and I was in no condition to reject it. "I bet you Amanda," I said. "If you win, I have to spend two whole months being her best friend."

"Ouch, that's a little harsh, but OK, fine. And if you win?"

I rubbed my hands together, an evil scientist at work. "You'll love this. You'll have to be her boyfriend for two months. Not that you could get her if your life depended on it. But you have to try. And if she has the good sense to say no, you'll have to ask her out every day in a place in Baldwin's hallways where I can overhear it. All of it."

Sam's jaw dropped. "That's evil!"

"What's the problem, Sam—it's not like I'm going to get invited on the winter break, is it? No way in hell, isn't that how you put it? I might as well buy a squash racquet now, right?"

Sam rocked with laughter again. "That's true, I forgot . . . OK, then, you got yourself a deal."

"I already know that I'm going, but if you want to wait until I'm on the beach with them, or wherever it is they go, that's cool by me."

Even as we were shaking hands, I became aware of the massive stupidity of my boast—the ridiculousness of our bet. My mother has always warned me that actions taken in anger lead to our undoing, but I have always had a nasty habit of ignoring my mother's warnings. Before I could recant, someone pinched my elbow. "Mimi, hey!" It was Amanda, standing with her mouth approximately a millimeter from my eardrum and hollering right into it. It looked as if she was trying to figure out if her feelings should be hurt. "What's up? I thought you were going to stay in with your dad!"

"I was—uh, I did—but then, well, he likes to go to sleep right after *News Night*. Sometimes the issues really bring him down?" I refused to meet her expectant blue eyes.

"Yeah, I know what you mean." Amanda pursed her lips in sympathy. "That exposé on the lives of Russian mafia girlfriends was such a total downer, didn't you think? I, like, practically burst into tears. Wasn't it so sad?"

"Yeah, totally. Totally sad."

"That's why we decided to come, too, to boost our spirits! What a relief you made it, too! And how about a high-five, because guess *what*? Courtney went wild at Key Food and bought all the supplies to make fat-free ice cream sundaes! The girls are in the kitchen. Come on," she said, tugging at my wrist. As I turned away from Sam, he mouthed something at me and winked. It wasn't until I entered the kitchen and saw Ivy unloading a bag of fat-free chocolate syrups and low-carb whipped creams that I deciphered Sam's silent message:

SOCIAL SUICIDE.

September 23
7:43 a.m.

Dear Diary,

Dear Diary? ("Dear Sam" is probably more appropriate, but I'm supposed to be keeping a diary, so . . .) Hmm. Is that how you're supposed to start a diary entry, or is that just the way it happens on low-budget sitcoms? Does anyone even keep a diary in real life? I'm going to have to come up with a better sign-in. Starting off with "Dear Diary" is serious cruising for a bruising—if this notebook lands in the wrong hands, there's no way its contents will go unread.

September 23
7:48 a.m.

Hi.
(How's that? Any better? Not much.)

What's up, D-man?

(Double lame.)

How's it hanging, Mr. D?

(This is embarrassing. I haven't gotten any sleep and I'm cracking bad jokes for my own benefit.)

I'm supposed to scribble in here to keep track of my initiation into the Coolie crowd: Sam's orders. You'd think he could come up with better reading material, but whatever. (Hi, Sam! Nice shirt! Ha!) In a way, I feel less self-conscious about the whole journal-keeping exercise when I know that someone else will be reading it. Just like writing letters, huh? Hmm. Not quite sure where to begin. It's fair to say I've made significant progress. Just twelve hours ago, I was at a Joan Baez sit-in with Tasti D-Dork, and since then I've clinked champagne bottles with Albert Del Nino's wife—not bad for my first twenty-four hours at Baldwin, right? Not that great, either. I now have three months to convince the weirdest, scariest, and coolest girls in New York City that they want me to join their inner ring. Total cinch, right? Right? Hello? Come on, Dr. D. I need some support.

The bet itself is a bit of a blur: Sam and I made it last night, at Nona's bash. Jesus, I can't believe I'm up so early. Is it possible I only got four hours of sleep? All right. No offense, but I'd better get this diary thing over with, so here goes. After long hours of tossing and turning, I've decided that the only way to crack this clique is to be incredibly systematic about everything. Sam agreed (hi again!). So, hmm, plan of attack. I guess my main goal is to remember who the Coolies are. What if there's another group at Baldwin whose members look like a tribe of apes applied their eye makeup? That could get very confusing. Come to think of it, maybe I should spend this weekend learning how to wear eye makeup. Note to Mimi: Buy something black to smudge all over your face. But first shower. Or not (I doubt any of the Coolies are in the Clean Girl Club). No, first figure out why there's an open bag of Fritos stuck under your pillow. Or no, even that can wait. Night, night, D-Lover. Or morning, morning. Or morning, night. Whatever.

Civilization for Beginners

Proud to be one of the first progressive schools in America, Baldwin is constantly reviewing its curriculum, hoping to stay one step more progressive than everybody else. They have an antigrading policy, which basically means that if you get a 45 percent on an algebra test, your teacher will pencil "Getting there!" or "Very interesting interpretation!" on your paper. In short, there's no such thing as failure, only "room for growth." Sam told me that the teachers' "year-end reports" resemble those album reviews that spill a thousand adjectives without ever telling you if you should buy it or not.

Sometime in the early nineties, the school combined the English, history, and fine arts departments with the intention of "debunking the Dead White Man Learning Curve." As a consequence, most Baldwinites graduate knowing everything about Andy Warhol's lovers and the best turpentine for thinning out oil paint but nothing about the difference between Socrates and George Washington. I thought of my mother's two-books-per-week workload with some gratitude right then.

Presiding over our World Civ class was a man named Stanley. For a teacher, he was fairly young, in his mid- to late twenties, with a slim build and corn-colored hair that was already starting to thin on top. While his face was pretty nondescript (with the exception of sharp blue eyes that never blinked), his outfit was truly loud: an argyle cardigan, red bow tie, and construction-cone orange chinos. His speaking manner was gentle, sometimes inaudibly so.

The class's "agenda" involved our exploring a different "zone" every month (Stanley found the word *country* offensive). After learning about the zone's history, poetry, and pottery, the whole class took a field trip to Montague Street to eat at the ethnic restaurant most similar to the featured zone. I was glad that September's zone was China because I love, love egg rolls.

"Did the Ming dynasty come before or after the Ting dynasty?" Frank Abrahams called out, interrupting Stanley. (Stanley discouraged hand raising and the feudal ageism it connoted.) Frank, who had been preparing for college entrance exams since the womb, had a different binder for each of his classes and took at least a dozen pages of notes an hour. (There is one in every class, even at the most progressive school in the nation.)

"Which one came before?" Stanley repeated in his radio therapist murmur. "I'm curious, Frank, why do you bring that up?"

"I'm just trying to get it straight in my notes?"

"Do we Baldwinites reduce history to dates?" Stanley scanned the classroom imploringly.

"Uh," Frank blushed, "no?"

"No *way*," a kid named Arthur Gray—I remembered him

from the orientation meeting—added emphatically. Arthur was sitting next to the hottest guy in the class, a broody arty type named Max Roth.

"Correct!" Stanley cheered, missing Arthur's sarcastic eye roll. "Why worry about details when you can concentrate on . . . on? Anybody have an idea?"

Even I knew that the correct response was "aura," Stanley's all-time favorite word, but before Frank could volunteer it, there was a loud clunk in the back of the room—a clunk that had nothing to do with either the Ming or Ting dynasty.

Turning around, I saw Nona's dreadlocks dangling like a waterfall over her desk. Vivian began hissing, "Nona! Nona!" so loudly that everyone except Stanley, who could lecture through nuclear fallout, was staring at the most popular girl in the sophomore class. Nona seemed to be unconscious, her face smooshed against the graffitied surface of the desk like a melting scoop of ice cream.

Lily Morton, a model of efficiency in her Sacramento Kings sweatshirt, yanked at one of Nona's dreadlocks. Then, receiving no response, she levered herself forward to hoist Nona upright.

That was when we saw her face. Her beautiful face. But it wasn't that morning: her skin was drained of all color, and her eyes were bugged open but rolled upward, with only disgusting egg-white blobs showing. Someone screamed. It was Courtney Sisler, second in command to Amanda in the Tasti D-Lite crew.

"Stanley, Stanley!" She was totally freaking out.

"Shh!" Lily made a slicing gesture against her throat, but it was too late. Chaos had erupted. Stanley knew something was up.

"I'm going to get the nurse," Courtney whined. "Please, can't I? This girl needs help! I think she overdosed!"

The rest of the morning was straight out of an emergency room drama, what with the stretcher, the sirens, and the weeping fellow World Civ students. Zora Blanchard even called a "crisis" assembly in the twelfth-floor gym (there was an African dance recital going on in the lobby), where she treated us to an improvised lecture on "communities of healing."

The wildest thing happened right after lunch. I'd been hanging out by the school's entrance, answering the theater crowd's questions about the drama in World Civ, since none of them got to see it in person. Though it was obvious that none of my interrogators had ever spoken to Nona before, they were all talking about her possessively, even competitively.

"This summer was particularly hard for her," one blobby girl observed. "With her parents splitting up and all. And that story they ran in all those magazines—that must've been really tough."

"My dad saw her in his AA meeting," contributed a short girl with frizzy orange hair.

"But tell us," a kid named Nathan urged me, "is it true that Stanley thought she was dead?"

"You should have seen Stanley—" I was about to elaborate when a screeching sound silenced me. The instant the white stretch limo squealed to a halt in front of the school, Gayle Del Nino materialized and headed straight for the main entrance. She was wearing a low-cut fringed suede dress that displayed her retired-supermodel calves splendidly, but her skin was drained of all color and it looked as if she'd smeared a marker under her eyes. Probably just waterproof mascara.

"Hold on," I said, and ran after Mrs. Del Nino. I had to see what was going on.

She crossed the main lobby and burst into Zora Blanchard's office. The door slammed closed just as Mrs. Del Nino began shrieking expletives about Baldwin and the irresponsible nitwits who ran it.

School let out early after another crisis assembly, leaving Sam and me to analyze the Fall of Nona Del Nino over falafel.

"Oh, whatever," Sam scoffed. "She'll just be locked up in one of those country club rehab centers upstate for a few months, where she'll get engaged to some recovering sex addict, and then, once the shrink breaks that up, she'll reemerge just as fucked up, the only difference being that now she goes to an all-girls school on the Upper East Side. It happens all the time at Baldwin, Mims, a classic rite of passage around here. Regular as the changing of the seasons."

I was traumatized, but Sam kept insisting that Nona's breakdown improved my chances with the in crowd: "They have an unexpected opening, so start scheming fast."

I thought him heartless to mention our stupid bet when the health of the most powerful girl at Baldwin was in jeopardy.

"Sam, this is *not* the time for social scheming. If you were there in World Civ, you'd understand. I'm still totally shaken. In Houston a few years ago, Rachel overdid it on cocktails at a bar mitzvah. She had to go to the hospital, and we all thought she wasn't going to pull through. But this is something complete—"

I would have continued if I hadn't looked across the table to see Sam smirking.

"Sam, must you *always* be such a jerk?"

To tell the truth, over the weekend I'd resolved to call the whole thing off, but right then, with Sam making fun of my distress, I had no choice but to grit my teeth and hold my tongue. The bet was on.

But Nona's collapse really had rattled me. Before the World Civ debacle, I'd felt ready to dip my toes into the mysterious waters of Baldwin, but a bona fide drug overdose was beyond my experience. Would I really find no niche at Baldwin—was I fated to pal around with Amanda, whose overdoses were limited to Diet Coke and fat-free marshmallows?

When I came home from school that day, my missing luggage was waiting inside the entry hall, but I was too traumatized to unpack with any enthusiasm. The next morning in World Civ, my numbness persisted. As Stanley, pretending nothing had gone wrong the day before, lightheartedly impersonated a palm reader to enliven our discussion of Confucius, I felt incredibly sad. I wasn't the only one to sense a void in the back of the class. Vivian's eyes were more raccoonlike than usual, and Lily had worn a black sweatshirt. In Creative Writing that afternoon, I saw that Pia and Jess were somberly attired as well.

"Mimi?" Kim came up to me toward the tail end of this extremely boring inner-selves-exploring session. Though she was approximately eighty-nine years old, Kim was another teacher who rejected "hierarchical dishonesties" by using her first name. "Can I have a word with you after class?"

"Sure," I squeaked, crimsoning as every single person in the class turned to look at me. I had no idea why I was in trouble.

"Mimi," Kim whispered after my lucky classmates had filed out, "I just wanted to tell you how much I *loved* your prized possession essay—so original, comparing your cat to a cheeseburger like that! It was so clever."

"Oh, thanks?" I said. Was she joking? I had composed the essay about Simon in exactly twelve minutes the night before, while detailing the Nona episode to Rachel on the phone. "Is that why you wanted to see me?"

"You have such a *voice*, Mimi, such a *perspective*. So, I hope you don't mind, but I took the liberty of xeroxing your essay and passing it along to Lily Morton, who's the sophomore editor at the *Baldwin Bugle*. They're looking for new underclassman talent, and I thought you'd be absolutely—"

"You *what*? You showed that essay—the essay about my *cat*—to Lily? Lily Morton?" Lily Morton, as in daughter of domestic goddess extraordinaire Margaret Morton? Cool-girl, Nona-intimate, no-nonsense Lily Morton? Lily Morton read my essay in which I compared my cat to a double cheddar cheeseburger—with a pickle on the side, no less? I blinked at the laptop-size amethyst hanging from Kim's neck and considered all the ways I'd like to strangle her. "Why didn't you just shoot me?" I muttered.

"Now, Mimi, no need to be so modest! Embrace your gift of

expression—use it, don't abuse it! Lily liked your essay so much, sweetie, that she asked me to invite you to stop by the newspaper office after school today. Isn't that *wonderful*?"

An hour later, I was standing across a big drafting table from Lily, who looked, if possible, even less glamorous than she had that morning in World Civ. She had a pencil stuck behind her ear and red ink stains all over her fingers.

"I'm so sorry," I faltered. "I've never been more humiliated in my life. Kim's a total freak show, and she feels sorry for me because I'm the new girl. I only wrote that stupid essay about my cat and the cheddar because I thought the whole assignment was so stupid . . ."

I must've babbled for a full five minutes, but Lily never once looked up—she was too busy frowning over a headline sheet, murmuring different possibilities to herself. I felt like a human scab. Only after I'd edged to the door, mumbling, "OK then, glad we cleared that up" under my breath, did Lily drop her red editing pen.

"So do you want to write for us or not?" she demanded.

"Do I—? God, I don't know. Sure?"

"Great," she said unenthusiastically. "What's your journalistic experience, anyway? Do you primarily cover pet shows?"

"Pet shows? Well, hmm, I've never—"

"It was a joke, hello? The cat?"

I was saved right then by the office door springing open behind me.

"Hi, Lily, hey!" a girl bearing a remarkable resemblance to my new editor exclaimed.

Lily's eyes hit the page again. "Oh, hey, Tammy."

"Hey, Lily, I was wondering if you had any openings on the Features page yet? Like, I was thinking I could do love horoscopes or something? Because this summer in Provincetown, I read a whole book about it? On astrology?"

This Tammy girl had the most annoying voice I've ever heard, plus she was very near panting.

"Sorry," Lily said, not sounding it. "All filled up again—better luck next year. Blame it on the new girl," she motioned to me. "She snagged the last available space. She's writing a column on outsider impressions of this crazy place we call Baldwin."

I beamed pathetically. I was?

"Oh, OK. Shoot! I thought high school would be different, but I guess I'm still always one step behind, huh?"

"You sure are," Lily allowed.

"*C'est la vie*, that's what my mom always says! So what about getting a coffee, huh, Lily? A mocha frappe? Or, if you're busy, I could just, you know, get you one?"

"Actually, new girl and I—" Lily looped the table, then, laying her hand on my back, started to tell Miss Annoying about our longstanding plans. "We actually have appointments to get fake IDs this afternoon." I looked at my new editor in disbelief. "We're going to some NYU student's lab. At four-thirty, so we should get a move on, huh, new girl?"

I nodded, too thrilled to care that she had no idea what my name was. "Didn't he say we should get there by four-fifteen?"

"Oh!" Tammy simpered. "Fake IDs, how neat! Do you think I could get a fake ID, too?"

"I am *so* sorry, Tammy. Unfortunately they don't take walk-ins, so I had to make this appointment *months* ago. The waiting list is longer than Princeton's, apparently—this place is so professional that they give you a fake blood type and everything. They even ask you about organ donation to make the licenses completely authentic." Rather than deal with the wreckage of Tammy's face, Lily turned to me. "Four-fifteen, did you say? Shit, we're going to have to take a cab."

"A very fast one."

We hailed one on Clinton Street. I had no clue what was going on as Lily pulled her cell phone from her backpack and got to business.

Identity Crisis

OUR CAB BLAZED ACROSS THE BROOKLYN BRIDGE, bouncing between lanes like a little white ball at a Ping-Pong tournament. I was terrified, but I noticed that, no matter how wild the driving, Lily's posture remained impossibly stiff. She wasn't the most fashionable or beautiful of the girls, not by a long shot, but she was self-confident in a strangely powerful way. She had this talent for making me doubt my whole existence, even when I was sitting six inches from her, close enough to notice that she smelled icy, like expensive men's deodorant. I made a mental note to chuck the geeky For-Teens roll-on I'd bought just before leaving Houston.

"Got it? Good!" she barked, ending her second phone call.

The cab screeched between a beat-up Miata and a red van and I flew forward, slamming my hands against the glass divider. To curb my dizziness, I looked down at the floor, the only thing in the cab (apart from Lily) not spinning at an insane speed. Then and only then did I remember the heinous burgundy cowboy boots I'd forgotten to remove that morning. For about the tenth time that day, I wanted to jump off a cliff.

I had tried the boots on for my dad only out of pity, but when

Quinn cruised into the apartment earlier than usual, wearing nothing but tight jeans and a muscle T that showcased his perfect six-pack, I got too flustered to deal and left for school. I hadn't even noticed my fashion felony until World Civ.

This was just great. Here I was, alone for the first time with Lily, the heiress to the most powerful finger food empire in America, and I was decked out in deep red cowboy boots that were several sizes too large for my already gigantic cruise ships (as my sister called them). I crossed my legs to hide one beneath the other—the best compromise I could manage.

"Look, I *know* we weren't planning on going until tomorrow." Lily sounded really annoyed. "But plans change, all right?"

She pressed her phone between her right shoulder and right ear, freeing her hands so that she could remove a black leather Filofax from her backpack. Without looking at me, she plucked a University of Delaware ID card from one of the credit card slots and tossed it at me. Though I tried to handle the laminated card as casually as possible, I'm sure it was beyond obvious that I'd never so much as touched a fake ID before in my life. Luckily, Lily was paying absolutely no attention to me.

"Not bad," I said, examining the picture of Monica Reubens, who looked exactly like Lily, only with chin-length hair and a huge zit on one of her cheeks.

Lily covered the mouthpiece and shrugged. "I got it done eons ago—almost two years. With my birthday this weekend, I'll be twenty-three, so I decided to get an updated version. Bouncers get suspicious when you get *that* old. Oh, hold on—" she said to me, cutting herself off suddenly to scream into the phone. "*You* call Jess, then! She's probably doing something idiotic with Preston—but whatever, find her! She needs to come. No ifs, ands, or buts. Got it?" Lily snapped the phone shut in indignation. Her mother's entrepreneurial gene was beginning to surface. "Jess has the *worst* taste in men," she murmured afterward, more to herself than to me.

We looked out the windows in silence for several traffic lights. By the time Lily remembered my existence again, we were already on the Lower East Side. "You know, I didn't even get your name."

"Mimi," I said, wishing my big red boots would evaporate like Monica Reubens's zit had. "Mimi Schulman?"

Lily scrutinized me. "Cool," she declared.

"Cool?"

"Your name. Mimi. I don't know any others."

Could've fooled me. When we stepped out of the cab at Comida de Maria, apparently the fake-ID bodega, Pia was already propped against the deli window, her face assuming the bored-looking scowl that I, in my brief time observing her, already identified as her trademark. Her long dark hair was arranged in some complicated-looking up-do, and her arms were crossed over a full-length black leather coat that must have cost considerably more than my parents' car in Houston. She had on a pair of stiletto boots that made my Annie Oakley getup even more embarrassing.

"I really appreciate your being here on time," she said, greeting us with a grimace. "Thanks to you, I've been verbally molested by seven different guys."

"Oh, spare me, would you," Lily said. "You wouldn't be wearing that push-up bra if you didn't *love* that shit."

Pia made a tsk-tsk sound and stomped after Lily into the deli.

"We have to pretend we're just regular customers," Lily advised in a low voice. "They're super anal about getting busted by the cops, so no loitering. Pretend we're shopping for a dinner party."

"In *this* dump?" Pia curled up her lip in disgust.

Muting the Spanish soap opera on TV, the man behind the counter carefully monitored our efforts to locate paper towels and American cheese. All three of us were relieved when the store's sensor ding-donged twice, signaling Jess's arrival.

"Here we are," called Jess from the other end of the aisle, breezing into the bodega with Vivian trailing a few steps behind her. Jess looked too fresh-faced and celestial for that grimy setting, but Viv was right at home.

"Fresh from Rollerblading? Or was it Buffalo wings happy hour at Applebees?" teased Pia without breaking into a smile.

Vivian smacked her lips and poked a twenty-five-cent bag of miniature cinnamon glazed donuts. "Mmph, I bet those are *so* good," she murmured.

Pia snatched the doughnuts and like a magician made them disappear into her purse. I gaped at her, and she seemed to notice me for the first time. "Who's *this*?" she asked, not overly kindly.

Viv, as if cued, glared at me from behind Pia.

"Oh, this is the new girl," Lily said. "Her name's—"

"Mimi," I said before she could forget.

"I remembered," Lily said. "It's a good name."

I smiled desperately at the four girls. None smiled back.

"This had *better* be important," Jess snapped, looking rumpled in a man's undershirt and tight gray pants. "Preston's parents are out of town for tonight only, and we were having a pretty good time."

Lily ignored her and accosted the guy behind the counter. "We're here to see Hernan," she announced.

From his side of bulletproof glass, the potbellied man eyed us suspiciously. Once assured that we were authentic fifteen-year-old brats and not undercover detectives, he led us into the storeroom.

"Try to look tired in your picture," Lily told me as I stepped behind a curtain. "It ages you."

In the back of the dark corridor stood a little man—Hernan, I assumed—with a camera that looked exactly like Dad's beloved 1976 Polaroid. Twenty minutes later, the five of us emerged with new laminated identities—all for the startling price of seventy-five dollars each. When I confessed that I didn't have that much cash on me (I've never had that much cash on me in my life), Pia just shrugged and forked over the money for mine, too. She then looked at Jess—the only one besides me who didn't have an ATM card—and asked, "Shall I?"

Jess, sheepish, shook her head: "No, thanks, Viv's covering me today."

Pia told me I could pay her back "whenever." I felt awful, but I could tell Pia wasn't even trying to be nice—she just plain didn't care. Sooner or later, I'd have to hit Dad up for more lunch money and gently inform him that the fifty dollars a week allowance we'd previously settled on might have to be adjusted for teenage inflation.

But the embarrassing loan was worth it. I was Carmella Rothman, hailing from Eau Claire, Wisconsin. Carmella Rothman looked exactly like an exhausted fifteen-year-old with two black eyes.

"Lemme see that," Vivian said, grabbing my freshly pressed card. "You know who you look like? It sounds crazy, but in this picture you sort of remind me of that Russian model who's the next big thing."

"That is just *so* not true." Pia looked appalled. "Hello, have you ever read a fashion magazine in your whole life?"

My face burned. So *this* was how she extracted payment for the seventy-five-dollar loan, by humiliating me and saying I looked nothing like a professionally pretty woman?

"I just read the new *Loaded*," Pia went on. "She's *so* not Russian, she's *Ukrainian*." She slit her eyes, looking from me to the picture. "But you're right. There is a resemblance. And P.S., your boots are completely the shit."

"Oh." I gulped.

"That's the highest compliment in Pia's book," Lily told me under her breath.

And just like that Carmella Rothman's cheeks matched her dark red leather boots.

NYPD Blues

WE WERE SITTING UNDER THE BROOKLYN BRIDGE, halfway through our third round of Corona Light, when the cops rolled up. Talk about unexpected guests. We didn't even have a chance to toss our bottles into the river.

The car door slammed shut and a very large law enforcement officer thundered toward us. My mind was reeling. One week in New York and I was going to court. Even if I stayed out of jail, at the very least I'd be shipped back to Houston, where I'd be forced to watch Maurice experiment with drywall solutions and sample nasal inhalants while my mother fretted about my super-ego. Myrtle would take over my bedroom and borrow my razor to shave her armpits. It was all over. And worse—I'd blown my one shot at big-city popularity. Sam would laugh in my face. My father would never forgive me. I might never see Quinn again. I felt a coma coming on.

And I wasn't the only one losing my shit. Pia's Tupperware-tight jaw had dropped to her faux fur neckline. Vivian whispered, "I think I'm gonna pee." And Lily actually moaned in distress. Only Jess was reacting calmly. From the corner of my eye I saw her rolling up her T-shirt to expose her impressive abdominal rack. I *had* to start working out, or at least getting off the subway one stop early.

The cop was ugly and hairy and huge. Completely ignoring Jess's superior midriff, he planted himself in the middle of our cocktail party. His partner leered from the passenger seat.

"Afternoon, ladies—or should I say *girls*?" It wasn't a friendly greeting. "Forgive me for crashing your party, but you should know better than to hold private meetings in public places. Especially in daylight. What have we got here?" He snatched my beer, sniffed at the bottle, screwed up his face in disgust.

OK, we got the point. Light beer was nasty, but so was his waistline. He was a walrus on two legs.

"Let's see some identification!"

This was getting really scary. We hadn't had our IDs for an hour—we hadn't even used them at night. No one moved. Someone had to do something. I wanted only to run for my life. My heart racing beyond belief, I opened my eyes huge and batted my lashes. "Mistah," I drawled, switching on the Texan twang I perfected not in Houston but as a child in New York watching *Dallas* reruns with my dad. "Ah'm tahrubly sawhruh, but won't ya tell us what on *er-yuhth* we're a-doin' wrong?"

I actually said "a-doin'," I'm not kidding. It was so un-me. Though of course I was shaking in my boots, a tiny part of me felt as glamorous as the star of every single thirties movie that my dad and I watched way too many times. I felt like Marlene Dietrich and Barbara Stanwyck and Mae West all rolled into one. I felt— drunk. What had I eaten that day? Could the answer really be just a pumpernickel bagel in the morning? "We were just having a nice cool refray-yush-munt, Officer—isn't it so *hawt*?"

"You girls aren't from around here, are you?" Lieutenant Fatass asked, skyscraper shoulders sinking just a little.

"Oh, no, suh, we've nevah be-en to a big city like *this* before," I said. "We're from Petunia, Texas—our glee club won a competition. A jambuhree?"

Instead of chiming in, my new friends stared at me as if I'd dropped into Brooklyn Heights from Saturn.

"It's our church group," I continued. "We just won a big statewide pageant. And this is our prize—an all-expainse-paid trip he-uh-ere, in the—the *greatest* citee in the greatest cuuhntry in Amaireeca!" The more I slurred my words, the more terrified I felt, especially after remembering midway through saying "expainse" that Carmen Rothman hailed from Eau Claire, Wisconsin, not Petunia, Texas, and that Petunia, Texas, was not only not the name of a real town but didn't even sound remotely—

"Well, ladies, I hate to break it to you," the officer interrupted, shaking his bloated head, "but we've got some stricter open container laws here than in, where'd you say, Tulip?"

With a peaceful hand motion, the officer dropped his notebook—just like that. After that, the officer tucked our unopened six-pack under a chubby arm. Plucking our bottles out of our hands, he poured the contents out onto the sidewalk and tossed the bottles into a dumpster.

"Welcome to the Big Apple," he said, shoving his massive

body back into the patrol car. "I'd stay with Coca-Cola if I were you." After exchanging a few words with his partner—poof!—he vanished. And that was it. Our criminal records remained clean.

When I recovered consciousness, my palms were sweating and I wanted to pee all over the sidewalk. With a final tremor of fear, I raised my eyes to the shining faces surrounding me.

"Oh. My. God."

"That was *so* cool."

"Mimi, you said your name was?"

"Oh. My. God."

"You deserve, like, every Oscar there is."

"My sister's having this performance art event on Lorimer Street this weekend. You *have* to come."

If real life had turned into an inspirational teen movie right then, I was playing the geeky bespectacled tuba player who miraculously puts on a strapless dress, picks up the electric guitar, and rocks out at the homecoming dance. The hot drummer would be checking me out with new ideas about my desirability, my working-class friends out on the dance floor would dissolve into tears, and the entire crowd would be repeating my name over and over like some yoga chant, and I'd live on in my fans'—and the hot drummer's—hearts forever.

It was that good, I swear. I couldn't *wait* to tell Sam.

September 20-something-or-other (Sorry, I am too tired to keep track.)
8:55 p.m.

Hey there, D-Baby. Can I just say, there's nothing like a New York autumn? There's something about the way the air smells, sort of like cinnamon. And people on the streets all look so nice, too, as if they've all just ripped off the tags of their new fall clothes and couldn't wait to put them on. Tell me, D-Dogg, are you feeling the love out in Diary Land?

Now, to get right down to business: It brings me great pleasure to report that, while I'm not exactly the Queen Bee of Cool just yet, I do know this chick by the name of Carmella Rothman who isn't doing too badly for herself. She was invited by the Coolies to get her photo ID updated and didn't faint once.

Carmella and I were both surprised at how much less intimidating the girls are up close and in person. Like take Vivian. The girl famous for her ultra-inaccessible musical taste also happens to carry a beat-up Carnegie Hall schedule in her handbag—how cute is that? I mean, even I know that's compromising. (It popped out while she was fishing for her wallet. She looked around to make sure nobody had seen it. I think I did a pretty good job of playing dumb . . . and I think her inviting me to a party in Williamsburg that her sister's throwing this weekend was her way of paying me back for it. Or maybe it's just that I'm awesome. Ha, ha.) Much more to say, but I'm socially spent for the moment. Just take my word that everything's going hunky-dory.

The Contender

THE NEXT MORNING I WAS FEELING PRETTY groggy. I squirted my dad's Visine into my eyes, showered, and made it on time to the pre-Baldwin breakfast that Sam and I had arranged at the Yemenite café. "Better start drafting 'Roses Are Red' odes to Amanda," I said with a smirk, handing over the notebook. "Less than a week, and I'm already *miles* along the road to eternal coolness."

"Whatever. Listen to this. It's the most amazing thing since Michael Jackson released *Off the Wall*," Sam said, handing me his headphones.

"Did you order yet?" I said, ignoring his offer. I was too excited about my world-class triumph to concentrate on anything else. I spent, I admit it, most of that meal replaying every detail of the previous day: how instead of being dragged to Rikers Island, we ended up playing drinking games in Pia's parents' Columbus Circle Trump Tower penthouse until three in the morning. (When I'd called my dad to tell him I wouldn't be coming home in time to catch *Ninotchka* on cable, he'd rather bemusedly expressed happiness that I was making friends so quickly.)

The Pazzolinis were diplomats, which as Pia explained meant

simply that her parents traveled a lot to countries I've never heard of and could murder people without getting arrested. After the lardy policeman had driven off, Pia had changed her attitude toward me 180 degrees. At one point she even said in private, "I have to tell you, Mimi, it's a relief that the cute new girl at Baldwin is actually cool."

"So you can act like a dumb southern chick, big deal," Sam said after hearing my replay of yesterday's highlights, including Jess's confession about how serious she and Preston were getting, Vivian's repeated invitation to the party in Williamsburg, Lily's comradely "Can't wait for your article!" exclamation, and so forth. "You think the cool girls can't act, too? They can act like they like you as long as it's convenient, and I'd say escaping a night in juvie's *extremely* convenient. Why shouldn't they invite you to Trump Tower for a few bottles of champagne that the Italian government paid for? That doesn't mean they'll ever call you again. Or even say 'hi' in the hall."

"Sam, you are *such* a spoilsport," I said. "And P.S., I'd appreciate if you wouldn't call them the cool girls. It's really reductive." Sam clearly hadn't learned a single thing about women since the fourth grade.

"Look, Mims," he said, leaning toward me. "I don't want you to get your hopes up, that's all. I feel like I shouldn't have even made that bet with you. It wasn't fair. There's no way the new girl could know that there's no chance in hell of breaking through the iron gates that protect Nona's crew from regular-guy riffraff like you and me."

"You're just getting nervous because that's exactly what *is* happening," I shot back. "And you're probably feeling a little antsy about becoming the squash team's new mascot."

"Uh, not really afraid of that. Can we resume our friendship and talk about something else besides the brat pack?"

"Like . . . ?" I tried to sound bitchy.

"Like . . . how about . . . New York? There's a fine topic for us. Let's discuss."

I gave in and, haltingly at first, told Sam my opinions about the unspoken laws governing . . . the subway. "Tell me this. When people step off the train to let others out, why do they squeeze in on the platform so close to the door? They're just blocking the people they're supposed to be helping out. And why do people slide over every time the person sitting next to them gets up? How different can two seats really be?"

By the time we'd paid for our teas and started strolling toward Baldwin, I was talking at a more speedy pace, railing on about the city's cramped supermarkets: "If they can figure out a way to have such big gyms and restaurants, surely some genius can put in a Key Food with more than three aisles."

Sam was shaking his head and chuckling appreciatively, causing me to forget all about how annoying he'd been acting earlier. "Oh, wait," he said, stopping about a half block from Baldwin. "Remember those pictures I was telling you about? From our end-of-the-year school play in fourth grade?"

"*Charlotte's Web*? Yeah?"

"Well, I brought them," he said. "Come here."

And so we sat on a bench and flipped through a whole stack

of snapshots Sam had unearthed over the weekend: me in a pig costume and Sam all done up as Templeton the rat. The two of us stooped over the largest bowl of Cheerios mankind has ever known. Chasing a beagle in the dog run at Washington Square Park. Toting our matching lunch boxes to the first day of third grade. In the final picture, Sam and I are maybe five or six, and we are walking across the Brooklyn Bridge with our arms entwined—skipping, it looks like. I am wearing a Superwoman costume, cape and everything, and Sam is dressed as Spiderman, and together the two of us look fully equipped to rescue Manhattan from all evildoers.

Wow. I felt overwhelmed and oddly moved, looking at these images for the first time (my mother's way too disorganized to chronicle our lives in photographs). Sam and I really *were* best friends once upon a time. And my return to Baldwin was significant for that if no other reason. "Sam," I started to say, glancing over at him and seeing how little he'd changed after all. "Sam, I—"

But before I could finish my still unformed thought, someone called my name from across the street. I looked up and it was Jess, waving both arms above her head. I glanced at Sam, who shrugged. "A bet's a bet—you've gotta prioritize." And so I left the stack of pictures on the bench and trotted across the street to join my day-old friend.

After school that afternoon, my dad, Quinn, and I had just settled into the couch for a "work break" to watch the director's cut of *On the Waterfront* when the phone jangled. I was annoyed because a) young Marlon Brando—bubble butt notwithstanding—is the hottest man on the planet and b) the word *waterfront* reminded me of yesterday's amazing triumph.

"Hello?" I said in a not-very-excited voice.

"Mimi?" Two innocent syllables made my temples throb. Downing crantinis the previous night had made for an extremely grueling day at Baldwin, and Amanda's aerobicized voice was the last thing I could handle. "It's Amanda! Hey! How! Are! You!" Every word hit my skull like a bullet and I thought of Sam's taunt: *"Mimi and Mandy, sittin' in a tree . . ."* As soon as Quinn left, I'd search the Internet and make up a mock wedding invitation with both their names on it. If Sam continued to harass me, maybe I'd even post it on Baldwin's "Thoughts and Dreams" bulletin board.

"Oh, hey, Amanda," I replied in one of those parental please-can-you-lower-your-voice voices. "What's going on?"

"I HAVE THE GREATEST EVER NEWS OMIGOD YOU'LL DIE IT'S SO GREAT!" she bellowed back. "I MEAN, NOT REALLY GREAT BECAUSE COURTNEY'S YOUNGER SISTER HAS MONO, BUT FOUR HUNDRED NEW TICKETS WENT ON SALE AND I GOT TWO EXTRA TICKETS TO THIS AWESOME FOLK HIP-HOP CONCERT THIS FRIDAY NIGHT. THEY WERE SOLD OUT FOR MONTHS BUT OMIGOD OMI—CAN YOU TOTALLY NOT BELIEVE IT AT ALL?"

There were two major problems with this invitation, not counting the volume at which Amanda issued it. The first was that Vivian's sister's avant-garde costume party in Williamsburg was also on Friday night. The second was that I'd sooner have all my teeth extracted with no anesthesia than hear live "folk hip-hop" with Amanda.

"Holy shit, Amanda," I said, and at her gasp added, "pardon my—French? But Friday night, well, like, you know what I told you last week? About my dad and his . . . *depression?*" I turned up the juice here, pronouncing the word like "scabies." "It's getting worse. He's *beyond* bummed about my mom, and I don't know what he'd do if I ditched him. Gosh, I guess I could sneak out during *Night News,* but he's just *so* lonely."

My confidence produced exactly the desired effect. "No, Mimi—gee, I'm the one who's sorry, wow. That must be way tough. And I would *never* ask you to sneak out, gosh! That'd be awful—what if he woke up in the house and realized he was all alone? You'd be *double* dead, huh?"

Across the room, my father's gorgeous assistant was swaggering toward me. He paused and held up a page of the Arts section with the word "PIZZA" written in red Sharpie. In the same instant, call-waiting beeped.

"Amanda, I've gotta go," I whispered, cupping my hand over the mouthpiece. "My dad's just stumbled in from a bar, and I'm worried about what he might do."

"Oh, *Mimi.*" She gave a loud Hallmark-card sigh as I clicked over to Sam.

"Uh, hey," he said, sounding appropriately sheepish and apologetic. "Sorry if I was a little rude this morning. I was just sort of—whatever. Anyway, I thought maybe, to make up for it . . . Well, I bought some Ben and Jerry's, and I was wondering if maybe I could come over to watch some movies? There's this director's cut on now? Of *On the Waterfront*? Which is one of my very favorite movies?"

"Mine, too!" I exclaimed, though I doubted for the same reasons. "That's exactly what we were sitting down to watch!"

"Oh, great, great. Well, then, can I—I'm actually passing through the neighborhood. So maybe I could stop by sometime?"

"Sure, why not? Come whenever."

"Oh, great. Great. How about, I don't know, now? Because I'm actually, uh—" He stopped talking and the buzzer sounded. "Right outside."

Chubby Hubby Hangover

THE VERY NEXT MORNING—not that I realized it was the next morning, since I was busy being sound asleep—the phone went berserk. ZZZ ZZZ. ZZZ ZZZ. If I could make the Zs any bigger, like the size of five pages, I would. Believe me: we're not talking about just ringing, the sound most phones make. Ringing would be perfectly normal. Pleasant, almost. But Dad had gone out and purchased one of those techy phones with the megaphone buzz of a bloodthirsty mosquito. ZZZ ZZZ. ZZZ ZZZ. A mosquito the size of a beach ball.

"Christ!" I jerked up. My stomach ached after the three pints of Chubby Hubby that Sam and I had inhaled into the wee hours of the night. Did Tasti D-Lite hurt Amanda's tummy like Chubby Hubby did mine? Pia swore that stuff made people fart. ZZZ ZZZ. ZZZ ZZZ.

ZZZZZZZZZZZZZZZZZZZZZZZZZZZZZZZZZZZZZZZZZZZZZZZZZZZZZZZZZZZZ.

Rolling over to yank the phone off its cradle, I saw Sam conked out on the floor. Late the night before—or should I say early that morning—he had fallen asleep by the foot of the couch, his hand draped over my ankle. The first time he'd placed it there, I'd assumed he was reaching around for something that he'd left on the couch—the remote control or an errant AA battery. But instead of fidgeting, he just curled his hand around my ankle, and there it remained, six hours later, in the exact same position.

"Hello," I groaned, kicking Sam's arm down to the ground. He let out a megasnore. I noticed that the movie channel was still blasting at full volume.

"Honey, good morning! Oops, are you still under the covers?" It was my mother, sounding totally unlike herself. "Wakey-dakey time!"

I almost puked into the mouthpiece. Leave it to my mother to call ass-early on Wednesday morning, the one day of the week when I have two free periods in the morning and, if I miss assembly, don't have to be at school until 10:35. "Ugggh . . ."

"Now, honey, I want to check up on your outside reading and see if you've gotten a chance to look at that book about the Nepalese trekkers yet. It's *so* arresting."

"Mom, do you know what time it is?"

"I'm all too aware of it, sweetie pie. Remember, it's an hour earlier here! Where does the time fly, right? I don't have much time to chitchat. Maurice got me up at the crack of dawn to help him with his new stretching series, as a matter of fact. He really damaged his coccyx while building a doghouse last week."

A doghouse? What in God's name—? "Did you wake me to talk about Maurice?"

Another trademark Mom move: disturb a loved one's slumber for no apparent reason. If she didn't have time to chitchat, why couldn't she wait an hour? And why did she always have to mention her disgusting new boyfriend—even the term made me sick—in the first paragraph of every conversation? I missed Texas less every day.

"Well, in a way, yes. So listen up, sweetie, I couldn't wait—I just had a bit of fun news."

"Mims," Sam had risen with the imprint of a pizza box crossing his cheek. I made a chuckling sound, which my mother interpreted as encouragement. "I've gotta go," he whispered. "My mom will kill me."

I nodded sympathetically and pointed at the phone, indicating that I was about to Kill My Mom. She hadn't stopped talking and I hadn't started listening. Until, that is, I heard the words "Maurice" and "Myrtle" and "moving" and "in" and finally, the clincher: "together."

"WHAT?!?"

"I know, honey, sudden, huh? But we've been so *happy* together, especially since Ariel went to Austin. The rhythms are just jibing—what can I say? We felt it was the right time to make a few changes in our own lives, too, you know? A little tit for tatty?"

Listening to my mom just then, I was amazed that she had finished junior high, much less become a tenured college professor. It sounded as if she were asking me if I wanted to go pee-pee. And I did not.

"Tit for tatty? What are you talking about, Mom? You and Maurice are moving in together? And what about Myrtle? Are you going to get her monogrammed bath towels and put pictures of the three of you strolling in Hermann Park up on the mantel?"

"Now, honey, you know I would never buy monogrammed bath towels! They cost three times the—"

And then I lost it. Did I *ever* have any say in the earth-shattering decisions my mother was always going around making? "Mom, I've only been gone, like, five days! You just couldn't wait, could you? How great! How terrific, Mom, how just *fantastic!*"

This outburst was strange but unstoppable: Anger is totally un-me, especially at seven-sixteen on a Wednesday morning, but my mom really pushed all the buttons.

Especially when she responded as if I'd just FedExed her three dozen yellow roses and a Ferrari with a NUMERO UNO MAMA vanity plate. "Oh, Mims," she burbled. "Thank you for that—thank you *so much*. For your honesty. I am *so* glad to hear you owning your emotions. You're so much more mature than Ariel—she just took her phone off the hook, can you imagine? And oh, speaking of Myrtle, she's thinking of applying early to Barnard, so we were wondering if she could bundle up with you and your dad for a few nights next month? The Geophysics department's having an open house over Columbus Day—"

For all her superficiality, my sister was not without her moments of brilliance. I did what I should've done three minutes ago—what Ariel would've done immediately: I slammed down the phone.

Half an hour later, Quinn found me at the breakfast table, spooning dry instant oatmeal into my mouth directly from the single-serving envelopes. I was so bummed, I didn't even care what Quinn would think (but never too bummed to notice his sinewy forearms). The table was strewn with balled-up

Kleenexes and another empty tub of Chubby Hubby, my fourth in the nine hours since Sam had arrived.

"Mimi! What's happened?" Quinn cried. Shit. Why didn't I remember that I shared this room with a hunk before turning it into my personal disaster zone? Insult to injury, et cetera. "OK, let me guess," he said. "I love a good puzzle."

"Be my guest," I replied through a rather buglelike blow of the nose.

Quinn wrinkled his nose at me. "Got it," he said. "Brando."

"Huh?" What was he *talking* about? "Brando?"

"Marlon. You're devastated that he's passed away, but there's no use shedding tears. It happens."

"You don't understand," I struggled to explain.

"I'm sorry for kidding around," Quinn said in a more soothing tone of voice. "If you want to talk about it, I'm all ears. And eyes and intestines and butt cheeks."

I blew my nose, rubbed at my eyes.

"Even if you won't tell me, I do understand this: we are *not* letting you leave this house without a quick fix-up." He pushed a knotty hank of my hair behind my ear, then flicked something away from my nose. "Look—an oatmeal flake!"

This cheered me up for exactly one tenth of a second. Quinn was the last person on earth I wanted feeling sorry for me, to say nothing of picking oatmeal crumbs out of my snot. Cohabiting with the object of your affection isn't all it's cracked up to be, trust me—especially if said object of affection doesn't know that he loves you yet. The whole setup can significantly reduce the chances of his spontaneously ramming his tongue down your throat while you're sobbing at the breakfast table with oatmeal stuck to the mucus on your cheek.

I buried my nasty red face in my palms. "I think I just need to be alone."

"I was the new boy at school once, too," Quinn said. "I know it can be tough, especially when you're a little different." He walked behind my chair and started rubbing my shoulders.

"It's not that," I balked. How mortifying—he thought I was having adjustment problems. My whole body was tingling. Quinn was touching my shoulders. It was indescribable. "School's not the problem. It's fine. I'm already popular. I'm writing for the newspaper."

"Then what is it?"

I looked up at Quinn's face and something happened. That gorgeous lock of dirty-blond hair falling over his left eye, his dark bow-shaped lips—I saw only kindness and compassion. All I wanted was to spill open my heart to him, red eyes and maple and brown sugar and flying snot and all. I realize it's idiotic to unleash your problems on your dream guy, but I wasn't exactly thinking straight right then.

"My mom—dad's ex-wife, or almost ex-wife . . ." I hesitated. "Well, she called me this morning and told me that she's letting her boyfriend Maurice move into my old house with her and—"

"Do you mean—"

"And Myrtle—that's Maurice's know-it-all daughter, who spends all her time on the Internet reading about molecules—she's probably going to move into *my* room. Can you believe it? She was once caught writing nasty things about herself on the bathroom wall in junior high, and now she's going to spend all her time rifling through my personal possessions."

"Oh, Mimi!" Quinn understood. "This is a case of serious suckage."

"I'm not even going to get a chance to hide my valuables from her creepy graffiti. I'd call Ariel, but she's in Austin and so wrapped up in her Vanilla Gorilla vs. Kappa Kappa Gamma drama that she probably doesn't even notice that Maurice is the world's grossest vitamin-pusher." I stopped to sniffle. "Even if she did, she'd—"

"We have to put an end to this," Quinn cut me off. "Maybe we should tell your father—perhaps he could intervene?"

"That would be a good idea"—I chuckled bitterly—"except if he ever found out how serious Mom and Maurice have gotten, he'd be too shocked to wiggle his left pinky, let alone 'intervene.' I don't know if he's told you this yet, but he's still pretty hung up on my mom. It's a *total* disaster, it's—"

Before I could finish, Quinn shushed me. I followed his eyes to the doorway, where my father stood shaking a still-wet photograph with a pair of rubber-tipped tongs. "What gives, kids?" he asked. My dad stunk at solitude. He couldn't stay in the darkroom for ten minutes without wandering around in search of company. He had the worst case of ADD of anyone I knew. I was pretty certain that was the only reason he hired assistants—not to assist, but to entertain.

"What've you got there, Dad?" I gave him my best well-adjusted-daughter smile.

"Oh, nothing special, just a portrait I took the other day. A friend of the Judys asked me to do a session and I figured I could use some practice in the studio."

"I helped out with lighting," Quinn added. "She wasn't half bad. An actress. Fiona, right?"

"Veronica," Dad said, a little too quickly. He eyed the print with a distinctly gooey expression.

"Let's see," I said. I hoped Dad couldn't tell I'd been weeping.

"Here she is," he thrust the photograph out at us. This Veronica woman was about forty, or a well-preserved forty-five, and had chin-length black hair and sparkly eyes that were either blue or green or hazel (the picture was black-and-white). She was gazing dreamily into the lens—at my father!—with her head tilted back slightly. I was about to wonder if my dad had a thing for this Veronica when it hit me: Veronica looked like my mom, or how my mom would look if she ever actually put on an ounce of makeup and bought the clothes Dad was always begging her to try on. And I mean *exactly*. Dad didn't care about this Veronica; it was Mom he was thinking about.

"Not bad," said Quinn.

"Nope, not bad. Not at all," Dad agreed, talking not about the photo but the model.

My father was many things, but over my mother was not one of them. What was I going to do? There was no way I could tell him that Maurice was moving in with her. Into her bed. Into Dad's old bed. Nor could I tell him that Maurice's pimple of a daughter, Myrtle, was joining the party and setting up shop in what used to be *our* home. Imagining Myrtle's drool swirling across my pillow, under my covers, soaking my mattress, I wanted to hurl all four pints of Chubby Hubby straight across the room.

September 24 or 25 (I'm lousy at dates)
10:14 a.m.

Salutations, dearest of Ds. I recently had my first dream about my new chums, which seemed like a landmark of some sort. It's like what people say about learning a foreign language—you know them only when you can speak them in your sleep. And my darling Freudian mother has always said that the more you dream about something, the more it becomes part of your waking life. (Help me here, Sam. You know what I mean, right?) Anyway, a few nights ago I woke up at three in the morning after this crazy dream about being in the heart room at one of those children's science museums with Pia. It must have to do with something I learned the other day: Pia's a closet science freak! Up until a couple of summers ago, she used to spend her Julys in science camp. Lily told me she's also in advanced chemistry with all seniors, but when I asked Pia about it she tried to downplay it by talking about how much she likes goofing around with Bunsen burners.

I'm confused about everything. About Quinn, about my dad and mom, about Baldwin and my new friends, if I can even presume to call them that. I'm confused about Maurice, and Myrtle, and the weird homespun rainbow scarf Judy #2 brought down to me last night. No one ever told me tenth grade would be this much of a maze.

Billyburg Baby

I ALWAYS SPEND SO MUCH TIME ANTICIPATING events that I can't help but be disappointed by the events themselves. That's what I was thinking about on the L-train to Williamsburg Friday night, as (for the tenth time) I consulted the mirror in my lip-gloss kit to apply a final coat of mocha liquid eyeliner. The eyeliner went on smoothly, but I still suspected that all the Artists—to say nothing of the Coolies—would scorn the vintage plaid miniskirt that I'd spent forty minutes safety-pinning. It took me almost as long to choose my tights. (In case you're wondering: pinstriped, major control top.)

Then there was the hair (I stood in the mirror until finally figuring out how to get one of those pouffy Katharine Hepburn rolls on top), cover-up (no amount of concealer could weed out that zit garden on my chin!), shoes (dark violet Mary Janes), and the purse (I emptied out some satchel-type thing of my dad's). All told, at least two hours of work, longer than I'd spent on any Baldwin assignment or even my debut article in the *Bugle*, a (not overly) personal column about the differences between Baldwin and my old school in Houston.

I was having one of my more decent-looking moments, but

still, that didn't guarantee that I'd have any fun. That was always how it happened: The longer I fine-tuned my outfit, the less time I ended up wearing it. I'd be home for the eleven o'clock news.

My optimism didn't exactly surge as I pushed past a couple of guys loading a white van with band equipment on the street, then squeezed inside a large, derelict warehouse. I didn't recognize a single person—everyone there looked like an extra from *The Man Who Fell to Earth*, decked out in Day-Glo unitards, with silver eyeshadow smeared from cheek to chin, and slicked-back hairdos. Avant-garde screeches (it wouldn't be fair to call the clanging of pots and pans "music") drowned out all the conversations, and the only snippets I overheard—"Bert's having his colon irrigated" and "I'm *so* over Iceland!"—intimidated me more than the ambient noise. Wow. These freaks made my Baldwin classmates seem totally Laura Ingalls Wilder.

I didn't see my new friends anywhere, just two rocker guys sipping lime green liquid from science beakers and a slight woman tweeting into a microphone for a crowd of exactly five people. I'd predicted a much more Goth scene, but what do I know about New York? I cursed myself for not having met up with the girls before the party so that we could make an entrance together—not that such a plan had been suggested.

"Mimi?" I heard a voice behind me. "Mimi Schulman? Is that you?" A male voice.

I turned around and almost slammed into the dark, mysterious, and very cute boy from my World Civ class, the clever one with perpetually mussed hair. Max Roth: the quiet cowboy of Baldwin's tenth-grade class, not to mention its most attractive member. Whenever nobody knew the answer, Stanley would point his finger and cheer, "Let's hear it, Max!" The sleepy-eyed boy in the back row was never not right.

How did someone so cute know my name? "Oh, hey, Max!" I was relieved that the warehouse lacked overhead lighting, which might draw attention to my flushed cheeks and the oily chin situation. "What are *you* doing here?"

"I do installations with one of the guys giving this party—Dimitri," Max said. "He's officially a neon artist, but he's been branching out into large-scale sand-and-rocks projects lately."

"Wow, that sounds totally cool. What kind of stuff do you two do together?" I hoped the dark room also concealed the fact that I had no idea what he was talking about.

"Well, you know Dolby sound in the movies? How there will be different sounds intended for the left and right ear? We're trying to make Dolby visual art, but with really giant pieces. Dimitri's been doing the left and I'm doing the, ah . . ."

"The right?"

"Right." Max laughed nervously. "Sorry about that; I get distracted at parties and find it hard to have real conversations. I'm much more at ease in World Civ, ha."

"Yeah, me, too." I nodded sympathetically, then—noticing the irresistibly braidable length of his eyelashes—threw in, "Your work sounds really cool. My dad's a photographer, so I'm used to all these freaky artsy types wandering around my house."

I couldn't believe that I had just used the expression "freaky artsy types" with the brooding genius of my World Civ class. There should be federal laws prohibiting me from leaving my bedroom.

"I know who your dad is—I saw some of his stuff at an ICP show."

"ICP?"

"The International Center of Photography. It was a group show and they had a few of his old pieces. I'd love to meet him sometime. I've been getting into big-scale collage installations lately, using digital photographs that I blow up really—"

"*There* you are! We thought you'd bagged on us—oh, hey, Max."

Max shrunk back as Lily swooped down on us. The rest of the gang appeared right behind her. Pia, whose olive skin glowed under the warehouse's phosphorescent light, looked particularly angry and glamorous in skintight black leather pants and only a lacy camisole-type thing, also black, on top. Jess, resplendently blonde as ever, was wearing the same preppy sweater sets she sported at school every day, only slightly tighter and lower-cut. Her eyes, as usual, surrounded by thick smudges of eyeliner, Viv looked carefully scrappy in a cutoff Ramones T-shirt and shiny tasseled combat boots. Only Lily was underdressed and unfabulous, with her dirty-blond hair slung back into a ponytail and her dirt-stained sweatshirt looking as if it hadn't been washed in a week—no, make that a month.

"Fabulous outfit," Pia said in place of hello. "*So* Riviera, circa a long time ago."

"Thanks," I said. Someone handed me a drink. "Yours, too. Is that—black patent?"

"Hey, hey, my, my," Jess said, jabbing my shoulder and lurching forward.

"Jess's *very* wasted," Lily apologized, pulling the disheveled blonde off me. "Though we have no idea how, since we all got here together."

"Omigod!" Jess yelped suddenly. "Preston!" Removing from her tiny handbag a phone no larger than an Am Ex card, which was lighted up blue and vibrating, she careened toward the exit.

"Jess, come back here! Stop!"

With Lily pursuing Jess, Vivian swung a protective arm around me. "Mimi," she said, "it's high time for the introductions. My sister was *so* intrigued by what you did under the bridge the other day—I described you as the greatest thespian of the sophomore class. You know she does spoken-word performance pieces?"

"Mia is *very* cool," Pia said. "Unlike Preston, who expects Jess to accompany him to every single professional sporting event that passes through Madison Square Garden! Ugh—there's a lot I'd do for love, but *not* professional basketball. Thank *God* Francesco's not American!"

"C'mon—she's over there!" Vivian pointed across the room at a girl standing motionless on an egg crate. She was wrapped in aluminum foil. Something bright yellow—a feather, maybe?—stuck out from her forehead. "Let's go."

"OK, just hold on a sec," I said, glancing back over my shoulder. "I was talking to—"

But Max had vanished, absorbed into the crowd of pale-faced twentysomethings, leaving me to trail behind Vivian and Pia across the immense former sugar-cane refinery.

"Hey, Mia," Vivian called up to her sister when we'd finally made it across the room. "This is Mimi—the one I told you about. I told her you wanted to meet her."

Up close I understood Mia's legendary status better. She wasn't pretty exactly, but she had mile-high cheekbones and the most intense eyes I'd ever seen. No wonder every guy at Baldwin wanted to get with her.

Mia didn't budge. Not only did she not reach down to shake my hand, she didn't smile or even blink; Vivian might as well have introduced me to the Statue of Liberty. "Whoops." Vivian shrugged, as if her sister's nonreaction was completely normal. "I guess she's not breaking character yet. C'mon, we'll find her later." As we resumed zigzagging through lines of crates used as couches, Vivian clarified: "It's a new piece she's working on, called 'Newfoundland Winter.' About space and stillness. She rehearses a lot."

Soon after we'd colonized three adjacent crates, Pia drew a silver cigarette case from her purse, which contained rolling paper and what bore a startling resemblance to marijuana. She pushed her thin thighs tightly together and began to roll a joint.

"My parents are in town next weekend," she told Vivian with that haughty eye roll that I had already come to recognize as more habitual than bitchy. "They're having this huge party at our place in the Hamptons—it's always *such* a hassle."

"Whatever," Vivian said. "You know their parties rock. Our

pilgrimages out east are always totally worth it. Are they going to let you bring Francesco?"

"Shh!" Pia narrowed her eyes at Vivian. "Well, duh, Viv, Francesco does work at the embassy, so he'll probably be there, but not as my date. How many times do I have to tell you not to broadcast my personal life to everyone and their mother?"

I was feeling very left out during this exchange, perhaps because Pia had turned her back to me. Once the joint was lit, though, I mustered the courage to squirm back toward Viv and Pia. Across the room, past several unshaven hipsters who were engaged in a mile-long game of Twister, I spotted Max leaning against a concrete wall. When he saw me see him, he raised his arm and waved slyly. Adorable.

"What's up, Mims?" asked Viv.

"Nothing," I said. Part of me wanted to tell the Coolies how cute I thought Max was, but I had no desire to humiliate myself. Because weirdly, though the Coolies all seemed to get action, unlike Rachel they never talked about it until after the fact. There was no dignity in obsessing over a guy—especially a fellow tenth-grader.

"This shit is killer," Pia announced, a huge puff of smoke exiting her impossibly small nostrils.

"Hell yeah," Vivian agreed, and took a hit.

Watching the girls pull at the joint, I took mental notes so I'd know what to do when my turn came. The thing was, I hadn't actually smoked all that much pot before, as in, actually, ever.

"Here you go," said Vivian, handing me the joint. It looked

wet and limp, like the worms that used to swarm the sidewalks after big rainstorms in Houston. Not, in other words, all that appealing.

You would think that this would be a big moment for me. And what was I thinking about as I brought it to my lips? That I was doing something illegal? No. That I was about to smear grease all over my brain, risking writing truly horrible columns and never getting into a college anybody's heard of? No. That I was going to look like a big fat dork who barely goes near smoked salmon, let alone smokes pot? Bingo.

Luckily, right then a cute indie-rock guy appeared out of nowhere and sat down on Viv's crate. He was wearing a bomber jacket and a baseball hat that said VERN'S FISH. Viv snuggled up to him in a way that implied, well, something.

I sealed the joint with my lips and pulled. The warm smoke filled my mouth and tickled the back of my throat. I swirled the smoke around there, let it swish up against my teeth and sink into the pores of my cheeks. I started coughing, and as soon as I had stopped I blurted out, "This is definitely weird." I regretted it the moment I opened my mouth. "Weird pot," I corrected myself, taking another toke. "The stuff we have in Texas is way different," I lied, and began coughing again. "Total embarrassing inexperience" might as well have been tattooed on my forehead.

"We don't have all night, Mimi," snapped Pia. "Give it up."

"Sorry." I started to hand her the joint, but she put out her hand and pointed behind me. "Not me. It's his turn."

And who was huddled over me? None other than Max Roth,

his sweatshirt hood cinched around his face. He looked adorable—and amused. I noticed that there was a tiny cat embroidered on his sleeve, bright orange like my baby Simon back in Houston. I glanced admiringly back at Max: Anyone with cats on his sleeve won major points with me.

"Thanks, Mimi," he said, accepting the joint and drawing it expertly to his lips.

"What was the stuff in Texas like?" he asked after a couple of tokes.

"Well," I stalled, trying to think of suitable adjectives. Unfortunately, the only word I came up with was *green*.

"Green?" Max's eyes crinkled.

"Mimi's so busted!" Viv exclaimed, slapping her knee. "She's a pot virgin, ha!" With the exception of Lily, everyone else cracked up even more at that. I had to join in, lest I seem even more of a schmo, but I couldn't help thinking that Viv enjoyed her joke a little too much.

"It's cool, Texas," Max finally said, ending the laughter and my displeasure. "Even the bad seeds need somebody to hang around with who can be a good influence."

OK, so he'd made total fun of me. But every cloud has a silver lining: He'd called me *Texas*.

I was relieved when Lily returned right then. "No, thanks," she said, when Max offered her the pot. "I'm pretty fond of my gray cells, actually. Listen, guys." Wiping her nose with her sweatshirt sleeve (*Margaret Morton's daughter?! Up-the-nose drugs?* I couldn't help thinking), Lily looked at Pia and Vivian with a serious expression. "Preston called again and I lost Jess. I think she's gone. She must have hijacked somebody else's car service."

"Talk about determination," Vivian said.

"Shit," said Pia. "You think she's going over there? To his pad?"

"Well,"—Lily consulted her cell again—"you tell me. It's a quarter to eleven. You think she's going to the gym?"

Even while the joint continued to circulate, no one looked too happy, not even Viv, who had the cute fake rock star slobbering all over her.

"This is a mess," Pia declared.

So she said, but pretty soon Mia, with a crowd of perform-ance-artist friends, drifted over to kick off the evening's next scheduled activity: walking through the desolate streets of Williamsburg and plastering cryptic flyers reading only NECK FACE on street signs and wooden posts and every abandoned storefront we could find. Which, all things considered, wasn't that boring. I think I even had fun.

I got home around two-thirty. I wanted to watch TV, but not enough to wake Dad, so I settled for logging on. There were some e-mails from porn companies, an offer for a free diploma from an accredited university in Arizona, and an e-mail from Rachel: *Mimi*, it read, *will you please come visit SOON? I'm DYING down here without you. Having a long-distance boyfriend sucks but hav-ing a long-distance best friend sucks even harder—*

That's as far as I'd read when an Instant Message from

Amanda—electronically known as SqshGrl85—popped up onscreen.

SqshGrl85: Mimi! What's up!

Fuck me. Would she ever go away? I double-clicked Amanda's greeting into cyber oblivion and returned to Rachel's message. *The only person who would take your place in our "She Said/She Said" column was Sheila Hero*, Rachel wrote. *She agrees with everything I ever write and it's so friggin' boring people are starting to call her Sheila Zero.*

SqshGrl85: U R quite the night owl tonight. What have you been up to?

Again I clicked Amanda out of sight. Back to Rachel. *In other news, Aaron Traister has stolen one of his mother's diamond tennis bracelets and has since disappeared. Some people think he got shipped off to military acad—*

SqshGrl85: Listen, R U free next SatRday? Courtney + I are organizing a sailing outing for next weekend.

There was no getting rid of her. I'd have to finish Rachel's letter some other time.

Mimicita86: Hey there.
SqshGrl85: So, R U in?

Mimicita86: I'm actually going out of town next weekend.

SqshGrl85: Awesome! Where 2?

Mimicita86: Hamptons. Pia's having some people come out there. Small thing.

SqshGrl85: Glam!

The annoyingness of the word "glam" killed any concern about hurt feelings. (And the pesky "!" didn't exactly help matters.) Amanda had no right to be mad at me—it wasn't like it was my party, not that I would've invited her if it had been. I had been so overjoyed when Pia had mentioned it a few days before, it was almost embarrassing to recall.

Mimicita86: Glam? More like just old people.

SqshGrl85: Well, I'm still soooo J.

The screen went blank for a moment before the words "That's J 4 jealous. C U soon XXOX" ended our online chat. I shut my laptop and thought about Amanda. Irritating, definitely, but not stupid. She knew that I'd ditched her and moved to more "glam!" horizons. Well, good. Why should I learn how to restring a squash racquet when I could party with the international jet set?

Give me one good reason.

Colloquium of Cool

THE NEXT WEEK AT SCHOOL PASSED WITHOUT much to write home about. The individual days blurred together, filled with playing hide-and-seek with Amanda (I was always hiding, she was always stalking), staring at Max Roth, making small talk with the Coolies, fine-tuning my next "Texan in Gotham" column for the *Bugle*, and, believe it or not, doing homework. For the first few weeks, I had dismissed academics at Baldwin as a joke, but even though the assignments were experimental, they were still, alas, assignments. And some of them—like my English assignment to write a personal letter to Gustave Flaubert about my reaction to *Madame Bovary*—took some serious thought. That, along with my mother's insistence that I read a book about a former businessman's spiritual self-discovery in Tibet, made it doubly hard to focus on my weekend in Bridgehampton.

When Saturday morning finally rolled around, I was beyond excited for my trip, which we'd all spent all of lunch on Thursday discussing. I'd already blow-dried my hair and set aside a discreet cosmetics bag. I must've logged on like fifty times since returning from school the previous afternoon, but beyond more special offers from Amazon.com and the usual bevy of

Viagra alerts, I had No New Messages. Rachel hadn't even written back to my long, heartwarming reply. Probably too busy with cozying up to Sheila Zero.

I had just closed my laptop yet again when Sam had another case of bad timing and rang our bell unannounced. No sooner had I opened the front door a crack than he stormed into the brownstone bearing fifteen varieties of Middle Eastern appetizers: hummus, baba gannouj, tamarasalata, the works.

"I got grub," Sam said, shoveling a mega-proportioned glop into his mouth.

"None for me." I shook my head. "My appetite's taken a nosedive."

"What*ever*—you're always starving, Miss Piglet, and anyway you'll need extra energy today, because I'm taking you to a special music conference at the NYU gym."

He looked so pathetically psyched. I hated to disappoint him, but I was going to turn into a whale if I didn't watch it. "Sorry, no can do," I said, going into the bathroom to examine the evenness of yesterday's application of the self-tanner that Pia had recommended. "I don't even have time to eat, much less hang out with any zit-faced music nerds—no offense. I was actually on my way out the door." I squinted. Definitely *un peu* bronzée, and not in a zoological striped way, either. Pia really did know her products. Too bad I couldn't afford this one more than once every five years.

"Oh, were you?" Sam said, his face appearing above mine in the mirror. "Whither, if I may be so bold to inquire?"

"Whither? Sam, you are *such* a loser sometimes."

I peered at my belly closer, and yuck: my skin color actually resembled Sam's ginger-colored 'fro much more than Bo Derek's skin in *10*, but maybe it was just the exposed light bulb that was doing such unflattering things to me.

"Yeah, well, what's your answer, then?"

God, he stressed me out! Instead of answering, I pushed him aside and returned to the kitchen, where I yanked a huge bag of whole-wheat pita from the pantry. This was a situation that demanded some serious snacking.

"Yes? Ahem?" he said, tapping his Nike against our Persian carpet. "Your final answer?"

I ripped my pita into jagged pieces and drove them into the hummus. "I was going to go . . . out of town," I said, my face stuffed with food. The hummus had red peppers in it—my favorite kind, and the hardest to find.

"Where? To a Tupperware party in Darien with Amanda?"

"What? No, to Bridgehampton, actually. Give that back!" I don't know why, with a whole huge bag of pitas in front of him, Sam had to steal mine. "What are you doing?" I snapped. "That's totally unhygienic and canine."

"Chill, Mimi," he said, inserting a piece of my pita into his mouth. "Isn't it a little late in the day to go to Bridge—ah! You mean to the Pazzolini estate? Did you hear that they bought the house next door and demolished it, just because it ruined their view? How absurd is that?"

The absurdity of it almost brought tears to my eyes. It was nearly noon on a Saturday, and Pia hadn't even called me yet. At first I tried telling myself that she was running late, but at this point, who was I kidding? Was it too late to be awaiting her call? "Yeah, I *had* heard that, thank you very much. Obviously."

Sam detected the quaver in my voice, because when I looked up that same evil grin was playing across his features. "Oh—I see! Little Miss Popularity got dissed, did she? The Coolies are catching rays without her, is that it? Ah, yes, come to think of it, I *did* see Pia's chauffeur fetching the whole crew yesterday afternoon. What, were you at the school nurse, missed your ride?"

I couldn't believe that someone I had once called my friend— my *best* friend—was mocking my obvious, intense distress. It was too much, it was—inhuman. "I did *not* get dissed." I thought hard and fast for an excuse, finally coming out with "I had to spend last night with my dad!"

"So what'd they do, invite you and then quote-unquote 'forget'? Ah, the oldest trick in the book." He wagged a reproachful finger at me. "Tsk, tsk, Mims, not telling me. You forget—you vowed to tell me *every* single detail of your path to popularity. How else can I keep my Coolie log? You haven't written a single word since your NECK FACE exploits last weekend."

"Whatever—as if you're keeping a real log! And as if I'll ever tell you *any*thing ever again, if you're always going to laugh at me. Honestly." Hoping to terminate the unpleasant conversation, I popped four large kalamata olives into my mouth like aspirin.

"But, Mims, of *course* I'm keeping a log. How else can we track your progress?"

I hadn't realized there were pits until I started choking.

Sam pounded me on the back and a kalamata pit shot toward the terrace, upon which I burst into tears.

"It's OK, Mims. It's cool, you're all right. Danger averted— shh. Here, let me throw them away. Give them to me." He took the half-masticated olive in his hand and held it there.

"It's not that," I said, snuffling, "It's just that you're so mean to me, Sam. Did—oh, I am so hungry. I really am hungry," I said finally, burrowing into a large portion of pita. "You're so mean, Sam, so mean!"

His face sank to the level of the kitchen island, and Sam became putty. A mere mention of his male insensitivity and Sam cut the crap—he was actually pretty liberated in a way. Before marrying the obnoxious Mr. Geckman and deciding to grow old at Metropolitan Opera benefits, Sam's mom had been a big women's rights activist, and she had trained Sam well in respecting the ladies.

An hour later, instead of sipping champagne on the shores of the Atlantic, I found myself trolling through a huge auditorium crammed with "listening booths." The electronica convention was pretty much as I'd predicted, swarming with bald pariahs in torn undershirts and postal worker pants and huge firing-range headphones, all nodding their heads to some unknown melody. These were people who took their fun very seriously, as if they were going to be tested on it. Everyone in the convention hall looked as if they'd seen more than a few episodes of *Star Trek,* and I'd bet not a single attendee had ever been on a date.

Not that I had, but still.

Even though I was the only girl there without either dyed or shaved hair, I had to admit that my mood had improved a lot. At least I wasn't staying in bed, drowning my sorrows in high-fat frozen desserts, my normal modus operandi on days like this one. I even sort of had fun just watching Sam have fun, if that makes any sense. "Hey, listen to this!" he kept crying out, or, "Omigod, look, that's DJ Quicksand!" By the end of the day he had collected enough neon concert flyers to paper the Holland Tunnel.

The only weird incident occurred at the end of the afternoon, outside the Scrappy Sissy label's listening booth. "I'll go into my own," I said while Sam jammed to the beautiful sounds of arrhythmic screeching.

"No, they're all full—this one's special," he insisted, dragging me inside yet another booth. "Fallen Fauna's totally indie, and they just got screwed by their biggest act, so they've only got this one booth."

So we entered the booth and stood there, leaning toward each other, sharing the headphones with one ear each. I couldn't make out any sounds over Sam's breathing, but I wasn't complaining: I'd heard enough simulated meows that afternoon to last a lifetime, and at that point I wanted only fresh air and the sweet silence of car horns and sirens. My mind drifted for I don't know how long, because all of a sudden I realized that the song had ended and we were still just standing there.

"Uh, Sam?" I said, wriggling free of my earphone half. "Hello?"

He jumped as if I'd just thrown water on him, and our foreheads collided. Both of us out of sorts, we struggled to leave the narrow black booth at the same time. As we walked to the door, I noticed that the nine adjacent booths all had big placards reading SCRAPPY SISSY above them. I shrugged. I just totally didn't understand anything about anybody.

We spent the rest of the afternoon chilling in Central Park. The zoo had already closed, so we settled for buying pretzels and lounging in the Sheep Meadow. Sam had dared me to stuff the entire pretzel, mustard and everything, into my mouth and swallow it in ten seconds while whistling the tune to "Dancing Queen." I was about to win the dare when I heard "MIMI!!!! Omigod!"

Directly behind an old lady tossing stale bread to a flock of pigeons, who should it be but Amanda? Of course. I *knew* she played tennis up here every Saturday, but still, Central Park was a huge place: Why did my luck have to be so rotten? She was flailing her arms and bounding straight toward us like a lost child on the beach who has finally found her parents.

"Looks like you're not so unpopular after all," Sam snickered, savoring my misery. "Maybe there's a round-robin tournament you can join."

I was so annoyed—either by Sam's sarcasm or Amanda's existence—that a piece of pretzel caught in the back of my throat. I started to choke for the second time that day.

"Are you OK?" Amanda gasped as Sam began to pound my back again. My, he must be very adept at burping babies.

"Mmm hmm." I nodded as another cube of pretzel roosted in

my throat. I bent over and spat a mouthful of dough onto the ground.

"Hey!" Amanda backed away, careful to keep her pristine sneakers out of range.

"Hey!" the old lady bleated. I thought she was objecting to my public spitting, but when a cluster of pigeons descended at my feet, I realized I'd robbed her of all her companions.

"I thought you were going away this weekend?" Amanda said. "What about the party in the Hamptons? At Pia's?"

In calmer circumstances, I could have spun a decent excuse, but with Sam and Amanda both staring at me and all the birds skittering around me like demented flying rats, I drew a blank.

"There was a last-minute snag," I blundered finally. "My dad made me stay at home because, er, he had an unexpected house-guest." It was so totally obvious that I was improvising, and not all that well, either. "He thought I could show her around," I added in desperation. "Some girl he photographed for this fashion shoot?"

I hoped that would be enough, but Amanda was still watching me, her face as gray as an earthworm. Sam shot me a look of revulsion, as if he'd never lied in all his life.

"He's a photographer," I pressed on. "My dad. It's his job."

"Oh yeah," Amanda said, kicking the ground with the toe of her squeaky-clean tennis shoe. "I think you told me that before." And then she looked right into my eyes and asked, "So where is she?"

"Where is who?"

"The model? You know, your houseguest?"

"Oh." I gulped, then pointed randomly toward Columbus Circle. "There." My trembling finger stopped right on a four-hundred-pound woman in argyle leg warmers. "See her?"

"Wow, *she's* a model?" Amanda gaped. "A *fashion* model?"

"Yeah, for some new, uh, 'supersize it' campaign? She's *supposed* to look like that, can you believe it? Just think—if we all traded Tasti D-Lite for banana splits, we could also be supermodels!"

"Yuck-o!" Amanda shivered. "That'll be the day!" She laughed delightedly. She must have really wanted to believe me, because she immediately proceeded to invite me to join the gang that night for a video slumber party.

"Can I come?" Sam said.

"Girls only—but you can bring that, uh, model, Mimi, as long as she promises not to eat my dad's Spanish serrano!"

"Gee," I said. "Sounds great, but I told my dad I'd meet up with him. We have to take our houseguest to this, uh, buffet. In Queens."

Amanda shrugged, then glanced at her watch. "I'd better get running. I was supposed to be at my PSAT tutoring session ten minutes ago."

She made the universal "call me" sign and started walking away.

"Can we just pretend that didn't happen?" I asked as Amanda's blond ponytail bobbed out of sight.

"No." Sam shook his head. "I would ask you what that was all about, but I don't need to. Now that you've gotten through your nervous breakdown, we might as well talk honestly about this whole deal. Am I to understand that the bet's off and you're playing by your own rules? Perhaps you recall that we're keeping a popularity log?"

"Haven't we already gone over this, Sam?"

"I was trying to this morning, but unfortunately you started choking. Now, listen to me. We agreed to keep a log, Mimi, so that's exactly what we're going to do. But you have to be straight with me."

"But Sam—"

"Look, Mims, maybe you were right this morning. Maybe this whole bet thing's stupid and mean. After all, given the way they treated you this weekend, it's clear that you and the girls have developed a truly meaningful friendship, and I would *hate* to obstruct your blossoming intimacy in—"

"Stop it!" I flared up. I couldn't stand that smug expression on Sam's face, or his sarcasm. Why was he always so, so obnoxious? Right then, I felt more determined than ever to prove him wrong. I couldn't give up yet. I'd invested way too much already. I *knew* I could get in with them. And besides, now that the girls had betrayed me, I felt less guilty about dishing out so many details of their lives, Dear Diary and all. "What if I *promise* to be honest?"

Sam frowned.

"What if I swear? C'mon Sam, honesty's my middle name!"

Sam kicked a chunk of heaved-up pretzel far into the distance and finally grinned at me. "You wish."

We started laughing. Some secrets I'll never give away.

Pot Luck Breakfast

THE ONLY REDEEMING THING ABOUT DRAGGING your ass to Baldwin on Mondays is checking your school e-mail account (technological lazyass that I am, I still haven't figured out how to access it from a remote computer). After a long weekend away, your in box is usually crammed with interesting items. Beyond the expected acupuncture seminar announcements from Zora Blanchard's executive office, there were usually a few random greetings from student organizations and maybe an actual note or two.

This explains why, rather than cross the main lobby and risk an encounter with my so-called friends, I paid the computer lab a visit during my first free period. I needed *some* distraction from the massive plummet in my social standing over the last forty-eight hours.

Six messages were waiting in my in box, but the screen could fit only the first five, three of which were junk, and the remainder of which were from Rachel, carbon copies of the ones she'd sent to my home account that contained details of the Lone Star Hair with Flair Fair she went to "for kicks" this weekend. Even though I'd already scanned the e-mail the night before, I actually reread about how good old Richard Eagins—a former class-mate we used to call Mr. Potato Head—got so hammered that he let a lady named Maybell give him a mohawk in front of a thousand strangers. "He looks more potatolike than ever," Rachel wrote. "He actually has *spores* on his head!"

I clicked on the arrow that would lead me to the next page, where my sixth e-mail was waiting. Figuring it would be yet another copy of a note I had already received from Rachel, I was shocked to discover otherwise. It was from Max Roth, or PainterRoth00. Well, this was certainly a first. Why on earth was he writing to *me?* Good thing nobody else was in the computer lab. For some reason I didn't feel like examining, I found myself seriously freaking out. The letter wasn't as juicy as Rachel's account of Richard's public shearing, but still it was from Max, who had Rachel beat in the sexual attractiveness category. Plus, I appreciated knowing that *someone* at Baldwin (besides Amanda, who still Instant Messaged me on an hourly basis, and Sam, that is) had registered my existence. "Hey, Mimi," it said. "What's going on? Nothing new here, just procrastinating . . ."

And so on. Max was no Shakespeare, but then very few boys composed emails like my friends and I did. I was musing on this gender gap when I heard my name. I leaped up in my seat, and my left foot thumped forward into the surge protector, which I guess I managed to unplug or break. The monitor went black, and I turned around feeling like a total dumb-ass.

"Hey, Vivian," I murmured, totally nonchalant and above-all-that as I rose from my chair. She was wearing more eye makeup than most drag queens, which, let's face it, looked a little silly that early on a Monday morning, but not as silly as it would have on a less stylish girl like me. She seemed to have just emerged from three days at some basement rave: no traces of her weekend of sun and fun clung to her sallow complexion. Of all the girls in the group, Viv was the quietest, the least forthcoming, for better or worse—definitely the hardest to face in my current condition.

"What's going on?" she asked.

I just shrugged and made for the door. Unfortunately, Vivian stood directly in my path. "What's going on, Mims?" she repeated. "I was just coming to find you. Do you want to skip out of here for a cigarette break? I'm *so* not in the mood for school right now. I was supposed to read this book for French culture, but I couldn't get past the first page. It was so annoying. All about the gazillion love affairs some old woman had. Totally gross, not to mention inappropriate."

I tried to keep my expression flat and unemotional. *Play it cool, Mimi*, I told myself.

"Actually, they're affairs she *supposedly* had," Viv corrected herself. "The book might have been a little more believable if her author photograph weren't so repulsivo. No way I can go to class and survive a forty-five-minute-long discussion of some wacked woman's sexual fantasies. The only thing I'm prepared to say is that I spilled Diet Coke all over it and some of the pages aren't even readable."

I couldn't help it: "Gosh, must have been a hard weekend, struggling through such a heavy book?" I scowled.

"I am pretty tired, yeah," she admitted.

"Must be pretty rough, lying out at the pool all day."

In response, Vivian played dumb—and quite well, I might add. She was definitely well practiced in popular-girl bitchery, and her smile kept on widening. "Hey, *I* know." She lowered her voice. "All we have next is assembly—aka, free period, right? Why don't we go grab some Turkish coffee at that place around the corner? I could *totally* use some caffeine."

The Williamsburg party had introduced me to this basic expression in the Baldwin lexicon: "Turkish coffee" was code for pot. I couldn't believe Vivian was actually going to light up a joint at eleven-thirty-five on a Monday morning. It was so bright-lights-big-city generic.

"Sure," I said. I couldn't believe how weak I was, but I couldn't help it: I liked her, and maybe I was also a little lonely for cool female friends like Rachel. Or maybe my ridiculous eagerness came from my curiosity to try pot again (if only to prevent further respiratory disasters at future social gatherings). "And we've got lunch next, so that gives us, like, two hours."

"Totally—lucky I already ate, huh?"

An hour later, we were sitting on my couch in the Village, fairly to totally high. All had gone well until then: I'd exhibited forgiveness and restraint and all those qualities my mom always praises in Myrtle, probably just to make her biological children feel inadequate. We had smoked under some scaffolding on Court Street a block from Baldwin. Then, when it became obvious that sitting through a biology lab double period would pose serious health risks, we took the train to my house. The one thing I hadn't lied to Amanda about this weekend was my father's photo shoot—though he was, of course, photographing organic soaps in a studio, not overweight live-action models. Now that he was shelling out five figures for his precious younger child's education, he actually had to go out and make money. He tried to make me feel guilty about his "selling out" to the catalog market, but personally I thought it was good for him to leave the house every once in a while. I mean, really, there are only so many days you can waste doodling rabbit ears on snapshots of dead movie stars.

Vivian and I had been plopped on the couch for about an hour, flipping hyperactively from one cable station to the next before finally settling on this crazy talk show about women whose husbands have left them for their children's babysitters or other trusted members of the household.

"So what did you do this weekend again?" Vivian asked me midway through this highly entertaining program. "I can't remember."

And just like that, all my sorrows welled up in me again. I felt a little shocked, given the bitchiness of my earlier weekend reference, that Viv would revive the subject. Still, I managed to answer as casually as Vivian had asked. "I went to this electronica symposium at the NYU gym," I said. Uttered out loud, it sounded incredibly lame.

"You *did*? I was dying to go to that symposium!"

The funny thing about being stoned is that people become more themselves, if that makes any sense. Vivian, despite her creds, had always seemed too dorky for authentic popularity— too enthusiastic. Viv had made some truly hilarious comments that morning, like when the talk show host had invited members of the at-home audience to call up if they'd ever caught their siblings in bed with their husbands, and Vivian had gasped, "Omigod, how *horrible!*" On the other hand, maybe she was just insecure about having a sister even hotter than she was.

"Yeah, right. Everyone there had antennae and multiple eyebrow piercings—Sam was the best-looking guy in the whole place, if that's any indicator!" I pointed at the antacid commercial on TV: a creepy-eyed bald man clutching his stomach and leaning against an eighteen-wheeler. "The rest of them all looked exactly like that dude."

"Sam doesn't have a girlfriend, does he?" Viv asked.

"Huh?"

"I just thought he might. He has such . . ." Viv flicked her eyes to her feet ". . . nice coloring."

"Are you kidding?" I asked. Surely she was.

And as predicted, Viv nodded and laughed. "Well, he does have stellar taste in music," she said. "And hanging out with you sounds *much* better than getting molested by a bunch of eighty-year-old European sleazebags. One of the guys who was there, my dad actually sued last year for securities fraud, and there he was, living like a total king. And then there was this disgusting hedge fund president who went to China and came back with an eighteen-year-old bride. And he had the *nerve* to say we looked alike. But whatever . . . I'm so jealous of you. You'd better invite me next time, mkay?"

Even stoned I thought this was a pretty rude, salt-rubbing comment: not just as a reminder of all the glamorous events I'd missed, but of her father's fame. I did my best to answer acerbically. "Yeah, Sam's great. He's kind of nerdy, but at least he doesn't disinvite me to parties and then crack jokes about it. At least he's reliable." Somehow, thinking about my parents, and about Sam and Rachel and best friends and my childhood in New York, depressed me, and for the millionth time in forty-eight hours, tears rolled down my cheeks.

"Oh, sweetheart, what does *that* mean?" Vivian scooted toward me on the couch. "Tell me what's wrong. You've been so distant and weird all afternoon. Have I done something?"

So I did it, I described every last detail of my dull as hell—not to mention agonizing—weekend. I'm even pretty sure I remembered the part about logging onto e-mail 1,800 times and cursing Pia twice as often. Vivian coaxed this record of my shame from me with sympathetic nods. It was funny: Usually she seemed the most distant and checked-out of the bunch, including even Pia, but that Monday afternoon she was treating me just as I'd always wanted my emotionally deficient big sister, Ariel, to—considerate, kind, confiding.

"When did she invite you, again?" Viv asked.

"Last weekend," I said. "Right after the Williamsburg party. And she acted as if she meant it."

"Now, Mimi, I'm *sure* she did—obviously. Pia's just careless sometimes. You know—she expects the whole world to turn on her pinkie."

"Well," I sighed, "*that*'s why I was weird this morning, in a nutshell. I felt totally, I don't know, rejected."

"*I* get it now," she said afterward. "I feel *so* stupid. I'm seriously glad you told me, Mimi, because there's something about

Pia you have to understand. She's not mean, she's really not. It's just that Nona going into rehab really threw her for a loop, you know? They were best friends, and Pia's just kinda lost her grip." Vivian clapped her arm around my shoulder and gave me a little shake. "Mimi, listen. We had no idea. I *completely* forgot she'd invited you—I'm totally absorbed in my own troubles right now, and so are the rest of the girls, but I swear no one meant you any harm. We like you, Mimi, we really do. We were all talking about you so nicely all weekend, Pia most of all."

"You *were?*" I asked, smiling and sniffling at the same time. "She *was?*"

"Yes. And, come to think of it, your amazing boots. Insider tip: I'd keep an eye on those guys. I know four devious ladies who are trying to figure out ways to make off with them."

Dear Diary,

I have no idea which day it is, or even which month. I guess I could look at the newspaper, but that would require energy.

Truth be told, I spent the first few days of this week in a depressed fog. Perhaps it came out in my last entry that Pia's "forgotten" invitation to the Hamptons was a serious downer. On the popularity meter, I felt as if I'd hit the lowest possible level, hovering around the molten core of the earth.

But, turns out I was just wasting time feeling sorry for myself. Viv told me that it was a mistake, and I know that's a clichéd excuse, but I actually believe it.

Nona and Pia, apparently, had a "special" friendship that none

*of the other girls shared and turns out that Nona had sent Pia an
e-mail that really upset her. She was supposed to come back to
school soon, but the doctors decided she needs to take some time off,
and they're sending her to some boarding school in Bumfuck,
Massachusetts, where there's a farm on campus and the nearest
liquor store is forty minutes away—by car. To top it off, Nona's
totally bummed about it. She wanted to come to Baldwin and do
outpatient therapy in the city, but her parents are so mad at her
they don't even want to lay eyes on her. So that pretty much explains
it. And Viv swore to me that next time they make an excursion out
of the city, I'm getting an invite by certified mail.*

Love,
A much happier Mimi

The L Word

My TALK SHOW SESSION WITH VIVIAN REALLY got that next week off to a better start than I'd expected. Sure, I was still touchy about the previous weekend's ditchage, but Vivian had done her utmost to make sure that my wounds healed fast. I don't know *what* she said to the girls, but before the week was up, they had welcomed me into their crew, so I had trouble holding a grudge. This time, there was no seesawing or backtracking: I was officially in with the popular croud.

We'd get create-your-own salads together at lunch, and after classes let out we'd huddle by the little brick wall outside school, firming up that night's social schedule. They abandoned me only once, on a Thursday afternoon, when the four of them took the Metro North to visit Nona at her treatment center. I felt kind of flattered when Lily explained the delicacy of the situation, and agreed that it might be uncool to rub Nona's replacement in her sober face.

Amanda, meanwhile, refused to take the hint. She kept haranguing me to visit her father's country house on Cape Cod with her. "It's *so* fun! There's a candle factory where you can watch them pour the wax right up close. And it's just down the road from an amazing outlet mall!"

I looked at Amanda with a distaste I had difficulty concealing. She was wearing a red and white striped polo shirt and big silver hoop earrings that gleamed only slightly less brightly than her teeth. She and her whole squash crew—Courtney, Mary Ann, Ivy, and Sophie—looked identical in every setting, ready to canoe or ride horses. My new friends, on the other hand, all had their own styles going. Pia favored haute couture, Viv goth, and Lily grunge (or just gunk), while Jess wore sexy cardigan-and-jeans combos that might have seemed boring if her breasts weren't so gigantic. In this company, I could wear whatever I wanted, even the most outlandish of my father's vintage finds. It was liberating, getting dressed up to go out with girls who had such different—and yet somehow complementary—styles. I could experiment much more than in Houston. Like almost everyone in my old high school, Rachel, for all her Jewishness, was an even WASPier dresser than Amanda.

In short, all was smooth sailing until the following Tuesday evening. I was sitting at the kitchen table, staring at my biology notes and cursing Lance, our bio teacher, for insisting that biology at Baldwin had to be as hard as it was at any other school. Why oh why couldn't we forget about the studying for tests every other day and just make short animated films about mitosis instead? Dad was in the kitchen, too, working on a batch of blueberry pancakes. We were both pretty lost in our own worlds, when the phone rang.

"Mimi! What the fuck are you doing home?" It was Pia, on a polite day. I heard squealing in the background. "We're all at my place. Get dressed. We'll swing by in twenty."

Before I had a chance to answer, she slammed down the phone.

Dad's head swung around from the stove. A glop of batter dotted his cheek like a Marilyn Monroe mole.

"What's going on?" he asked.

"Uh," I spluttered, trying to figure out how I could possibly ditch our hallowed Tuesday breakfast-for-dinner tradition, throw on a slinky outfit, and be out the door in twenty minutes. "I'm in *deep* trouble." I held out my notes and screwed my face into a constipated grimace. "There's, ah, this big biology review session at this kid's house, and I was supposed to deliver a spiel on the nervous system and it totally slipped my mind. And now they're all waiting for me uptown!"

Dad flipped a pancake. Slowly. You could tell he was thinking something.

"They sound *super* stressed out! Don't ask why, but they're counting on me."

"Well, young lady, I guess that means more pancakes for me." He wagged the spatula in reproach.

It killed me when he tried to cover his disappointment with that funny-guy routine, so I got up and gave him a jumbo hug, but that only intensified my bad-daughter guilt.

Smushing between Jess and Lily in the back of Pia's dad's stretch limo, I forgot all about it. I'd been worried that I was overdoing it in my super-clingy low-cut purple top, but the rest of the girls (except Lily) were decked out like a Versace print campaign. I fit right in.

"Where the *hell* are you going?" Pia rolled down the limo's divider and let the chauffeur have it. "If you take First Avenue, we're not going to get there for *weeks!*"

Several U-turns later, we were all nestled in a banquette in the back room of a club called Peppermint Pete's. The decor was immaculate: marble floors, thick velvet seats, white linen table-cloths. Even with all the shirtless female employees offering lap dances, the joint was incredibly classy. Everyone in the place—by which I mean all the preppy businessmen downing whiskeys at the surrounding tables—was staring at us.

I had just figured out that we were the only nonperforming females in the joint when I noticed that once again Jess was rolling the bottom of her shirt up over her flat stomach. I'd never met a girl who thrived on male attention more, in whatever context.

"Stop!" I lunged at her. "We're *customers,* not strippers!"

"Chill out, Mimi, seriously." Pia signaled. "Could someone get her a drink?"

As if psychic, a bouncy-breasted lady bopped over and handed me a Freaky Fizzy, a special mixture of Midori, Amaretto, and about three other liquors I'd never heard of. The comparative modesty of my own chest had initially made me feel insecure, but two sips of my Fizzy and I remembered that my breasts, however unimpressive, were at least all natural. Yep, the Fizzies sure got me into the spirit of things, and I was happier than I had been when my Houston luggage finally reached the bottom floor of our brownstone. Soon I was dancing with Lily in one of the aisles, swirling my hips and avoiding the leer of a bald giant in blue-tinted sunglasses, when I spotted several familiar male faces across the room: Preston, Jess's boyfriend, and a horde of his cheesy-looking friends.

"Lily, oh my God!" I said, ducking down. "Preston's here. We can't let Jess see. She'll flip."

"Why? She told them to come."

"Oh." Did I ever feel like an idiot.

The guys seemed pretty uptight when we joined them a few songs later: Half of them ordered Diet Cokes. I knew less of Jessica than any of the other girls, and I couldn't figure out how such a beautiful girl could fall for a lout like Preston. He had broad shoulders and nice blondish brown hair, yes, but his eyes were too close together and his front teeth too far apart, which made him look more than a little stupid. Not only that, but he seemed incapable of conducting a conversation in a normal tone of voice: Everything he said, he shouted.

"What is this?" I said. "The prohibition era?"

No one laughed.

"We're not really in a position to get sauced," responded a sort-of redhead in baggy pants. "It's early-decision application time. We're kind of stressed out."

"They're all seniors," Lily told me. "College apps. Hey, where's Blow Job Harry?"

"He's coming later. He had other plans," said another guy, bringing a ginger ale to his mouth suggestively. Blow Job Harry was a Baldwinite known for having his way with Baldwin women. It was weird. Monday after Monday, girls trudged into school admitting that they'd gone down on the kid over the weekend. Nobody knew how he did it. At any other school, Blow Job Harry would've been a total reject: He didn't play a single sport and in fact had probably never exercised, judging from his emaciated physique. He was about seven feet eleven, with plenty of freckles and front teeth big enough to launch a rocket off. But Harry was also hilarious, self-confident, and extremely clever, and at Baldwin—a place renowned for its open-minded coeds—these three qualities more than compensated for his physical inadequacies.

"I'm beat," the ginger ale drinker said, "I just finished bull-shitting my way through the Princeton essay. Call me anal, but November one is *right* around the corner, and if I don't get in early, my dad will probably revoke my trust fund." He looked a little too attentively at me, then leaned into my neck. He was so close, I could feel his breath against my skin. "What are you wearing?"

"My perfume? I got it in Texas. It's called—"

"No, I mean your shirt. I was admiring the fabric. It's very sexy."

My expression surely revealed my repulsion, because right then the baggy pants guy came to my rescue. "Ignore him. He gets like this when he's stressed out. We shouldn't have let him get so close to sophomore girls."

"Oh, but it's OK for the sophomores to hit on each other, is that it?" the lecherous Princeton guy shot back, gesturing to where Pia and Viv sat tickling each other's arms.

"What's *that* supposed to mean?" Jess issued an offended gasp.

"All I know is that I'm lucky to have already landed the best sophomore *ever*," Preston bellowed, drawing Jess even closer. "Jess, baby, can I tell you something?"

I was still thinking about the bizarreness of such a preppy guy using the word "baby" when Preston dropped the bomb-shell: "Jess"—his voice couldn't have been louder—"I know I've been a real head case lately, trying to get all my shit together for school, but I've been meaning to tell you, well . . . I think I love you, Jess. I've only had two beers, so I swear I'm being serious. I've never been in love like this before."

There was silence at all six adjacent tables, and even the leather banquette stopped squeaking. The only sound on the whole earth right then was the pulsing techno remix egging on the waitresses.

"I love you."

He said it again, just like that, right in front of all of us, at a cheesy club where the fanciest thing on the menu was deep-fried mozzarella sticks, about as unromantic as you could get. The strange thing was, Jess seemed genuinely touched. A tear gleamed at the corner of her eye, and her head dropped into Preston's beefy chest. "Oh, Preston!" she simpered. "Preston, I—"

I'm totally not making this up. When Preston mentioned the

nearby five-star hotel where he'd conveniently booked a room, Jess was too wilted to protest. Preston's friends exchanged winks and jabs and I felt sick to my stomach. I couldn't believe the whole seduction scenario had played out in front of so many unrelated Baldwinites. Jess could be too good-hearted for her own good.

The rest of the girls and I soon detached from Preston's posse and proceeded to the Pazzolinis' New York pad, which was located uptown in the Columbus Circle Trump Tower. Not only did Pia's parents have one of the most luxe apartments in the place, but they had an adjoining guest suite. By the time we rolled in, we were totally, ecstatically wasted. When I called my dad to give a progress report on my biology project, I discovered that my central nervous system wasn't functioning all that well.

"These people are *such* nerds," I told him. "Yeah, I know, but we've got a few more hours of work left, and Ms."—I coughed— "said she wouldn't even feel comfortable sending me in a cab at this hour."

"Well, Mimi, I can come up in a cab and get you if it makes you feel any safer," Dad said.

"No, Dad, it's OK, I wouldn't want to put you out like that."

"Really, Mimi, I don't mind at all. What I do mind is your staying out all night with someone I've never even met."

God, he sounded lonely. Why else would he get all Curfew King on me? "Dad, can I help being conscious about school?" I think I meant another word, but it was all slurring together. "Hey, what's that on in the background, Dad? You having a little party over there or what?" (I was hoping to distract him from the very unacademic sounds on my end of the line.)

"Nope, not even close," he sighed. "Quinn and I are just watching *Grand Hotel*—your very favorite film of 1932, right?"

Ever since the split, my dad pulled stuff like that all the time, declaring every single thing he saw "your favorite"—"your favorite" root vegetable, "your favorite" reality show, "your favorite" brand of green tea (not that I even drank green tea)— as if trying to prove that he knew more about me than I did. He couldn't go to the grocery store without purchasing "your favorite" quilted Kleenex or running into "your favorite" homeless man at the West 4th Street subway station. Dad's declarations had exactly zero basis in fact, and their frequency made me wonder if maybe he was losing his grip.

"Oh, Dietrich, right?" I said after a too long pause.

"No, no, *Garbo*, silly!" His voice perked up—if there's one thing he loves it's correcting me about my favorite things. "She's a good-looking lady in this film, isn't she, Quinn?"

"Yup!" Quinn intoned.

I was feeling semi-sad as I walked sluggishly down the hall, imagining Quinn drooling over another woman: I didn't stand a chance against an eleventh-grader, much less Garbo. I walked into the luxury bathroom to find Pia and Viv lounging in the hot tub.

"What is this? Some sort of fantasy sequence?" I asked.

"Hop in!" Pia commanded.

I turned to Lily, who was sitting with terrible posture on the black marble toilet, covered in enough sweat gear to warm the Statue of Liberty. "Go ahead." She made a sick face. "I'm not into germs, that's all."

Lily was even less into nudity, I could tell, and I couldn't help feeling slightly uncomfortable myself. "Can I borrow a swimsuit or something?" I asked after a pause.

Pia laughed and a bubble landed on the center of her tongue. "Swimsuit? Hello, does this look like the Speedo outlet?"

I would have preferred to join Lily in her decency, but there wasn't any extra space on the toilet seat. Besides, the one good thing about having friends who weren't self-conscious was that they probably wouldn't be paying much attention to my not exactly stellar body. To them it had about as much shock value as a pile of laundry.

"Are we going to have to drag you in here?" asked Viv. "Because I will if I need to."

"No need," I said, slightly dismayed.

And so, clutching a melon-colored hand towel, very gingerly I peeled off my purple shirt and stepped into the swirling water, one foot at a time.

Blame It on the Margarita

Bio CLASS PROVED PRETTY DEMANDING THE NEXT day, which came as quite an unwelcome surprise, especially since I'd stayed up very late drinking bubbly in the bubbles. I was not prepared to ask much of my brain that morning.

Over the past few weeks our biology lessons had been getting easier and easier as our teacher, Lance, sunk deeper and deeper into depression. A mere month ago, back when *l'amour toujours* with the French teacher Claudine had Lance's confidence soaring, he had made us learn stuff: memorizing the function of mitochondria, labeling the different parts of lungs, reading articles in *Science* magazine, and all sorts of inconveniences. But ever since Claudine terminated her *petite affaire* with him, Lance had us spending our class time playing Science Scrabble or coloring in pictures of fauna, while he sat at his desk and stared sadly into space. For a simpering accordion enthusiast, Lance was a good-natured guy who didn't deserve this kind of heartbreak.

To rub salt in Lance's wound, Claudine started giving private French lessons to Stuart Francis, a teacher in the language structures department. They'd meet in the cafeteria, for all the world to see. I guess when Lance caught wind of the *nouvelle* develop-ment, he went from sad to mad and resorted to taking his angst out on his sweet students that morning by springing a pop quiz on us.

I was the last to reach class, but it had taken me forever to get there. Around five a.m., I had taken the subway from Fifty-ninth Street back to the West Village, and after a brief nap and a noble battle with my wardrobe, I chose the one train that stalled for fifteen minutes between the Wall Street and Clark Street Station. So when at last I stumbled into Lance's bio heaven, I was surprised to find not the usual mayhem but orderly rows of silent, wide-eyed students. From his seat in the back Sam shot me a look of extreme anxiety.

"Glad you could drop by, Mimi," Lance growled as he flung a sheet of paper at my desk. "I hope you'll be able to finish in time."

I experienced all the telltale symptoms of total panic: dry mouth, shaky wrists, churning stomach. I could barely under-stand the exam questions, let alone ace them. I looked down at the paper, empty except for a single question: "What are the functions of life?"

I couldn't believe my luck: overlapping lesson plans must be the *only* good thing about switching schools. I hadn't exactly been knocking myself out studying at Baldwin, but I remem-bered this answer from my ninth-grade science class in Houston; I'd probably still retain it at the ripe old age of eighty-seven. I'd always remember MRS GREN. "Movement, Respiration, Sensitivity, Growth, Reproduction, Excretion, Nutrition." Ta-da!

That accomplished, I lay my head on the cool tabletop. I started reminiscing about the hot tub party, which gave way to a delicious vision of Quinn beckoning me across a crowd at some Chelsea gallery opening when a bell jostled me awake half an hour later. "Thank you, thank you," Lance said as he collected our test papers. He cleared his throat and shuffled to the door, where he stopped at a gray trash bin and dunked our exams right in. We all watched with startled interest. "Now you know that it pays to be prepared for life's more miserable possibilities," he said, and walked off before anybody could respond.

"That sucks," Sam said as he made his way over to me. "I totally aced that sucker."

It was time for assembly, which was a totally Baldwin phenomenon: a daily schoolwide get-together in the second-floor lobby where students announced meetings and birthdays and other such earth-shattering events. Zora Blanchard, who could sip from her ever-present coffee mug and speak simultaneously, then read off the names of people who had missed classes the previous day. After assembly, students were expected to approach Zora and explain their absences, a ritual I was not above sticking around to observe. Baldwin was just a barrel of comic relief. The truants' excuses ranged from "I was feeling depressed" and "I slept in" to "I felt like cutting." Zora preferred the more creative efforts, those along the lines of "I was so consumed with my tuna can sculpture that geometry class completely slipped my mind" and "I was feeling jittery so my shrink and I called an emergency double session."

I found a spot in the lobby near the yellow elevator (there was a yellow and blue one, for even and odd floors, respectively).

Across the lobby some of the cool senior girls were giggling and passing around a photograph that they were going to great pains to conceal. Judging by the high-pitched level of their excitement, I figured there had to be some nudity involved. Next, I noticed that standing next to the girls was none other than Max Roth. He was wearing a pair of Levis and a hooded sweatshirt, both of which were accented with a dash of white paint. His hair, too, had some paint stuck in it. It was kind of unfair, how hot some people were. Why must there be some things that seem to exist solely to remind you that you can't ever have them?

I ended up standing next to Amanda of all people, who squeaked and gave my wrist a little tug when she saw that I was next to her. Perhaps for this reason, assembly that day seemed even more excruciatingly boring than usual. Sarah Ramos, a sophomore devoted to wearing bright yellow raincoats indoors, raised her hand to describe her missing digital camera. Another kid lost his SAG card and complained that he couldn't audition again until it had been returned. Finally, lovelorn Lance, desperate for companionship, tried to recruit musicians—or, as he put it, "collaborators"—for his innovative new Klezmer band.

After assembly was over, I tried to break free of Amanda and her friend Courtney, but they were both still trailing behind me when I reached the opposite side of the room.

"Are you *friends* with them?" Vivian asked me when at last I managed to wave my all-American escorts away. I turned away from Amanda's and Courtney's retreating figures, surprised by the amount of scorn in Viv's voice.

"No, of course not," I answered, perhaps a little more emphatically than necessary, given that Amanda and Courtney might still be in earshot. A twinge of guilt shot through me—but why? It was true that Amanda and I weren't friends, wasn't it?

I couldn't dwell on my remorse for long, though, because right then Pia jabbed me in the side. "You still have those little Swiss army scissors your mom gave you, right?" she asked. "There's this tag on my sweater that I forgot to take off. Can you help a girl out?"

As I pulled my mother's survival gift from my bag, Pia scooped up her hair so I could perform the operation easily. Two seconds later, a $365 price tag had come undone and fallen to the lobby's linoleum floor. "Thanks. Now put on your coat. We have a little party to attend."

Torre's was only five blocks away from Baldwin, but it felt like three worlds. I'd been there only once before, with Sam, for lunch. It was this total dive in the North Heights, always empty except for the waiters watching soccer on the bar TV. We chose a table near the back, behind a beaded curtain that gave us a sense of totally unnecessary privacy.

"Let me." Pia signaled for the crotchety-looking waiter. "A pitcher," she commanded. "With salt."

The waiter raised his eyebrows and started to chuckle. "What, are your parents coming?"

"Look, I'm old enough to know I'm entitled to a light drink." Pia switched on her huskiest voice, then brandished her fake ID.

"I don't think so. I wasn't born yesterday, so unless you want to walk right out—"

Angelic Jess, who was oozing warmth and sunshine that

morning, took this opportunity to intervene and purred, "How 'bout we compromise with some virgin margaritas?"

I didn't really care either way. It was 10:55 in the morning—I would've been happy with a doughnut.

"And some queso, too?" Lily asked in her meekest voice.

"See, all it takes is a little smile," Jess said to Pia as the waiter happily waddled toward the bar, "and you'll get everything you need out of life."

"You call virgin margaritas what I *need?*" Pia was clearly enraged that her fake ID worked everywhere except the shittiest Mexican restaurant in Brooklyn. After a young woman who also worked there delivered our pitcher, Pia reached under the table and started rifling through her bag. "At least I came prepared," she said, bringing a flask of vodka up to the table-level and emptying it into the pitcher. Just seconds later, the first stern waiter returned, totally unaware of Pia's latest exploit. Impressive.

"So?" After waiting for the waiter to fill five pint glasses with lime green slush, Vivian turned to Jess. "What up? What happened to you last night? Is it just me or do I smell something in the air?"

Jess craned her head out of our booth, making sure that the place hadn't attracted any new customers. The coast was clear. "Swear to secrecy?" she said. "On your life?"

"Oh, get on with it!" Pia had yet to recover from the tequila diss.

"I'm serious," Jess insisted. "I'm not saying a word until each and every one of you swears."

Left palms were raised as Jess sucked in a deep breath: "OK, here goes," she said, studying her lap. "Well, last night, I . . . after we left you guys, I told Preston I loved him and, well . . . I'm a new woman." That was as far as she got before plunking her forehead onto the table and letting out a piggy squeal.

"You did it?" yelled Vivian. *"IT?"*

Jessica raised her face off the table and nodded. After taking a chug of her drink, she returned to the table. "I'm sort of freaking out," she said into the tablecloth.

Vivian proceeded to grill Jess about the big night, demanding all the hows and whys and wheres and what-it-felt-likes. Jess remembered the bulk of it: It took place on the couch in the hotel room, to a mix CD that Preston had burned especially for the occasion, and it felt swirly and gooey and delicious and didn't hurt at all—or maybe a *tiny* bit. "He was *so* sweet to me." She sighed.

After Jess and Preston completed the deed, Jess told us she passed out in his arms and slept beautifully—practically a first. She woke up in the morning to find him serving her a cup of seven-dollar hot chocolate and a fresh loaf of ciabatta from room service, both of which she was too jittery to touch. "All that intensity," she concluded, "and I *still* made it to school on time!" She stretched her arms out above her head. "I don't even know what to say. Everything feels so different."

No one said anything for a minute or two; we were all just soaking it in. The whole conversation was making me feel especially fidgety: not only had I never had sex, but I'd never even contemplated it. It seemed as far removed in the future as mortgages or gray hairs.

Jess sighed, then started to speak again. "And the most amazing thing about the whole night is it could happen again anytime now. I'm telling you, life is completely different. You guys don't realize it, but you're so *innocent*."

"God. Francesco is *so* controlling, I swear," Pia said, changing the subject before Jess could keep saying patronizing things. Francesco was the twenty-four-year-old wunderkind assistant spokesman at her father's office, Pia's secret boyfriend. I'd never met him, but Vivian once showed me his picture in the 100 Hottest Bachelors spread in *Hamptons* magazine. "He's been completely insane all week," Pia went on, "which is pathetic considering that at the time he didn't even know that I hooked up with Guillermo last weekend."

"Guillermo?" Viv asked.

"Duh, my dad's sub chauffeur. So last night I told Fran about Guillermo because, well, why not? We're *supposed* to have an open relationship—"

"Pia." Jess's voice quavered. "I actually hadn't finished about Preston and me. Because this morning, right before school—"

No one was paying attention to Jess, though: The pendulum had shifted to Pia, just as she had intended it, I'm sure.

"But Fran *totally* lost his shit, pulled a total Ike Turner when I told him. He started sweating and talking about 'taking a course of action.' I mean, whatever! He knows our theories!"

"Your theories?" I offered tentatively.

"It's nothing scientific," Vivian turned to me and explained. "It's just something my sister told me a long time ago, and ever since we've all adopted it as a total golden rule. We think we should try to hook up with as many people as possible, you know? At our age, it's totally crucial to build experience."

"*And* expertise," Pia added.

"Speak for yourself," Jess said. "Preston's the only experience *I* need. I mean it, guys, I think I want to marry him."

We all rolled our eyes: Jess's naïveté was extremely endearing, especially in the context of her jaded friends. I could tell from the expression on her face that she meant it, she really did want to spend her life with Preston.

"Enough about Preston, dear. We're *delighted* you lost the big V, but spare us the twelve-part miniseries, all right? Pay no attention to her, Mimi—Jess is perpetually suffering from Deadbeat Dad syndrome. Everyone knows that girls whose daddies dump them spend their whole lives searching for a replacement; that's *so* Psych 101. But anyway, as Viv was saying, Mimi, there's no such thing as only one guy—"

"What are you talking about, Pia? My dad has absolutely nothing to do with this! You're just jealous because you have no idea what it's like to find someone you really love, and it's no wonder, the way you treat your closest friends! I can't even *begin* to imagine how you act to your boyfriends!" Jess shuddered, and her face flushed with color until it was almost purple.

"Oh, Jess, don't be so melodramatic," Viv retorted, suddenly acerbic. "We *all* know what it's like to fall in love. We just try not to make a habit of it every semester, with, like, every athlete in school."

"Come to think of it," Pia plowed right over this interruption, still addressing me, "the theory works better when you *don't* like the guy. That way, you have less to lose, and you're not too distracted to focus on technique. If you don't start practicing now, you might turn out like Jess here—changing the vacuum bags and doing it military-style with the same boring investment banker three times a week until you die. But back to what I was saying before. The only reason I told Fran was because Guillermo was *incredible,* above and beyond anything I'd ever experienced with a man before . . ."

"Pia, why do you always have to ruin everything?" Jess whimpered, tears splashing onto the table.

Ouch. I wasn't quite sure what was going on right then. But Viv and Lily seemed as accustomed to Pia's brash interruptions as to Jess's emotional outbursts. If I had never met them before, I might assume that the two girls were veering toward major meltdown, but these explosive tensions didn't seem to ruffle Lily or Viv much. Lily was being quieter than usual, that was all. As for me, I just felt uncomfortable: less with Pia and Jess's sparring than with the general topic of conversation. Sex was an arena I knew admittedly little about.

"Hold on, wait," Vivian jumped in, shielding Jess a little from our stroppy Italian princess. "Pia, you're not saying—you don't actually mean that you did it, too? With Guillermo and not even Fran first?"

"Vivian!" Pia was shocked. "What kind of skank do you think I am?—no offense, Jess. I'm a strict Catholic, God—I'd *never* have sex before marriage! No, all we did was—" She broke off, making an embarrassingly graphic trombone gesture with her hand. "Big deal." Everyone tittered except Lily—even Jess, who was way too nice to hold a grudge for more than thirty seconds.

"You OK, Lils?" I jabbed her under the table, realizing that the only word she'd pronounced since we'd gotten to Torre's was "queso."

Dip and crunch, dip and crunch—that about summed up Lily's response to Jess's news and Pia's blowup. The lewder the conversation, the bigger Lily's appetite for free tortilla chips. If things remained this down and dirty, she'd probably have to order a refill or two.

"What? Oh, sure." Lily laughed gruffly, plunging another corn chip into the speckled orange goo.

Meanwhile I was trying to be casual, talking only when necessary while doing my best not to imagine how the gang would react to *my* secret—the fact that, excluding a spin-the-bottle game one summer at Rachel's brother's high school graduation party, I'd never kissed a soul. Perhaps Lily was so quiet for the opposite reason: It wasn't her style to boast about stolen kisses, of which I was certain she'd had many.

After two drinks we paired off to slink back to Baldwin inconspicuously. Lily and I were the last to go, even though I was totally dead and unprepared for my computer animation tutorial.

"You were pretty quiet in there," Lily said as we turned onto Pineapple Street.

"Oh, was I?" I was looking straight ahead, trying to marshal all remaining shreds of cool. "I guess I'm just tired."

"You sure that's all?"

"Yeah, well, I guess when it comes to sex and all that, I don't have all that much to contribute. Not that I . . ." It dawned on me that there were no atoms of cool in me whatsoever. Not even a speck of cool dust in my entire organism. I decided to try another tactic. "What about you? I'll bet you've dated all sorts of famous peoples' kids, haven't you?"

"Yeah, right." Lily playfully kicked one of her sneakers in the air. "I try to limit myself to three celebrity dates a week, actually."

"You can tell me whatever you want. It's not like I'm going to spread any rumors, if that's what you're scared of," I assured her.

She looked surprised, almost as if she was about to laugh. "No, it's just . . ." She looked up the block, measuring how far ahead of us her friends were before continuing. I couldn't believe it; I was sure she was going to make some celebrity love confession.

"Spill the beans, will you?" I nudged her along.

"My mom tries to get me to date, I guess," Lily admitted at length, "but it's not like *I* have any say in the matter, or like any of the guys have any desire to know anything about me beyond my mother's pie crust secrets. But even that's a stretch—I mean, how many guys do *you* know who are interested in baking peach pie?"

"What are you talking about?" I didn't get it. Was she just being self-deprecating for my sake? But Lily wasn't the type to put on airs. She truly felt lousy about her love life.

"Maybe I just need to set my sights on older men," Lily went on, sighing softly. "If I could find some nice widower who goes in for household tips, maybe I'd finally have a shot at getting to third base before the age of fifty. Make that second."

So she was as inexperienced as I was. I was floored. Sure, Lily's no supermodel, but why would any guy with half a brain turn her away? She was cuter than just-cute, with giant brown eyes and a moon-shaped face sprinkled with the nicest freckles ever. And surely it didn't hurt to be the daughter of one of the most famous people in America. Talk about a house you'd want to hang out at after school. "You're just beating yourself up," I said.

"I wish!" Lily squinted, then slowed down to make sure we weren't catching up to the rest of the group. Half a block ahead of us, Pia had taken off her fedora and plopped it on Viv's head. Jess, who was on the photo staff of the yearbook, was taking pictures of it all. Apparently she wanted to chronicle every detail of the most important morning of her life thus far.

None of the resentments between Jessica and Pia seemed to linger, and none of the girls had the slightest idea of the virginity fest being held directly behind them.

"Mimi, I know I don't know you all that well, but maybe that's why I feel like I can tell you this. Can I trust you not to say anything?"

"Sure," I said. I realized I didn't sound convincing enough. "I swear on my dead body."

"Your dead *body*? What kind of swear is that?"

Why did saying the right thing always feel an inch—make that a mile—out of my reach? I tried again: "I swear over my mother's body."

"But I thought you didn't even like your mother that much."

"That's just in the past year, but fine, I see your point. My father's body, then. And his gravestone. And my cat Simon."

"All right, all right." Lily seemed appeased. "I know this is going to be kind of a surprise, but I haven't even . . ." Her voice dropped to a whisper. "I've never even kissed a boy." I couldn't believe it. "Can you believe that?"

Was it possible that one of the most envied girls in all of Baldwin—all of New York!—was a kissing virgin at the age of fifteen? I would never in a million years have guessed it, but I was happy to take her word. If even Lily Morton had never smooched anybody, maybe I wasn't such a freak after all. I wanted to put it in the *Bugle* and broadcast it to the world—it was *that* newsworthy.

"Oh my God," she said. "You should see your face. You're horrified, aren't you?"

"Not at all! I'm not. I'm just . . . surprised, is all."

Lily stopped and looked at me expectantly. Of course here was my turn to fess up and tell her she was in good company—or company at least. But I couldn't dare utter the words. It was one thing for a girl whose coolness was as official as a government bond never to have been kissed. If anything, it was almost charming. But Mimi Schulman, the weird new girl who's almost six feet tall and whose father goes accessories shopping for her? That was another story. I felt pretty confident that Lily would never hold my dorky past against me, but the other girls would definitely toss me to the curb like a cigarette butt.

"My mom says I'm a late bloomer," she was saying, "but I'm not buying that anymore. I'm almost sixteen. In some cultures that's old enough to be a mother of four."

"Uh-huh," I clucked. "That's your problem. We should send you down to Guatemala, where you can live in the Mayan ruins and get cracking on that teen pregnancy plan."

Lily laughed and gave me a goofy smile that told me everything was going to be OK, which was funny, because I'm pretty sure I was the one who was supposed to be telling *her* that.

"You're the only person in the world who knows that," she said. "I guess we have the margaritas to blame."

"Hey, watch out, girlfriend. That's my motto."

"What is?"

"Blame it on the margarita. I've been saying that since I was ten. It's a Texas thing." I grinned.

"Seriously—and I'm not just saying this because of my verbal diarrhea—but with the exception of Pia, I don't think anybody actually likes to drink margaritas first thing in the morning. Why do we all go along with her?"

"Because she'd have some Milanese henchman after us if we didn't?" I offered.

"You're right. *Pronto.*"

Then something strange happened: Lily stooped over to tie her left Adidas. Tying your shoe ranks up with the most normal activities in the world, but the thing is, I was pretty sure it didn't need any tying in the first place. Was she trying to stay behind everybody else, so we could keep at our tête-à-tête? Perhaps.

When she was done fussing with her left shoe, she moved over to the one on her right foot, and started playing with the laces. Which convinced me. She was definitely trying to stay apart from the pack. She was trying to be alone with me. How about that?

"So." Her cheeks were flushed from coming up from the shoe-tying project. "What are you up to today?"

"I have this ritual," I said. "There's this place I usually go to—it's called school."

"Ah! I have a similar habit." Lily laughed. "But what about afterward? I mean, do you have another ritual you need to take care of?"

"I might need to go to the bathroom, but after that my life is pretty open," I said.

"Well, I have this habit, and I'd be honored to have you tag along." Her brown eyes sparkled with mischief.

"What's that?" I said.

"It's called going home. Would you care to come check out my digs? Don't worry, I'm not going to kiss you there," she said. "You can trust me at least that far."

"We have history to back that one up." I stepped back as she play-punched my arm.

Just as I accepted this honor, Pia doubled back and raced toward us, then stuck her hat over Lily's ponytail.

"I hate this hat!" Pia said. "It looks like ass on every single one of my friends and me, too. Can you believe they charge two hundred and fifty bucks for this fucking hat?" Pia removed her overpriced accessory from Lily and returned it to her own head. Skipping and laughing, the three of us caught up with Viv and Jess.

"We need to get you a personal shopper," said Viv. "You're losing your magic touch."

"How dare you!" said Pia, lunging at Viv and making strangulation gestures. Pia tripped and her hat rolled into the street, and we all stood there for a while, laughing.

That day, I learned that it's always safer to order virgin margaritas, not margarita margaritas, on a fake ID, especially before noon on a weekday. I also learned that people will surprise you—even people with famous mothers.

Study Buddies

By THE TIME I GOT HOME THAT NIGHT, I was beyond out of it. Torre's, it turned out, was only Step 1 on my road to self-destruction. I know I'm beginning to sound like a total lush, but I'd like to point out that I'm in the middle of an official Adolescent Transition Period, which has not been eased by the breakup of my parents' marriage. I also have an *extremely* low tolerance, and when I imbibe even the teeniest amount of alcohol, my face turns bright red and the world starts to spin and I become indistinguishable from your basic corner hobo.

After school that day, Lily and I had taken the 6 train uptown to her house, supposedly to study for our English vocab quiz. Our teacher, Julia, had handed us a list of difficult words and told us to be prepared to "act them out" the following day. Julia, like most humanities teachers at Baldwin, was a disappointed actress and treated English class like an improv workshop whenever possible. The only word on the list she gave us that was even slightly act-out-able was *akimbo,* which means standing with your hands planted on your hips and your elbows thrust outward. But the other words—*transient, gulag, nascent*—were hardly made for miming. At this rate, our next class project was probably going to be a three-act play inspired by sentence diagrams. I made a mental note to write to Rachel about this. No doubt she was entrenched in some despotic Texan multiple-choice hell and she'd find my predicament supremely funny.

The Mortons' apartment left me speechless, and not in the way I'd anticipated. Sure, it's probably unreasonable to expect a greenhouse and an apple orchard and a stove the size of Versailles on East Seventy-second Street, but the clutter and chaos of the place looked much more like my mother's study than any of the "makeover mansions" featured on Margaret Morton's hit TV show *House and Home*. The only person there to greet us was the maid, Thelma, who was sitting in the kitchen watching soaps and snacking on cheese curls.

"I'm not allowed to set foot in here," Lily said as she creaked the door open to her mom's study, "but it's my favorite room in the house."

So guess where we decided to hang out? The room was dark and leathery, like a psychiatrist's office, except, instead of books, the shelves were crammed with videotapes, all of them labeled with the names of the extremely famous people who had given Margaret Morton invaluable entertaining tips, like "Boris Yeltsin's Favorite Borscht" and "Elizabeth Taylor's Low-Fat Picnics." On every surface there were exotic imported flowers, but—unlike on TV—most of them were wilted and half dead, and the water in all the glass vases was a muddy brown. Settling onto a frayed Persian rug that stank of mothballs, Lily and I sipped some nasty-ass liquor that she said her mother reserved for very special occasions. Once we'd settled cozily into the room, we began to talk about guys—or rather, our lack of them.

"You realize we're the only ones in the group who don't get action on a regular basis?" Lily said.

At first, the bluntness (and accuracy) of the comment depressed me. But then it hit me that Lily had included me in her definition of "the group" automatically, as if I'd always belonged to it. It was maybe the biggest compliment of my life.

"These things come in waves," I said, trying to sound as if I believed it. And then: "You know that guy in our World Civ class, Max?"

Lily nodded. "Yeah, what about him?"

"Oh, nothing. But isn't he so cute?"

And so went our studies. Every half-hour or so, we'd get back to the business of reviewing words for our theatrical vocabulary exam. "Abject," Lily said, and collapsed onto the rug. We were playing a game similar to "Roxanne," which Ariel had taught me and Rachel way back when in Texas. Every time I pantomimed a word correctly, Lily gave me a sip of the liquor, and vice-versa. We soon introduced a new rule: If you got a word right you got a sip and if you got a word wrong you had to take two sips.

In the early evening, we tried to raid the kitchen, but the lichen-covered takeout containers in the Mortons' fridge made my dad's meal options look fresh from the farm. We had no choice but to keep drinking and binge on dry fiber cereal.

To make a long story short, by nine o'clock that night, I was pretty, shall we say, dizzy. Or, as Julia might prefer, *vertiginous* (picture me spinning around like a toy top, only to collapse onto one of Mrs. Morton's stained custom-made ottomans). Somehow,

I wound up in the back of a long black Town Car that Lily had ordered for me, assuring me that her mother's account would be charged for the ultra-comfortable ride into the Village. When the car pulled up before my beloved brownstone, I thanked the driver, Bertrand, perhaps overenthusiastically, and implored him to add a 25 percent tip onto the receipt that I signed.

After turning crazy circles in our entry hall, I squealed with delight when I saw Dad, Sam, and Quinn all squeezed close together on the couch, watching *Jezebel*. "It's my men!" I exclaimed. "The Three Musketeers!"

I was too drunk to wonder—it only occurred to me later: What was Sam doing there, and when had he become so chummy with Quinn? My dad had always liked Sam above all my other friends, ever since we were little kids in the city together, but now they were behaving as if *they* were the childhood best friends, instead of me and Sam. I know it's bad karma to be stingy with friendships, but there's something more than slightly unsettling about suspecting that two of your most prized friends are conspiring behind your back. The last thing I wanted was to be left in the dust.

But whatever. There are worse things in life than seeing your nearest and dearest getting along so harmoniously. Also, Sam had mentioned that he wasn't getting along so well with his parents, so it made sense that he'd seek refuge at my pad—who would choose bickering with one's family over movies and takeout with another person's family? Come to think of it, I hadn't laid eyes on either grown-up Geckman since moving to New York.

Quinn wasn't particularly slick about looking me up and

down. I was enjoying the attention until I realized that he was only checking me out for damage. "You OK, Mimi?" he asked, peering at me like I was a lunatic on the subway.

I stood there, trying to decide whether or not I should join them on the couch. It was a major Catch-22: If I disappeared they would want to know why; if I sat down, they would smell why.

Before I had made up my mind, Quinn glanced at his wrist-watch and catapulted up. "Mimi, please, have my seat. I have to dash. My friend Fiona's having her opening tonight, and if I don't at least make a cameo, my ass is grass."

"Who's Fiona?" I felt a sharp stab of jealousy.

"A chick I went to college with. No Michelangelo, but a great girl nonetheless."

"What's she opening?"

"You're hilarious," Quinn said, chuckling and patting my shoulder.

I scowled in a way that I hoped showed that hilarity hadn't been my aim. Dad seemed as upset as I felt by Quinn's proposed departure. "You can't leave!" he protested. "We haven't even gotten to the red dress scene."

"Sorry, no choice. See you early in the a.m., all right?" Quinn zoomed out the door.

My dad's face crumpled as it had when Mom dumped him. The poor wonderful man, whose only sin was having loved her too much. I felt a little guilty just then: I had sort of lost sight of my salvation schemes since arriving at Baldwin. Dad had made all these great plans for us—visiting Historic Richmond Village in Staten Island one Saturday; riding the roller coaster at Coney

Island; spending a tranquil weekend on the banks of the Hudson—but I had been too swept up in my own social experiment to take him up on any of his offers. I was a bad, selfish daughter: My daddy deserved only the best, and all I ever did was let him down. And, remarkably enough, he never once complained.

My heart swelled in sympathy, and, forgetting my bourbon breath, I scrambled over to give my Dad a colossal hug. Then, not wanting to leave Sam out, I leaned my neck to the other side. He turned toward me so abruptly that his chin banged into my forehead. What I did next might sound really weird, but right as Sam said "Ow," I opened my mouth and bit him on the neck. It came as a gut reaction—like something a shark might do during a feeding frenzy. I expected him to jump back, but instead he just remained in place, his neck pressed into my mouth, like in some vampire flick. Totally freaked, I shot back up and pretended to be fascinated by Bette Davis's argument with her dressmaker.

A few minutes later, Dad got up to place his daily pizza-delivery order.

We watched *Jezebel* in silence, Sam and I both looking straight ahead, until the famous scene when Bette Davis's red dress scandalizes *le tout* New Orleans. "Oh, shit!" my dad said suddenly, hitting his forehead with his hand. "My pictures must have been soaking in the fixer solution for about two hours now. Shoot!" He jumped off the couch. "I need to see if I can revive them. I'll be in the darkroom—call me when the pizza gets here, OK?"

"Dad, the red dress scene's only just started!" I called back, but only silence answered me.

And so it was that Dad left Sam and me in the shadows of the living room, perilously close on the couch.

Feeling nervous and strange for no apparent reason, I sprang up and grabbed my backpack, into which Lily had inserted a "party treat": a brown paper lunch bag with a fancy chocolate bar, a pack of gum, and an unsealed Evian bottle containing some of the amber-colored liquid we'd been drinking that afternoon.

"Want some?" I positioned myself a few more feet away from Sam and passed the bottle over to him. "It's totally delish."

"Nah, that's cool," Sam said.

"You sure?"

"Yeah, I'm sure. And I'm also sure that you don't like that stuff either—there's no way. It smells nasty. Radioactive." He took another sniff and made an ugly face. "Gross. Let me try." He glugged at it, after which his face assumed the disgusted expression of somebody who's just swallowed an eyeball. "Sha-weet," he said.

"Shut up, Sam—what do you know about anything?" I said, reclaiming the bottle. "It might not be your beloved Arabic iced tea, but someone really famous gave this to Margaret Morton, and I happen to think it tastes all right!"

"Someone really famous, you say?" Sam looked at me sideways and shook his head. "You've really started to change, haven't you? It was just an experiment at first, but your new friends are actually rubbing off on you."

"Well, what's so wrong with that?" I violently shucked off my vintage loafers, which—like all shoes made for women and not professional logrollers—were about half a size too small for me. Rather than think about the blisters sprouting on every toe, I took another sip. "They're totally cool and they're really nice to me."

"Yeah, it was really nice of them to stand you up last weekend, wasn't it?" Sam pursued. "You have a conveniently short memory," he said, reaching down to the floor and pulling my black-and-white notebook from his military backpack.

"How did you get that?" I snapped, fearing he'd been going through my room before I got home. "Does my dad let you go in my room when I'm out?" I was outraged.

"Let's just say Roger's a man who understands free trade policy. Anyway, why do you care? Doesn't it belong to both of us? Now," he said, flipping my ridiculous pseudodiary open, "Wanna hear what you said about that only five days ago?"

"No, I don't, thank you very much," I shot back, but Sam was already reading:

"*Dear Diary, I don't think there's anything worse than what Pia did: inviting me out to the Hamptons and then retracting the invitation for no apparent reason. If Mom ever met her, she would definitely say that Pia has a personality disorder: I don't think I've ever met anyone so inconsiderate and ungiving. And bitchy—God is that girl bitchy—she makes Ariel look like Mother Teresa.*"

"Stop it, Sam," I shrieked, trying to grab the diary out of his hands. "You *made* me write that, remember? After Central Park?"

"One minute," he said. "I'd just like to finish this spectacular passage, if I may. And let me just say," he looked up at me from behind the diary, "this Coolie notebook contains some truly marvelous prose, Mimi."

My stomach was churning like a windmill. "Don't call it that!" Sam could be a real smug fucker.

"Now where was I?" he said, gazing back down at the page. *Pia might be a million times more popular than me, but at least I don't have a mustache. Last week she must have slept through her regular waxing appointment because she was sporting some serious facial hair. Either that or she had a sip of chocolate milk and forgot to use her napkin.*"

"Stop it!" I snatched the book away from him finally. "You're not supposed to use that stuff against me, especially when the whole stupid thing was your idea. I already explained it—Pia's going through a lot of rough stuff right now, but she has a heart of gold, she really does. And so do Lily and Vivian—totally. As for Jess," I said, letting out a low whistle. "Well, Jess just had a pretty big day, so we all had a lot to talk about. It really brought us closer, so I'm willing to leave that whole Hamptons misunderstanding behind me."

"Jess had a big day?" Sam broke in. "How so?"

"I don't think I should go into details," I said, taking the remote off the coffee table and aiming it at the TV. "Oh, look what's on, this one's *so* sad!" It was E!'s True Hollywood Story: The Last Days of JFK Jr. "Not that I know what JFK Jr. has to do with Hollywood. Beyond the whole Marilyn Monroe/Daryl Hannah—"

"Mimi, please don't change the subject. You're lying again, I can tell."

"I am *not* lying!" I said, tipping back my Evian bottle to polish off the remaining ounces of backwash. "It *is* weird that the Kennedys are all so—"

"I'm not talking about the Kennedys, Mimi, and you know it. What *about* Jess, huh? You remember the rules: full disclosure . . . or else."

Sam grabbed me beneath my armpit, right where I'm most ticklish, which explains why, while John-John prepared for his bar exam, I lost my will and spilled the beans about Jess and the Big V.

"Everyone's had sex," I pointed out.

Sam's reaction went all over the place: from riveted to confused to *very* uncomfortable. I felt strange, leaning so close to him, being tipsy, talking graphically about sex while Carolyn Bessette traipsed across the flat-screen in a series of ball gowns.

"Mimi, you know as well as I do that that's a load of crap. This is a big deal. Up till this point I don't think anybody in our grade has actually gone that far, unless you count what Arthur Gray says happened on his summer abroad program—and it still has to be determined whether or not he made that whole thing up."

"Arthur Gray?" I said, "Really?"

"Mimi, here's the thing. When somebody in that crowd goes and does something majorly out of control like that, it's only a matter of days before the rest of the girls at school make sure they've caught up. Especially because it's Jess. She's the nicest of the group, as you know, and all the lonely girls in school sincerely believe that they're friends with her, and so they'll want to have something in common, see what I'm saying? Which means . . ." he trailed off, affecting a smirk. "Soon as word gets around, all the insecure girls in tenth grade are going to be giving it up, hoping they can keep up in Baldwin's fast waters. In many cases they'll slink off with seniors and this won't affect me in the least. But, in at least one or two instances, they'll be partnering up with—"

"Guys in the tenth grade."

"Bingo."

I know this should have repulsed me, but for some reason all this talk about sex made me feel mad at Sam for leaping ahead of me, as if I were jealous of the experience he might obtain in the near future.

"That's pathetic if you need such circumstances to get lucky," I said, trying to sound uninterested and condescending.

"You've got to study your market, Mimi. It would be foolish not to."

"Whatever. You're full of shit," I said in conclusion, and after that we were just sitting there, millimeters apart, silent and awkward. I gulped, remembering Pia's policy about experience and experimentation. And just like that I said it, the ghastly, horrible, life-ending thing:

"I dare you to kiss me."

I don't know why such an insane proposition ever occurred to me. Maybe it was how much I'd drunk at Lily's, or how lame the "experience" conversation at Torre's had made me feel that morning. Or maybe it was just how close Sam and I were sitting on the couch. Or maybe, just maybe, I didn't like the idea of his kissing anybody else.

And so, possessed by some demon, I said it again: "I double-dare you."

Sam gawked at me as if I'd encouraged him to run over a dog with his bicycle. "Whatever," he shrugged. Then, before I had a chance to recant, he placed his lips against mine.

And kept them there.

The next few minutes were simultaneously the most slow-mo and frenzied of my life. I had no idea where to put anything and focused all my attention on not drooling. The lips felt sort of nice when I managed not to think about the person they were attached to. I couldn't believe that my first-ever kiss was with— no, no, a racing mind never did anyone any good at all.

We stayed like that for a while, eyes squeezed shut, lips exploring each other's mouths, noses, eyelids, our tongues lapping and licking while our bodies remained stuck in freeze-frame for several beats. It was pretty gross.

But pretty nice, too.

At some point, the doorbell started to ring, again and again, but the sound seemed to come from another planet. It took the pounding footsteps of my father, the slamming of the front door, and finally the "I hope you're in the mood for magic mushroom pizza, 'cause I ordered the party size!" to bring me and Sam back to earth.

By the time Dad swooped into the TV room with a large box and a fresh roll of paper towels, Sam and I were sitting on opposite edges of the sofa, looking anywhere but at each other, wishing we had about a gallon more of Lily's special potion.

"Mimi," my dad said then. "I've been thinking—I don't really know what's going on in your life these days, so I was thinking—"

"Nothing, Dad, absolutely nothing is going on in my life!" I kept my eyes fixed straight in front of me, and tried not to hear Sam shift on the other end of the couch.

"How about we—oh, I don't know? Go out to dinner sometime, just the two of us? Or take walks. How does that sound—father-daughter walks?"

"Father-daughter walks," I said, snuggling close to my father, "sound incredibly nice. Now pass the pepperoni, will you?"

October 15 (or just about)

I'm not sure who I'm writing this for, to tell the truth, but since Rachel hardly ever writes me back, this diary's about my only correspondent, so I might as well keep up the habit. So, it's been a big week for all the girls, especially Jess, who finally broke the seal with that lout Preston. The next time a guy confesses his eternal love in a crowded nightclub in the company of all his friends, remind me NOT to shack up with him right afterward. My idea of a romantic serenade has always been a little more, um, romantic, but Jess had no complaints about going all the way with Preston. Still, if I had the pick of any guy in school, he'd be pretty low on my list, but like they always say: there's no accounting for taste. At least my mom left my dad and not vice-versa—otherwise, accord-

ing to the girls, I might end up like Jess, completely starved for male attention, no matter how lame the male. Sorry to be so bitchy this evening, but, well, let's just say I've had a challenging couple of days and leave it at that.

What else what else what else—oh, here's another juicy item: Lily Morton, Miss I've-Met-Everyone-Famous-Alive, might as well be a born-again Christian for all the romantic experiences she's had. Damn. Maybe Margaret Morton should run a holiday special on how to attract a guy with home-baked desserts, just for the benefit of her daughter. Not that America's best homemaker's too concerned with the goings-on inside her own slobby penthouse, to judge by the shocking tour Lily gave me this afternoon. Blech! Underwear littering the bedroom floor—I'm not kidding! Which is OK if you're a teenager, but for a parent? Double Blech. But more on that later. I think I need to lie in bed and stare at the ceiling and contemplate other more recent traumas. Which, no offense, Dr. D, must remain nameless for the present moment. Hugs and drugs, Mimicita xx

Attack of the Killer Myrtle

"**W**HAT!" I ROARED INTO THE PHONE. My mother had really out-done herself this time. "You told her she could *what?*"

"C'mon, now, honey!" My mother clucked. Uh-oh: she used pet names only when she knew she was in trouble with me, which was all the time these days. "Why are you making such a fuss when your father doesn't seem to mind at all?"

I looked despairingly at the couch, which had preserved highlights in the form of grease marks, deeply embedded bread-crumbs, and the occasional tomato-sauce smudge of about eight-een consecutive pizza brunches. "Of *course* Dad doesn't mind—but that's only because he's the nicest man in the world! And I don't think he's going to be the one who's doing the babysitting. For the love of God, can you tell me how you're still managing to destroy my life from ten thousand miles away?"

"Now, sweetie"—there she went again—"we're only fifteen hundred miles away, so please, let's skip the conversational hyperbole. And another thing—well, you know our family has always been liberal about language, but Myrtle and Maurice are more traditional, so I'd appreciate it, I really would, if you could respect her upbringing for one teensy weekend."

"*Her* upbringing? What about *my* upbringing, Mom, which you're so totally dead-set on destroying? And *teensy*? TEENSY? It would be a TEENSY hyperbole to say that you're completely and totally out of line this morning!"

There was a long pause that I filled with huffing and my mother with sighing. "Simon says hi," she said finally. "He stands by his water bowl and meows for a good half-hour every morning, even after I've put food in it. I think he really misses you."

So now she was resorting to the old guilt trip. And it worked.

I felt a stab of sadness. My poor baby Simon, the most reasonable being left in that nuthouse. When I thought about everything I'd left behind in Houston, Simon was what I missed most, without a doubt, even more than Rachel.

"Anyway, hon," my mother went on when it once more became clear that I wasn't going to answer, "what I wanted to talk to you about is Myrtle."

And off she went. My mother was unstoppable once she'd made a decision, and for some unknown, satanic reason, she had decided that Myrtle, Maurice's seventeen-year-old cretin of a daughter, would be "more than welcome" to "crash" with me and my dad for an entire weekend—*this* weekend, since Myrtle was looking at Barnard and Columbia. In fact, today. She'd been planning on visiting in December, but then her interview had to be bumped up last minute, and Mom *would've* asked Dad, but you know how *tense* he's been lately, yadda yadda yadda . . . I couldn't believe it. I didn't even have a full twenty-four-hour cycle to prepare for my doom. I was cursed. I really did hate my mom so—

"SO, SO, SOOOOOOOOO much," I finished, meeting my

friends' eight sympathetic eyes. At least the Myrtle catastrophe gave me an urgent excuse to omit any mention of my tryout kiss with Sam the night before. With Myrtle thrust on the horizon, I'd almost stopped thinking about it, truth be told. Ugh, but still: I could've learned a Life Lesson (my mom was totally into Life Lessons) at a much lower price.

"This girl is an über-loser," I said for maybe the fourteenth time, with my every detail of Myrtle's odious personality—her magnetically charged orthodontia; her high-rise jeans; her hairball-collecting obsession—earning more laughs. I neglected to tell them that she's also annoyingly pretty. "She's here looking at engineering programs, can you believe that? Engineering? She's seventeen, only a year younger than my sister, and I'll bet the only guy she's kissed is her stuffed Tyrannosaurus rex doll!" I blushed at my false confidence, thinking of you-know-what.

"Engineering, no way—that's the worst! I would *never* become an engineer." Pia was practically bursting her seams. "Omigod, wait! I have the *best* idea—what say we show Myrtle the time of her life tonight, huh? We'll show her what *real* engineering's all about—social engineering! What time did you say her plane gets in?"

Pia's laugh was almost vicious enough to worry me. But not for long. I remembered the morning in Houston that I found Myrtle wrapped up in my monogrammed bathrobe, chomping on tortilla chips and dribbling salsa all down the sleeves. Pia was right. It was high time my mom learned a lesson about boundaries. I gave the thumbs-up to our leather-clad ringleader. "She should be at the house by four-thirty," I said.

"*Perfect*." Pia clapped. "Just in time for happy hour! Girls, go home and get feline, 'cause tonight we're making a field trip to Meow Mix!"

Meow Mix was one of the oldest lesbian bars in New York, and also, word had it, the hottest. Unlike the skeevy watering holes in the West Village known for attracting senior citizen dykes, Meow Mix drew a young set that danced on tabletops and wore shimmery vinyl halters. Preston sometimes took Jess there to watch her grind against various vixens. Jess, of course, would much rather spend her date nights at Upper East Side trattorias. (Have I already mentioned Preston's a total pig—and I'm not talking about his eating habits?)

After returning home and exchanging the barest of greetings with Myrtle, the two of us met up with my friends at this choice destination. We sat crowded around a small table surrounded by—surprise, surprise—women. I was disappointed to see that none of them looked all that feline. I was disappointed to find the crowd way less foxy than it had appeared in the photo spreads in the *Village Voice*. Even the Judys Upstairs could've passed for Miss Venezuela and Miss Brazil in there. Jess had wisely skipped the event. Preston's parents had retreated to their country house yet again, leaving the young lovers unsupervised.

"Well, Mimi, you've certainly integrated yourself into the megapolitan social infrastructure with remarkable efficiency," Myrtle said—she seriously did talk like that. And she really was wearing a humongous red turtleneck over white leggings, an outfit that she must have ordered from a catalog. I don't think it's legal to sell atrocities like that in stores.

Pia was staring hard at Myrtle, determined to flirt with her until she'd freaked the living daylights out of my unsuspecting houseguest. Why Pia had this mean streak, I couldn't say, but I was starting to wish she wouldn't inflict it on Myrtle. "So." Pia leaned way forward. "What did you say you're going to major in again?" Pia reached across the table and grabbed Myrtle's thigh.

I couldn't believe Pia was hitting on Myrtle—it was so completely embarrassing. Why hadn't I just taken Myrtle to the Carnegie Deli instead, like a normal, unpsychotic hostess?

"Biochemical engineering," Myrtle replied with a placid smile. She didn't seem at all bothered by Pia's advances, not even when my lovely Italian friend reached forward to tickle Myrtle's lower abdomen.

"Mmph, how *fascinating*," Pia purred, pouting her lips and gazing at Myrtle as if she were the hottest man on earth. Without releasing Myrtle's thigh, the diplomats' daughter deftly shoved her elbows together to showcase her cleavage. I couldn't tell if Pia was being sarcastic when she added, "I've always thought biochemical engineering was really cross-disciplinary and thrilling."

"Not really, but it sure is a great way to meet guys! The sciences are severely understocked with X-chromosomes, if you catch my drift, and all those long nights in the lab can get pretty steamy." Myrtle snarfed beer out her nose and giggled as Pia pressed harder into her leggings. "But don't tell my boyfriend I said that—physicists are a highly jealous breed of men!"

"You have a . . . boyfriend?" I asked, beyond flabbergasted. Huh? Here was Maurice's geeky-beyond-belief offspring rattling on about nights in the lab, winking and snorting up beer and not at all minding the hand that was tracing figure eights over her lumpy thighs. A *boyfriend?* Myrtle? "Since when?"

"Oh, you know, off and on since tenth grade. He's one of Dad's dissertation students, so we keep our liaisons under wraps, to avoid any unseemly domestic disturbances."

"She's kind of pretty," Viv whispered my way. I pretended not to hear.

"A dissertation student?" Pia, fascinated, removed her hand from Myrtle's thigh and looked at my houseguest with new interest. "Wow, how old does that make him?"

"Twenty-five," Myrtle said blandly.

"Twenty-five, really?" Viv looked impressed. "That's even older than Francesco isn't it, Pia?"

"I *love* older men," Pia said, unable to suppress a sigh. "They are so . . . *knowledgeable*, you know?"

"But of course." Myrtle nodded. "And may I particularly recommend physicists to your consideration? Of all the graduate students I've known and loved, they best understand how a woman's body's put together. Straight A's across the board."

Everyone tittered, and I began to wish sudden death on myself.

"I like this place," Myrtle went on. "Interesting decor, and quite a promising clientele to boot."

"Oh, really?" Pia smiled again, remembering her role. "So you're also into women, are you?"

Myrtle screwed up her face to consider the question. "Well, to tell the truth, there's not much I'm *not* into," she said. "Human sexuality's an astonishingly rich enigma, don't you find? But my

AC/DC experimentation has been limited, because, like I said, there are very few women in the sciences. But that's one of the reasons I'm looking into biochemical engineering programs in the Big Apple—the singles scene is far more educational up here!" In conclusion Myrtle snorted and blew a bubble of ale through her nose.

Did I ever need refuge. I scanned the room for a woman to dance with, but neither of the passably attractive ones at the bar even acknowledged me. Right then, a large gray-haired woman who had been slumped over the bar, nursing a Guinness, stood up and made straight for our table.

"Excuse me, girls," she said, "but I don't believe we've been properly introduced." She extended a very strong arm. "I'm Bea."

Only Myrtle reached out to shake Bea's hand. "Charmed, I'm sure," she said, just as a Village People remix came over the speakers.

"Anyone else feel the heat?" Myrtle asked, rising from her seat and wiggling her hips.

"You know what I'm talking 'bout, lady!" Bea whooped. "Let's hit it!"

"Wow," Vivian said as Myrtle and Bea pounded toward the empty dance floor. "I hate to say it, Mimi, but that girl's pretty cool."

"No lie," Lily agreed. "She wasn't what I expected at *all*. I can tell she's going to grow up to be a hot woman. Great bones."

"Maybe one day" was all I could muster.

"She's hilarious!" Pia exclaimed. "I haven't met anyone I liked so much *all year*," she added. "I like her tons."

"You're only saying that because you have so many common interests," I told Pia.

"Like what—older men?"

"No, duh," Vivian said. "Quantum physics or higher mathematics or whatever it is she was talking about—I wasn't following."

"What*ever*." Pia tossed back her shoulders. "No, I like her because she's bad-ass."

"Yeah, right. You're just happy because you found someone to go with you to science fairs," I said meanly, humiliated that Myrtle had made such a splash. It made me seem dishonest somehow. From Sam, I knew that Pia regarded her right-brain skills as something of an embarrassment, but Viv was the one who brought it up, not me.

"What do you know about anything, Mimi?" Pia said sharply. "Why don't you go get us all some beers—I'm sure Bea has a tab."

"Get your own beers," I snapped. "I'm not your servant, Pia, all right?"

"Oooh, *sorry!*" Pia narrowed her eyes at me. "What's gotten into you this afternoon, Mimi? What is it—are you jealous because your new relative gets more play than you do?" She pointed toward the bar, where Myrtle was ripping it up with Bea. "Inferiority complex?"

"Jealous of Myrtle? Ew, of course not! That's just so not possible. Besides, I get *plenty* of play, thank you very much!"

"Oh, really? Like when? At summer camp?" Pia drummed the table with her fingers. She looked languidly around the room. "Ahem, we're waiting."

"Pia, stop," Lily pleaded.

"I . . . I have a confession to make," I said suddenly. "You know how you all asked me about men and I was really quiet? Well, that's because . . ."

I had everyone's full attention. Even Pia let the cherry stem she was expertly tying with her tongue drop onto the table. "It's Quinn," I said. "My father's darkroom assistant? Well, I have a *huge* thing for him. And, well, I sort of think the feeling might be mutual. I mean—I *know* it is."

"Quinn?" Pia was hooting with laughter. "You mean that guy who's always at your house? The one who helps you mix and match vintage outfits?"

"Yeah, what's wrong with that? He's cute!"

"And he's also as gay as the Easter Parade, obviously!"

"Pia!" Lily gasped. "Get it under control!"

My mouth dropped. Even after the many unwelcome revelations of that afternoon, I wasn't prepared for Pia to mock me so ruthlessly. It was one thing to test Myrtle but quite another to mock my great passion. "Gay? Quinn? Are you insane? That's *so* not true—he's a walking Ken doll!"

"Yeah," Pia sniggered. "I'll bet he has a high old time shopping for Barbie!"

"Pia, leave her alone," Lily commanded. "That's the most ridiculous thing you've said all day."

"And Mimi's right—Quinn *is* cute," Vivian contributed. "Really cute!"

My cheeks were burning with rage. Call it a pet peeve, but I hated when people referred to me in the third person when I was right there. "That shows how much *you* know!" I spat out. "What I was *going* to say before you so rudely interrupted me was that last night, while we were watching E!, Quinn and I . . ."

"You did what while you were watching E!?" Pia continued to cackle. "Curled each other's eyelashes? Lip-synched *Cabaret*?"

"No, we hooked up, actually." I said it with such self-righteous satisfaction that I almost convinced myself.

"You *what?*" Pia's eyebrows hit the ceiling. "Yeah, right!"

"Well, I mean, nothing major, just a little kissing," I said. Then, as Pia's lips curled into an I-told-you-so half-smile, I couldn't help adding, "OK, er, I—it was, I mean, a *lot* of kissing. A lot of definitely heterosexual kissing! And, like, the only reason we stopped is because Quinn's so totally respectful and old-fashioned that he insists on taking it slow, you know? Also, my dad practically walked in on us with this pizza he—"

I don't know how much longer I would've talked if "I Will Survive" hadn't cranked up right then. The whole bar broke into cheers.

"Oh. My. God." Vivian said. "Look over there!"

Pia and Lily gasped in unison, and I whipped around to see nerdus maximus Myrtle, pelvis locked with Bea's, getting way into the beat. Several construction-worker women had assembled in a ring around them, clapping their hands and cheering them on.

There might just be worse almost-stepsisters out there after all.

October 25, Sunday
7:46 p.m.

So I actually had a good time with Myrtle. After her interview, she came downtown and met up with me at the Gray's Papaya on Sixth Avenue. We stood at the window counter and pigged out on hot dogs and gossiped about the Grossest Couple in America. Turns out Mom and Maurice have new nicknames for each other now. Bunny-Butt and Dr. Snack. Can you guess who's who? My other favorite detail is that Dr. Snack (OK, it's Maurice) bought a superexpensive tent and they set it up in the living room. Once a week they lug sleeping bags in there and have "camping night," which, Maurice is convinced, is fabulous for his achy back.

What else? Viv is becoming a little less opaque. After Myrtle went to the airport today, I was supposed to go shopping with Pia, but she flaked out on me at the last minute. Instead I ended up going over to Viv's. The plan was to brainstorm a project for World Civ, but we just ended up hanging out. And after like two seconds of coaxing, Viv told me all about Pia's dark dirty secret—her record-breakingly high IQ. I knew Pia was smart, but who knew she attended college classes and tutored underprivileged mathematicians on the sly?

Viv's bedroom was the coolest—one of her walls is painted bright Indian pink and there are framed photographs of rock stars all over it. They look nothing like the normal rock posters you get at regular stores. Viv explained she also collects pictures of buildings in foreign countries, and every time a birthday or holiday rolls

around, her parents get her a few. So, yes, she's spoiled, but, I
mean, her mother grew up in a tiny hut on some island in the South
Pacific and wants to give her daughters everything she never had.
If only Viv's parents could buy her a better report card!

Underage in Undercroft

A FEW DAYS LATER, AT TEN-THIRTY IN THE morning, I was crawling on the floor of the student lounge, where Her Royal Highness Pia Pazzolini had dispatched me to locate her cherry-colored suede shoulder bag.

Five minutes earlier, I'd been leaning against the wall outside school telling my friends about the happy conclusion to my weekend with Myrtle when Pia interrupted me with a crisp "Hon, can you pop into the lounge and grab my bag?" Before I could assert my human rights, she mentioned a special surprise flask stashed inside it containing some very pricey vodka. She knew this would get me to act: I was by no means pining to get drunk so early in the day, but I wasn't about to admit that to Pia. "It's in the front, by the shabby blue couch," she'd called after me. "Fetch it and meet us in the bathroom in five!"

The lounge served as a Baldwinites' official "hang-out space" (as Zora Blanchard put it), but only the lamest members of the community spent any time there. The whole room perpetually reeked of a week-old salami sandwich, and most of us entered it only in desperation, to stash or retrieve belongings. It was the communal closet of the high school, cluttered with textbooks, iPods, water bottles, old Kleenex packages, makeup bags, pencils, burned CDs, sneakers, anything and everything. One of Baldwin's many unwritten rules was never to take anybody else's stuff from the room. In return, you could trust that your own possessions would remain safe amid the mess.

I was rustling through a pile of jackets and wadded-up sweatshirts when I spotted a piece of red poking out from behind a brown shopping bag. I nudged the bag to the side, pulling at it, but it resisted. Peering closer, I identified the red object as a pair of parachute pants, and then I saw that the pants were connected to an actual person. Before I could back away, the pile of jackets quivered and Sam's tan quilted jacket shot out, followed by his face. The whole sequence reminded me of those fast-action films of tulips spurting from the earth.

Sam snapped off his earmuff-size headphones, looking flustered and delighted and morbidly embarrassed all at once. We hadn't spoken or even e-mailed since That Night. I know that after kissing somebody for the first time, you're supposed to look forward to seeing him again, but not when it's your best friend—trust me. If there was one person I did *not* want to look in the eye right then, Sam Geckman had to be him.

"Uh, hey, I thought I might catch some Z's in here. I haven't been sleeping too well lately," he said, and rubbed his eyes.

I stood there, frozen, stomach somersaulting. If only I could find that bag.

"So, uh, what's been going on with you?" Sam asked.

"Nothing much—just been busy, really busy lately." I shrugged, and right then I caught sight of Pia's bag near his ankle. "Would you mind passing me that bag, the red one, behind you?"

"No problem," he said.

"Sweet dreams." I took the bag from him, looking away as his fingers grazed my wrist, then mumbled an incomprehensible "thank you" and took off.

I walked out of the lounge quickly, unnameable anxieties welling up inside me. Outside the lounge, the lobby was uncharacteristically noisy. A group of junior guys had set up bowling pins in the middle of the floor and were hurling soccer balls at them. "Strike!" one of them, a skinny green-haired guy, yelled. "Strikers Island!" his friend said. The two of them ran toward the same spot and smashed into each other, making a loud belly-flop sound in the process.

The longer I'd been at Baldwin, the more I was beginning to believe that many of the students were normal people who just pretended to be otherwise during school hours. After only a few weeks, for example, I had no trouble picturing the green-haired bowler sitting down to dinner with his family, smoothing the napkin on his lap, saying "please" and "thank you" and chewing with his mouth closed.

Rather than watch the bowling game unfold, I continued down the stairs to the Undercroft, where the nicest women's bathroom in the school was tucked away. I found my friends huddled together inside the handicapped stall. I glanced from one face to another—Vivian with her smudged black eyes and ripped-up vintage Dead Milkmen concert T-shirt; Pia with her lip-curled, eye-rolling half-sneer and thick eyebrows; Jess with that porcelain skin and dark circles rimming her eyes; and Lily with her supersize hooded sweatshirt and hair that hadn't been brushed in a week—and recalled the awe I had felt at Nona Del Nino's party that night. *These* were the popular girls? *Nope, I'm sure not in Kansas anymore,* I thought happily, handing Pia her bag to kick off our midmorning cocktail party.

"Here, everyone, take one," Jess said as she distributed dainty cocktail napkins with the letters PHG monogrammed on the corners. "I took them from Preston's parents' bar when he wasn't looking." She giggled. "Someone gave them to Preston as a Christmas present—aren't they adorable? I've never had anything monogrammed in my life."

"Oh, spare us," Pia scoffed. "I've had my whole existence monogrammed, and believe me, the thrill wears off really fast."

Lily laughed. "Yeah, just ask my mom."

Only Vivian, lowering the toilet seat to sit, appreciated the decorative napkins. "These are priceless," she said, laughing. As she smoothed the napkin over her lap, I noticed the black polish on her fingernails was chipping off into stripes. It looked beautiful somehow.

Huddled in a circle, we passed the flask in one direction and the pint of orange juice in the opposite to enjoy our makeshift screwdrivers. So what if we only got about three sips of vodka each—it was the thought that counted.

"So," Vivian said, "did you all see what Gretchen wore to school today? The very same Liberty print Marni dress that Pia had on last spring."

As far as I could tell, Gretchen Foergeron's greatest defining personality trait was her unlimited clothing budget, coupled with her total lack of creativity. Pretty much everything she wore, someone more popular had worn the previous week. Still, Gretchen made no attempt to conceal her rip-offs and was always hassling Vivian about where she bought her shoes. Still, it scared me sometimes, how no one at Baldwin could do, say, wear, or even think anything without being scrutinized like an amoeba under the microscope in bio class.

"*What?* Only a dumb-ass would pay a thousand dollars for an outfit like that!" Pia looked ready to hurl.

"But didn't you?" I asked. Pia glanced quickly at her feet as I went on: "Or I guess it doesn't count when your parents pay for it, huh. You're *so* lucky—my dad has the gayest taste *ever*. He considers the *Wizard of Oz* costumes totally high fashion. And my mom pretends that buying me clothes compromises my sense of 'adult responsibility,' but really it's just because she's queen cheap."

"My parents don't buy me shit," Pia said, her mouth twitching. "That would require sorting out their own lives long enough to think about mine." She averted her eyes from mine, fixing them instead on the stainless-steel toilet-paper dispenser.

"Pia—" Lily began warningly. Viv bulged her eyes at Jess.

"Yeah, but having access to their credit cards must be the best!" I pursued. "Every time my friend Rachel got an A, her mom would let her go on a mini-spree at Neiman's—"

"Mimi, drop it," Vivian warned.

"What?"

And then it happened: Pia's face, usually pulled into that

tight scowl, went limp and sad. Her voice, however, remained sharp. "Oh, you might as well tell her," she said. "I mean, it's not a big deal, I don't do it on purpose or anything. And not that often, either. I just can't . . . I don't do it often at *all*, Vivian. Stop giving me that awful look!" A tear traced Pia's cheekbone as she added, "I swear I don't!"

That was all she said, but it was enough. I already understood. A parade of Armani tops and Prada skirts and Tse cashmere turtlenecks flashed through my head, and it was suddenly totally obvious that Pia wasn't just a lucky brat who dined on caviar and considered filing her own nails a summer job. Several memories floated to the surface right then: Pia flaking out on our shopping trip last Sunday, my cutting off the price tag of her new sweater in the middle of assembly. Was it possible—was Pia not just a genius, but a shoplifter as well? I was still putting two and two together when Pia dissolved into tears and swiveled toward the toilet.

No one knew what to say: We were all too stunned that our superconfident leader had lost control so suddenly.

"It's OK," Lily braved after a long silence that was punctuated only by Pia's weeping. "We're all a little messed up, Pia. I don't exactly have the most involved parents in the world, either—the only time I've ever seen my mother cook is in the television studio, and the only time she's *ever* complimented me is in women's magazines—and even then she doesn't use my name. She just says, 'my daughter.' God, I'm like the biggest, bulkiest disappointment of all time."

"I'm not exactly un-messed-up myself," Jess jumped in.

"Over the past week, sex has really screwed things up between me and Preston. I mean, I know sex changes everything, but I didn't think it would change everything this fast. We're supposed to be in love, but lately I get the feeling that I embarrass him. And I found his cell phone and couldn't help but notice that he and his ex-girlfriend Pamela are calling each other practically every night during Letterman."

"Did you tell him you saw?" I asked.

"No, I decided to let it slide. But I can't stand it when he acts like I'm asking him to walk on the moon when I invite him to Park Slope. He always makes the most pathetic excuses whenever I try to get him to hang out with my mom and me together. The worst was the other night, when he invited me to his parents' dinner party and then totally ignored me—he didn't even put up a fight when I left before dessert. I mean, he could've at least *pretended*. He said he was just tired, but I know for a fact that he went to a Dalton party later that night. I don't know—I just feel really bad about the whole thing, like I've ruined it. Us."

"Really?" Pia, still tearful, scooted across the stall to hug Jess.

"So it's my turn, I guess," Viv piped in. "Well, look, it's not exactly a state secret, but"—her voice dipped to a barely audible volume—"I suck at school. Even little things that should be simple, like reading a short chapter." She threw up her arms. "It can take me an hour just to get through a few pages. And it's not the easiest thing in the world, being no Einstein when you've got an aggressive mother from the Philippines who was raised to think that there's no greater offense than being a lousy student."

"You probably just need a personal trainer for a little bit," I said. "My friend Rachel used to go to a tutor three times a week, and she's almost as smart as Pia." I shot Pia a guilty look. "You know what I mean."

"Don't think I haven't tried. I can't even get a tutor to stay with me longer than a month," Viv said. "I don't even know if I'm going to pass World Civ this semester."

"Babe," Pia jumped in, "if you ever need help with anything, I can try to help you out."

"I'm not going to ask you to waste your time on my sophomore course load," Viv said. "I'm just going to have to give up hopes of getting into Harvard, even though Dad's a legacy."

"That's ridiculous," said Pia, invigorated now that the spotlight was off her problems. "After school tomorrow, I have to go up town to Columbia to meet with my professor. You're coming along so we can go over your World Civ work on the train. Afterward, we'll go to Tom's Diner and keep at it until it comes together. 'K? You're very smart, Viv. Seriously. Being good at school is just a skill, like gardening . . . or eyebrow plucking." She gave Viv an encouraging clap on the back. "So we're on for tomorrow?"

"Sure," Viv said, slightly awestruck.

Just as I'd always sort of suspected: Pia's bitchy aristocratic act was mostly a cover-up. She was actually, dare I say it, a softie. "You guys are so cheesy," I said.

The air in the stall thickened as all eyes shifted to me. It was my turn to confess. But where to begin? With the Quinn fib? My sloppy first kiss ever with my best friend from childhood? The sob story of my parents' breakup, the nagging suspicion that all my happy childhood memories were based on lies? Or, I've got it: What if I just announced that our whole friendship began with a bet?

"Well . . ." I exhaled. "Sometimes, I get acne on my back."

Nobody spoke for an entire Chinese dynasty. I felt like the rottenest person on earth for denying my very good friends access to my intimate secrets and fears, but what choice did I have?

"Let's see," Jess said finally. She pulled up my shirt to study the pink zit that had blossomed just south of my bra strap.

"You should really do something about that," Vivian said.

Suddenly, I felt a throbbing sting. "Ouch!"

"I just did something about it," Pia said. "I have an amazing product you can borrow, but in the meantime, nothing beats the good old-fashioned pop." She held up a pus-smeared square of toilet paper and smiled proudly.

November 3
6:45 p.m.

Dear Diary,

This revelation has been a long time coming, but I'm afraid to say that Sam is no longer your faithful reader. I hope you're not too dis-

appointed: He lost that privilege when he felt me up. Looks like it's just you and me, D. Anyway, not mucho to report. Headlines aren't exactly ablaze. The race to Cooliedom has pretty much slowed to a crawl, as it seems I've reached the finish line before the final hour. I mean, I haven't officially been given a trophy or signet ring or anything, but at this point it's safe to say that I know more about these girls than their therapists. Pia's a shoplifter, Jess's a toxic love addict (pardon the Mom language!), Viv's struggling not to fail out of a school that doesn't even give grades—and Lily, well, Lily still dresses like a bag lady—an athletic bag lady. The funny thing is, Lily isn't even good at sports. It's nice, being the most normal person in a group. But I'm not sure that's even the point. I never thought I'd find myself writing this, but I like these girls. They're pretty cool. They sure are a million times better than Amanda and her crew. Having too many problems is a lot more interesting than having none at all. At least that's what I was thinking when I ran into Amanda and Courtney outside of the subway this morning. Honestly, I have no idea how I thought those two were Coolies, even for an hour. Amanda was raving about a new low-carb breakfast bar she had discovered in an organic grocery store on the Cape a few weeks ago. Courtney was so excited that she went online and ordered an entire industrial-size crate of the apricot-almond treats. Yuck-o. Both she and Amanda were so busy trying to force-feed me that they didn't seem to notice how I'd always rather start the day with a screwdriver than a reduced-calorie orange juice! There's just one reason, to tell the truth, that I wish Sam and I were still friends: I would love, love, LOVE to see the look on his face when

he finds out he's lost the bet! I can just see him and Amanda, walk-
ing arm in arm toward the squash court, and later returning home
to a delicious, zero-carb dinner by candlelight . . .

X's and O's
And 40 extra calories

Mimi

Hamptons Heaven

"Well, duh, I never said he was a *real* celebrity, just the executive producer of the worst soap on TV." Pia huffed. "And God, he scores the skankiest women in world history." She passed me the binoculars so that I could see her next-door neighbor sunbathing.

"Yeah, just imagine if he went prime time!" Lily laughed.

"He does that thirty-minute soap opera, right? The one on right before the lunchtime news?" Jess asked. "*So* ghetto." She had joined the gang's Bridgehampton expedition at the last minute, when Preston canceled their usual Friday-night movie with some vague excuse about a mock Dartmouth interview with a junior associate at his dad's firm. Coincidentally, there was a dance at Chapin, the all-girls school known for having two *Seventeen* models in its junior class alone. Jess had decided to take off for a whole weekend—her version of "hard to get."

As for me, well, I couldn't believe I had finally made the Bridgehampton cut—I felt as if I had truly arrived. When Pia invited me the previous Wednesday afternoon, I had determined not to get my hopes up—just in case. I packed only the bare essentials, to be as unpathetic as possible should something go wrong again. I showed up at school Friday with my unobtrusive backpack, and was hugely relieved when Pia told me that the limo would be picking us up at three sharp, so I'd better be ready. And was I ever—with good reason. *Bridgehampton is total bliss,* I thought, peering through the binocs and hoping they obscured my goofy grin.

Across the equivalent of about twelve football fields—a huge lawn even by Texas standards—Pia's googly-eyed neighbor, as squat and curvy as an owl, was lounging by the pool. He was wearing only a shiny black G-string, which was a lot more than I could say for his blonde companion. This weekend already promised to rank among the best of my life. "Wow." I whistled. "I was never really sure what silicone looked like before. It sure, uh, stands at attention, doesn't it?"

"I know, can you believe it?" Pia hooted appreciatively. "But our executive producer friend won't have it any other way. He likes female beauty to bounce like a basketball!"

Lily let out a long sigh. "I'm bored," she whined. "All we ever do here is spy on your neighbors. It's worse than public-access cable."

"You're right," Pia said, just as the hired hoochie slipped on a single red spike heel and bunny-hopped on one leg toward her host, "but do *you* have any better ideas? It's totally dead here— there isn't a single party or even any lame barbecue all week- end. Guillermo says celebrity sightings have hit an all-time low. Like, nil."

"Then you mean we can't admire your tacky neighbors getting all hot and bothered over C-listers?" Lily rejoined sarcastically. "What is this world coming to?"

We indulged a collective sigh of despondency. It was the weekend before Thanksgiving, and we all wanted to rock out before holing up with our families for the holiday. I in particular wanted to have the time of my life, since that Monday morning, for the first time since moving to New York, I was going to Texas, where who-knows-what fate awaited me.

"Harry's in town," Lily suggested. "Maybe he knows something?"

"Harry who? Oh, you mean Blow Job Harry?" Pia grimaced, thinking of the senior with the totally mystifying Don Juan reputation. "Since when has Blow Job Harry known *anything*? Except, of course, where to find some hopelessly insecure fourth-grader to seduce?"

"Ew, gross!" Lily screwed up her face. "Pia, why must you be so *vivid*?"

"We'd have to be pretty desperate to hang out with Blow Job Harry," Pia declared.

"Yeah, it's not as if any of us would be caught dead with BJH in the city," Viv agreed.

"Is there any reason you object to referring to him as just Harry?" Lily cringed. "That's only his name."

Within the hour, Blow Job Harry had shown up at the Pazzolini estate. Out on the third-floor balcony, he busied himself pouring us goblets of delicious red wine as we watched the last soap opera antics in the adjacent backyard. The executive producer and his consort were eating Fudgesicles and playing canasta while we lay out on deck chairs, staying warm under cashmere blankets.

"So," Pia said, whipping toward me suddenly with a look that I recognized with a sinking feeling. She was like one of those Jekyll and Hyde drunks on television commercials for rehab centers, evil when intoxicated. "Any progress with What's-His-Name?"

"What?" Blood rushed to my cheeks.

"Oh, you know, your dad's employee, the one who made out with you so respectfully? Quinn, isn't it?"

"Mimi made out with her dad's employee?" Blow Job Harry assessed me with new interest. He looked like a human carrot. "Excellent."

"Yeah, and isn't he a bit old for you?" Pia pursued.

"He is not old at all—he's only twenty-six, and he's extremely well preserved. Besides," I told Pia, hoping to duck out of the spotlight, "it's not as if you're one to talk. Have you ever so much as held hands with any man under the age of thirty?"

Lily, as usual, kept Pia at bay. "Well, I for one don't get the whole older guy hang-up," she said.

"That's just because you don't know any better," Pia said.

The whole Quinn topic had wrecked my late-afternoon mellowness, so I was extremely relieved by the rustling noise from the main guest bedroom behind us. We turned to see a tiny, elegant woman in a houndstooth suit, a slick black bun planted on top of her head.

Her diminutive appearance did not prepare us for her gargantuan voice. "Pia, come here!" she thundered. "This instant!"

Pia, as timid as I'd ever seen her, slunk toward the woman she referred to as her "stepbitch," answering the signora's barrage of Italian insults in English: "We didn't take any of the Shiraz! . . . Thanksgiving isn't for another . . . cellar . . . Chardonnay . . . breadcrumbs . . . I'm *not* lying . . ." And so forth.

Edging several awful inches closer to me, Harry grabbed my wrist and hissed some words in the vicinity of my ear, including "crazy" and "psycho." I tittered uncomfortably and tried to scoot beyond Harry's grasp, especially after Lily shot me a rock-hard glare, betraying an ugly streak of jealousy. Huh? Could Lily be lusting after Blow Job Harry? My first reaction—bewilderment tinged with pity—faded into a vision of Sam's tongue poking into my mouth. The only thing grosser than fortifying Blow Job Harry's reputation was hooking up with the person you played hide-and-seek with when you were three, so I guess I was in no position to judge.

We frittered away the rest of the afternoon in the basement, playing with the air hockey and table tennis sets. Pia was held hostage the whole time by her stepmother, forced to study every movement of Clay Maraschino, the celebrity chef the signora had summoned to prepare the pre-Thanksgiving grouse. Vivian told me all about the signora's obsession with teaching Pia how to cook so that she could be married off to some nice viscount within the next five years. The signora totally didn't get that Clay was white hot, and that Pia was interested only in his abs, not his asparagus.

Which, by the way, was delicious—the asparagus, I mean.

The whole meal was out of control, with about forty dignitary types all assembled around one obscenely long table. It was definitely the most glamorous occasion of my entire life—I'm talking harpsichordists in the corners, candles all over the place, and about six forks lined up at each plate. Annoyingly, the signora had put out seating cards and separated the gang. Lucky Pia was near the head of the table, yukking it up with Clay, who kept prowling the table to see how we were enjoying the meal (though I suspected he was more interested in showing off his form-fitting chef's jacket, with good reason). Vivian and Jess got to sit next to each other. Only Lily looked even half as lonesome as me, but she at least was seated next to Tom Rubikoff, a totally cute *New York Times* reporter who had befriended the signora while working at the paper's Rome bureau.

My luck paired me with Saolo di Printopolous, an elegant businessman who had flown in from Milan and knew only one word of English: "fantastic." I thought he was especially enthusiastic until I asked him how long he planned to stay in New York. When he replied, "Fantastic," I accepted our insurmountable language barrier and turned to the superskinny lady on my left. The place card told me that her name was Fenella von Dix, and she supplied all remaining info. Fenella was a recently divorced, Tribeca-based artist working on a series of paintings that she said "fused renditions of lake life and Eastern typesetting." The whole time she was talking, all I could think about was how her chin was fused to her collarbone. I swear, I've never seen a more nonexistent neck *ever*. Somewhere between the raw beet soup and salmon roulette, Fenella launched into her third anecdote about a spa she'd traveled halfway across the globe to patronize. It was clear the woman did a lot more jet-setting than typesetting. But surprisingly, Fenella seemed to know who my dad was, and even to like his photographs, so she couldn't be that hopeless.

I wish I could say the same about the food. It was very expensive, but also very slimy and alive-tasting. And Clay's experimental cuisine wouldn't quit. It kept rolling out of the kitchen, and, for the first time in my life, I found myself seated at a meal with far more courses than I could tackle. By my eighteenth piece of unidentifiable something-or-other, all I could do was poke at it with my lacquered chopstick.

"Are you going to be here for Thanksgiving?" Fenella asked me.

"No, I'm due back in Texas. I'll be visiting my mother."

"Oh!" Her taut face lit up, the tendons in her overly tanned forehead straining like guitar strings. "Your parents are divorced? How *terrible*. Men are such absolute bastards, don't you find? Rudolph, my *God* . . ." And off she went, railing on about her "ex," as if I gave half a shit.

It always amazes me how 99 percent of people in the world care only about topics that relate to them personally. Some people ask you questions, but it's so obvious they're only waiting out your replies so that they can begin babbling about themselves again. Herself recently divorced, Fenella von Neckless was clearly only asking about my dad's marital troubles so that she could start complaining about her own. I swore to myself never to be this lousy at the art of conversation, even if one day I found myself a single woman with nothing to show for my life but a condo in Park City and an armload of jangly bracelets.

"When did they get divorced?" Fenella asked, cutting short her monologue abruptly.

"Separated," I spat back. Forgive my brusqueness, but I was not ready to start using the D word. "They're taking a break." I don't know why I didn't just leave it at that—maybe because I'd glugged enough Shiraz to fill Pia's indoor swimming pool, or maybe just because I thought that if Fenella felt entitled to air her dirty laundry, then I could indulge a little, too: All's fair in love and dinner parties or whatever. "I feel bad because I'm leaving my dad all by himself. He says he doesn't mind, that he's just going to watch Fritz Lang movies, but I don't think he's too thrilled. He hasn't ever done Thanksgiving by himself ever. I mean *ever*—and he's really festive."

I looked up, a little guilty, to see if Fenella was paying attention. Was she ever: before I could even lay down my dollhouse-proportioned fish fork (thank God for my Junior League lessons in Texas!), she had thrust her name card into my hand, a telephone number scrawled on it next to her last name. She was wearing, I noticed, large semiprecious rings on at least eight of her fingers.

"I completely understand," Fenella said, rubbing her sweater across my forearm. "Have him call me if he wants. I'm around. Busy as hell, but around."

"What? But I—"

"After spending one nightmarish Christmas watching the Food Network and spitting out all the goddamned Godiva chocolates my friends so generously gave me, I've resolved *never* to let the holidays get me down again," Fenella said, her chin bobbing to merge with her chest. "So now every year I go with a group of my friends to the Brooklyn Academy of Music. It's very casual—they have reggae music and some decent food. He's welcome to join. No big deal."

"Thanks," I said, but before I could wonder why a total stranger had offered to babysit my dad, Saolo, the Italian man to my right, grabbed my wrist and interjected an ecstatic "Fantastic!"

Most of the deluxe guests at pia's deluxe house cleared out the morning after the pre-Thanksgiving party, including Pia's insaniac stepmother, who had to rush back to the city for her private pilates instruction. Left alone, the five of us spent Saturday in dorky bliss, chilling out and doing homework in a den that looked like the Swiss ski lodge in the Audrey Hepburn movie *Charade*. At first I'd been embarrassed to read *To Kill a Mockingbird* in public, but I was consoled to discover that the other girls were doing assigned reading as well. (I so easily forget that the endpoint of Baldwin is the Ivy League.)

For lunch, we scrounged up leftovers from Clay's feast the night before. Unable to get too excited about cold oily fish products, I came very close to applauding when Lily invaded the Pazzolini freezer and unearthed a microwavable four-cheese pizza for the two of us to split. After lunch we went back to our original positions in the den. Losing myself in my book, I managed to forget where I was and fall completely in love with Atticus Finch (I'll be the first to admit it: I'm a sucker for wonderful daddies). Vivian, on the other hand, remained restless— "I *hate* reading," she sighed about a hundred times—and Jess grew more depressed as the day wore on. She had drunk-dialed Preston after the dinner party, and by six p.m. he still hadn't called her back.

Because we were such loyal friends, we decided to cheer Jess up by taking her to some model's twenty-third birthday party that was held at an agent's East Hampton spread. Simply because Blow Job Harry had told us about the party, Pia had predicted that it was going to be full of losers. She changed her mind as soon as we walked into the kitchen, where the gorgeous Clay Maraschino was holding court, talking to a group of twiggy blonde women while mixing Tabasco martinis.

"Oh my God," Pia gasped. "He's still in his uniform. *Sooo* sexy."

Vivian and I distracted Jess while Pia loped over to the kitchen and wheedled Clay into whipping up a chocolate molten lava cake for Jess, who still hadn't heard word from the evil Preston. "You should go eat it with her," Pia told Clay, then whispered into his ear. A few minutes later, Clay, at Pia's command, hand-fed Jess his masterpiece—without a spoon! You should have seen Jess licking the brown goop off her lips and sighing with every heavenly bite.

We had planned to get up early the next morning and make it to the city by noon, but the party didn't wind down until four a.m., and when at last we all straggled home, we slept like mummies. When we did finally get up, in the early afternoon, we unanimously voted to see a romantic comedy at the local movie theater rather than hit the road. Because I'd lived in Texas, I wasn't that overwhelmed by the eighteen-screen cineplex in suburbia, but the other girls thought the Hamptons movie theater was as foreign and beautiful as the Taj Mahal. "Didn't you love how there were no subway vibrations during the show?" sighed Jess, whose spirits had been restored 100 percent by the drunken message Preston had left just before dawn.

"And the seats!" said Lily. "Wide enough to fit two people."

I didn't make it back to Manhattan until ten on Sunday night. I'd planned on going straight to my room to pack for my trip back to Texas, but my dad had other ideas.

"Do I hear the Lady of Long Island? Come on in here and give us some love," he called out. I found him on the living room couch, watching an old detective movie with a silhouette that must have been Quinn the superhunk. All the lights were switched off.

"What's going on, Dad?" I asked. My stomach fluttered when the male silhouette turned out to be Sam. What was he doing there? Hadn't the rules of the game changed since we'd you-know-what?

Sam had a conniving side, scheming to weasel into the house when he knew I wouldn't be there, and of course my dad had no idea that anything had happened between me and my ex–best friend. Guys can be really dense.

"Hey, darlin'," Sam crooned in a way that could have given away our dark secret.

I repeat: guys can be really dense.

"Quinn around?" I blurted out.

"He's at his parents' house for the holiday," Dad said. "So I've been here all by myself all weekend. Sam called a few hours ago, wondering where you were, and I said I didn't know, as usual, but would he mind playing my surrogate son instead?"

I knew it: Sam was capitalizing on my father's feelings of abandonment to stalk me—or whatever. What could I do? Tell my dad I'd sucked face with his favorite substitute child? Not in a million years. Which explains why, when I went over to hug my dad, I decided to keep it cool by giving Sam one, too. Or a sort of hug—when I wrapped my arms around Sam's neck, I pulled my body back so far that three linebackers could've fit between us. I hoped I wouldn't feel like this with everyone I ever hooked up with.

"Sorry I'm so late," I said finally.

"BMW traffic jam?" Sam asked.

"Ever consider getting into standup?" I shot back. "You're a regular riot. Actually, we just got off to a late start. We stayed up really late last night and we didn't even get to eating breakfast until, like, three." I paused to open my messenger bag and drew out the place card, which I passed to Dad. "This is your party favor. I met this woman who said you should join her for her Thanksgiving outing this year." I realized this sounded like a setup, a prospect Dad totally shunned, so I added, "She knows your photography and is a big fan. She's an artist. Fenella von Dix? Maybe you've heard of her?"

"Maybe," Dad grunted. He folded the paper and placed it on the side table with extreme care. He was modest, but he'd talk to *anyone* who had nice things to say about his work. I hoped Fenella would catch on.

"Fun weekend?" Sam asked, clearing his throat.

"It was actually really great," I said, pointedly addressing my dad. "Sometimes being around so many people can be a bit tiring, but we all got along really well. It's like we have a special rhythm worked out."

"So now you're rhythmic?" Sam groaned.

"I had a wonderful weekend," I answered.

"I was hoping maybe we'd get a chance to hang out before you left," he said. "Maybe grab some Arabic iced tea or something? That place is open all night."

I looked at him incredulously. "Are you serious? You really think I have time to go all the way into Brooklyn when I haven't even *begun* to pack? Dream on, Geckman."

Maybe my tone was a little cold, but it was true that I was completely unprepared to leave for Texas at the crack of dawn. But no sooner had I entered my room and turned on a new hip-hop CD than the door creaked open to reveal one very flustered Sam. He walked straight through the room, brushing past me, and plopped right onto my unmade bed. "We need to talk," he said.

I sank into my pistachio-colored armchair and mumbled a very unenthusiastic "So talk."

"You really think you know what you're doing, don't you?"

"Sorry?"

"Running around with the Coolies, having sleepovers with the Coolies? What else, making friendship bracelets with the Coolies? Swapping secrets and lies?"

I thought of my backne with a secret smile. "Can we stop calling them that? They do have names, you know."

"Oh, do they?" This really seemed to tickle Sam. I can't believe I just thought the word *tickle,* by the way; Sam totally brings out the dork in me.

"Yes, as a matter of fact, they do. Look, they're my friends." I pronounced the last word with special care.

"I can't believe it," Sam said, shaking his head, his floppy ginger hair going this way and that. "Those are not your friends. The only one of those chicks who's halfway decent is Vivian, and even she's a little sketchy by association. I repeat, those are not your friends."

"Sam, thanks for stopping by. Is that all?"

"Rachel's your friend," Sam said. "Quinn's your friend." I looked down, hoping he wouldn't be able to tell that the mere mention of the Q word rattled me. "*I* am your friend." He let out a long, obnoxious sigh. "Look, this was supposed to be a fun back-to-school prank. This was *not* supposed to get all touchy-feely. Do you realize how stupid you are, thinking that a group of shallow bitches is actually going to come through for you? There's no reason why a smart girl like you should be falling for them." He stood up, clenching his jaw, and said, "This could get really dangerous."

"What are you *talking* about?" I said. "At Nona's party, you made it sound like they were cool—that you were friends with them, or at least wanted to be. What happened, nasty case of jealousy got you down?"

"That's it, Mimi, you got it." Sam shook his head and turned his back to me. "I'm out of here."

"Oh, no, you're not!" Before he could worm his way out, I

leaped to my feet, running to the door to block it. "Listen, Sam, and I'll say this once and only once: Just because a group of people who won't give *you* the time of day happen to like *me*, that does *not* mean they're shallow bitches. I'll give you that they're popular, that they get into trouble, that they're intimidating, but you know what? They're also really kind. So forgive me for hanging out with the only people at Baldwin willing to take me under their wing and be nice to me, because that's *exactly* what's going on here. They accept me for who I am, unlike some people." I shot him a steely look.

"It wasn't supposed to get like this," Sam sputtered, his face the color of a fire hydrant. "I wish we'd never even made that stupid bet. I wish we hadn't ever—"

"I wish we hadn't either," I cut Sam off, before he could voice the regrets I myself had been feeling so keenly these past few weeks. "I wish we'd never—done anything."

"Well, then why don't we just call the whole thing off?" Sam asked.

"Call what off?" I looked at him and realized that we had been talking about two different things.

"The bet—what else? It's ruined everything."

"The bet. Right. Yeah, definitely, let's. I'm all for it. Fine."

"Fine!" Sam repeated, a bit overexuberantly.

"Um, great," I said. I faced him. I was about to ask him if there was anything else, but then I realized I didn't want to know. "In that case, see you around?"

Sam winced; his face hardened again. Brushing him off like that had not been the right move, but what could I do? I was, to tell the truth, getting a little sick of his theatrics. I was also having trouble making eye contact with him.

"See you around," he growled.

"Yup." I moved away from the door. "Buh-bye."

Sam took one step forward, but then, rather than grab the doorknob, he took me by the shoulders. I should have fended him off, but instead I found myself falling toward him. The next thing I knew, Sam and I were rolling around my bed, deeply involved in one heavy-duty kissing session. Though I remained pissed off at Sam and worked up about life in general, I have to admit that I was enjoying myself: Each kiss felt like a satisfying whack at a punching bag. Every time I pulled away to glare at him, anger would well right back up in me and I would slam forward again for another angry kiss. With Sam. Beyond weird. And it all seemed as natural as thumb wrestling, or skipping down the street arm and arm. What on earth was happening to my life?

The two of us tumbled around like that for what seemed like hours, but in retrospect I have no idea how long the make-out session lasted—I was far too delirious to keep track of time. At one point, I rolled onto my side to face Sam. "No, no," I said when he tried to kiss me for the millionth time, but I was too exhausted to fend him off, so on we snogged. I was emerging from some haze and was determined to set things right. I gripped Sam by the shoulders, hoping to shake some sense into him. That's the last thing I remember.

"Mimi." Sam was shaking me. I had fallen asleep in his arms, clutching his freckled shoulders. "Look at the alarm clock."

It was five in the morning. I was a complete failure as a human. I had two hours to be packed and standing in the check-in line at La Guardia. Sam rolled over and dug his face into the pillow while I stuffed every semiclean garment of clothing I could find into the bag I had taken to the Hamptons. Most of the clothes were dirty and nicotine-soaked, but that was the least of my problems that morning. "I'm out of here," I said to Sam without looking at him. "And FYI, I'm still furious with you."

"Yeah, I could tell," he said. He didn't lift his head. "But just one thing, before you leave . . ."

"What is it? I'm running totally late—I've gotta get my dad up."

"Well, just that maybe you could consider brushing your hair? Right now it's just screaming F. H. U."

"F. H. U.? What's that, some kind of disease?"

"Hardly." He shook his head. "I'll give you a hint. *F* is for 'freshly.'"

"Sam, no offense, but I don't have time for word games. I'm on the verge of missing an airplane here."

"Fine, Bozo, here's another hint. *H* is for 'hooked' and *U* is for 'up.' *Now* are you starting to get it?"

Ugh. If I had eaten anything the night before, I would certainly have thrown it up on the spot. "Sam, get *out* of here," I hissed. "If my dad gets up to find you in my bedroom, your touching little father-son relationship might sour a little. I'm counting down from twenty . . ."

Well before I had even reached ten, Sam, his own hair a tousled reminder of how he had spent his evening, had sloped quietly out the door. I knocked on my dad's door. He was in the kitchen within minutes, totally dressed and as good-natured as if he had already finished his third cup of coffee. "I'll sure miss you, Mimi-bo-bimi," he said. "It's been so wonderful having you here with me, really wonderful."

I could tell from his trembling tone that he was about to tear up, so I made an additional effort to reassure him. "I know, Dad, it has. And you'd better believe I'll be back before you know it! Now let's go get me a cab, OK? We'll both be in for it if I miss this plane."

We found a cab outside in a matter of seconds. "And while I'm gone, Daddy," I said, as I climbed into the car, "promise that you won't do anything I wouldn't do."

He held up his right hand and laughed. "Mimi, I promise—I don't think I could if I tried."

In the dim light of the taxi, I pulled my powder compact out of my shoulder bag and examined my hair. Even in the murky three-inch area of the mirror, I could tell that Sam had a point. My bangs were matted against my forehead, while the rest of my hair stuck out skyward. Good God. I might as well have hung a JUST BEEN FELT UP sign off my nose.

Lone Star Lame-O

I CAN SUM UP MY TRIP TO TEXAS IN two words: "totally" and "sucked." Stepping off the plane to find my mom racing at me like Old Yeller right before he's shot, I immediately yearned for my father in our calm, quiet brownstone. What I wouldn't do to be spending the holiday weekend watching TV with my poor lonesome dad. Having drooled on my sweaty shirt from the airport in Queens to approximately mid-Arkansas, I knew I needed to clean up before encountering my mom. I dragged myself to the economy-class bathroom and splashed nonpotable water over my face. Once fully conscious, I did my best not to think about what had happened the night before, and instead tried to concentrate on the mission at hand: keeping my cool. I closed my eyes, and when I opened them again, we were already taxiing down the runway.

"Hey! Mimi! Over here!" My mother bellowed, as if I couldn't see her jumping up and down right in front of me.

I drew in a deep sigh and braced myself for my mother's extreme, manic, low-on-meds hyperactivity. From a distance of half a continent, I'd forgotten the whole opposites-attract aspect of my parents' relationship. Without my mom, my dad would still be working at a one-hour photo lab, and without my dad, my mom would still be revising the four thousandth draft of her dissertation. She motivated; he tranquilized. It worked. Or, I guess, it used to work, until she abandoned him for Texas's number one hypochondriac. Could I ever get past Mom's cardinal sin? Did I want to?

"Well, brava!" Mom started clapping very loudly when I suggested we go straight to the parking lot because I hadn't checked any bags. "If there's one thing I've taught you in life, it's *never* to give your possessions over to the airplanes."

"Doubles your travel time," I muttered beneath my breath, in anticipation of her next comment. The fake Nice Daughter smile was applied to my face like a Band-Aid.

"Doubles your travel time," my mother said as we proceeded into the parking lot. We found her excessively sensible tan sedan with no difficulty, and my mother was still so proud about my carry-on-luggage foresight (to tell the truth, I hadn't had time to pack anything more) that she almost forgot to nag me.

But never for long. When we got to the parking booth, instead of paying the attendant, my mother turned toward me and began fiddling with the collar of the men's shirt that I had spent my few sentient moments on the plane ride stuffing under my vintage lace sweater just so. "Darling," she said, "is this what they call the new New York teen look?"

The woman deserved the Nobel Prize of Annoying.

"Mom, can't this wait till after my nap?"

"Honey, what's gotten into you?" she said, pumping on the brake.

"I'm just tired. I *said* nothing's wrong—I'm just not in the mood to chitchat about it, as you would say."

"'It'? What's this 'it'? If nothing's wrong, then explain your 'it'!"

"Mom, sorry to interrupt this interesting conversation, but there's a whole huge line of cars behind you. Do you think you could just pay the woman so that we could go?"

It always boggled my mind when my mom chose to criticize how I dressed. Not only was she the most irritating woman of all time, but she was very probably the least fashionable. Nothing angered me more than her comments about my clothes, which had been *much* more stylish than hers even when I was in diapers. I found it bizarre to remember that only two days ago I had waved goodbye to the signora—a woman who dressed better for the gym than most celebrities for the Golden Globes. How abruptly I was tossed into the couture tsunami that was my mother. Above her black leggings—just tight enough to remind anyone who cared (and many who didn't) that she, unlike the signora, didn't believe in gyms—she was sporting the lamest shirt ever: I WASN'T BORN IN TEXAS BUT I GOT HERE AS FAST AS I COULD, it read, with a cartoon of a large-breasted cowgirl tipping her hat underneath. It was truly the worst. My mother should've stayed with my dad, if for no other reason than he would *never* allow her to leave the house looking like such a complete moron. "That shirt's really something. Where'd you get it?" I asked.

"Myrtle just got it for me—don't you just *love* it? It's funny—even though we've lived here for a decade now, it's a different bag of beans cohabiting with natives. They've got such state pride! She also brought me an absolutely *adorable* 'NewYorkasaurus' T-shirt. I swear, that girl is too much. Oh, and by the way, I haven't had a chance to thank you for the great time you showed her up there, Mims! She couldn't stop talking about all the fun y'all had!"

What was up with my mom drawling out "y'all" all of a sudden, a regionalism she had staunchly resisted throughout our years together in Texas? Was she morphing into Maurice in his nerdy pseudo-cowboy language, too? This was too much to bear. "So, uh, how's Ariel? She back yet?" I choked out finally.

My mother pounded on the steering wheel. "Oh, Ariel, don't get me started. Still confused and underfed. Since moving to Austin, she's even started visiting *colonic salons*, of all the suicidal pastimes!" She said this with a perceptible shudder, as others might say "shooting heroin" or "selling her body on the Internet." "How on earth did I give birth to a girl who spends all her time trying to incorporate abdominal workouts into her mealtimes?"

"Can't wait to see her," I said with something other than sincerity. "Well, what about Simon?" I asked. "Is he back to normal at least?"

"Yes, he's back to eating cat food around the clock. And no abdominal workouts for that one. Every day of the year is fat cat day in his book."

"I think fat cats are sexy."

"Mimi!"

For the rest of the ride home, I focused on how happy I would be to see my big orange kitten, and vice versa. If not for Simon, I might never have made it on that plane at all.

Much to my surprise, when I walked into the house to see an even tubbier Simon curled up on the couch and Ariel doing a shoulder stand in the living room, angled so that she could watch MTV in the inversion, I almost wept with relief.

"Hey!" I called out to her.

"Shh!" my sister reproached me. "I could really damage my neck if my jaw moves too much in this position."

Nothing had changed after all. I beelined for the couch and buried my face in Simon's fur. He immediately started purring, my poor, neglected, adipose-laden sweetheart.

Simon made it almost possible to face Maurice, who wasted no time in telling me more about "ergonomic construction," his passion for building tables without measuring or using nails. "It'd be the perfect pastime if it weren't such murder on my lower back. But Doc Rosen assures me that manual labor helps relieve my carpal tunnel."

A few hours later, at our "pre-Thanksgiving dinner," Maurice was still rattling on about the same subject. "It's the simplest of principles," he droned over our nondairy stuffing (Maurice, big shocker, was lactose-intolerant). "All you do is eyeball the wood and get a *theoretical* idea of how it will fit together, and from that point on, it's all a matter of adjusting your needs to the shape of the objects. Unfortunately, my spinal condition allows me to work on the projects for only a few hours a day." And so on through the nondairy strawberry cheesecake. "I'm thinking about getting a customized brace."

I was having major trouble paying attention. Myrtle looked completely checked out as well. Even my mom, who'd never cooked a day in her life (the kitchen represented an "oppressive parameter of patriarchal society"), kept finding excuses to jump up and refill the pitcher of tea, which no one was drinking, because who wanted to remain awake while Maurice was talking? Ariel was counting out loud how many times she was chewing every bite. She wouldn't swallow before reaching fifty. "Forty-two. Forty-three. Forty-four."

"I've lost my appetite," Ariel announced after she finally swallowed.

"Pass it on over, then!" Myrtle exclaimed, reaching for Ariel's almost untouched plate.

Meanwhile, Maurice was still talking about a bird-watching tour that he was leading through Buffalo Bayou the following week, perhaps in a wheelchair. When Mom pressed Ariel to sample the baked brie, she looked appalled and jumped up from the table. A few minutes later, she reappeared in a black dress no larger than a hand towel.

"I'm hitting the nail salon—thank God the immigrants keep them open on national holidays." Ariel grabbed Mom's car keys off the kitchen counter. "Mimi, you're coming out with me tonight. I'll be back in an hour, so get ready."

"What? Where are we—"

The front door slammed shut, and seconds later I heard her little car start up. I was left to get dressed on my own and wonder what lay behind my sister's sudden hospitality. Ariel had never taken me out with her friends before, but then again I had never had a fake ID before, either. But Ariel had no way of knowing that, and she wasn't the type to feel guilty for ditching me with Maurice and Myrtle. Maybe it was something else, something new and flattering: Was Ariel finally beginning to acknowledge me as an adult? Ariel had always been slightly cooler than I was in a way that our age gap never fully account-ed for, but that afternoon in her room, while she did leg lifts and asked me for my totally and completely honest opinion about which pair of jeans made her ass look hardest (she had like twenty pairs, all identical), I could tell that she was *impressed* by my big-city weariness, especially after I confessed that hooking up with a guy the night before had cut into my sleep schedule. Though Ariel's response was limited to "Does this tank top make me look like Moby Dick?" I could still tell she was kind of humbled.

I have no idea why it took me so long to get ready for a night on the town with my sister, but I found myself frantically paw-ing through her closet, trying on several combinations of tops and bottoms, all of which threatened to cut off my circulation. How bizarre that I shared DNA with a girl with zero appetite.

Midway through this self-torturing process, I called Rachel and told her to get ready. She, too, was excited, but still tried to lay a guilt trip on me for not making time to see her alone. "I thought we were going to have We Time." Can I just say, for somebody so self-absorbed, Rachel required an awful lot of one-on-one time. Or maybe that requirement was a direct symptom of her selfishness. Anyway, I managed to get her off the phone only by vowing to ignore everybody else all evening.

"I promise not to pay anybody else any attention. Scout's honor," I said.

"OK," she said. "And don't think I'm not holding you to it."

I was still changing outfits when I heard a car honk and my sister's voice screaming my name. I had on a pair of baggy pin-stripe pants (mine) and an embarrassingly snug tank top (Ariel's). But there was no time to change, so I ran downstairs and hopped into the back seat of her friend Jocelyn's red Jeep Grand Cherokee. I was seated next to an extremely tan blonde girl who resembled a department store mannequin. Her forehead took up the space of three normal foreheads and her blue eyes seemed in danger of popping right out of her head. She looked like some botched plastic surgery experiment: the kind of girl who all guys found hot, despite her obvious repulsiveness.

"I *promised* Rachel we'd bring her, Ari!" I tried not to whine when I noticed that Jocelyn was making straight for the Marquis. "C'mon, it's only two blocks out of the way."

This was not something I could afford to mess up. Rachel and I were still in touch, definitely, but if our unbreakable bond hadn't exactly broken, it was certainly weakening. We talked on the phone all the time when I first moved to New York, but after about a month our conversations disintegrated into brief weekly check-ins. I sensed that Rachel blamed these lapses on me. And I couldn't entirely disagree.

Jocelyn U-turned across four lanes of traffic and seconds later crashed to a halt at Rachel's. I could see her buzzing around her bedroom as her window faced onto the street.

Things with my Best Friend Forever were rocky from the get-go. For one thing, even though I'd told her twelve times to be ready, Jocelyn still had to honk for approximately ten minutes before Rachel emerged from the house. When she did, she kept spinning around to wave goodbye to her parents. The other problem was Rachel's outfit. She was dressed for a mother-daughter luncheon at the Junior League, not a scuzzy bar with shower curtains separating the toilet stalls. "A million sorries," she said after hugging me, looking like she'd just robbed a Laura Ashley store.

"I just hope we can get in, is all." I tried to prevent my lip from curling at her floral-patterned dress.

The night started out disaster-free: The bouncer was busy plugging the jukebox back in when we arrived, so Rachel got inside without a fake ID. Though I was too exhausted to take advantage of the Texas Tea special—two dollars for a full pint of Long Island iced tea with tequila instead of whiskey—Carmella Rothman, my fake ID persona, still came in handy. With Carmella's help, Rachel bought about a hundred teas, and the first thing she whispered to me when the drunkenness kicked in was "Well? Have you noticed? I got highlights!" and tossed her hair back and forth. I was trying to come up with a response that didn't sound too condescending when Rachel exclaimed: "And I had my first orgasm, can you believe it!!!"

"Omigod, really?" I said. "With Dave?"

"Dave? With Steve. Who's Dave?"

"Oh—no one," I said. Steve: right, of course. Who *was* Dave? I grabbed Rachel's Texas Tea and took a huge gulp. "Steve's what I meant, duh. You know how I always get one-syllable names mixed up."

I was saved by the appearance of Chad Hutton, this guy from Ariel's class who was now a freshman at Tulane and home for the first time since college. He came up and looped his arm around my waist and led me, without even saying hello, onto the Marquis's grimy dance floor. As soon as the repaired jukebox kicked in to blast "Pancho and Lefty," Chad and I started to pretzel and two-step and spin and dip. I was having the most fun since La Guardia when Ariel suddenly yanked me away and shoved me into the ladies' room, where Rachel was waiting for me.

"What's *up* with you, Mimi?" Ariel screeched. "We're taking you home. You're *hammered*."

"I'm what? I am *not!*" I protested. "I'm way too hungover to drink! I just had one sip of Rachel's tea. Didn't I?"

I felt crazy, like someone who is trying to convince others she's just witnessed a UFO landing. "I don't know," Rachel said, refusing to meet my eyes. "Why else would you be lambada-ing with Chad Hutton, who as you know perfectly well—!"

"What do I know perfectly well?"

Ariel started to shake me. "Listen to me. I don't know *what's* going on with you tonight, but Chad is totally bad news, and I would *never* have brought you here if I thought you'd act like such a total skank! Remember what I said about your reputation, Mimi? Well, I have one, too, and it sure doesn't help my chances during Bid Week to have my fifteen-year-old sister getting down with Chad Hutton on a national, like, religious holiday! Everyone knows Chad and I hooked up all summer, so it becomes total, like, incest if you do the same!"

"Yeah," Rachel echoed, as if she and my sister were partners on a cop show and I had held up a convenience store clerk at gunpoint.

"But what about the Vanilla Gorilla?"

"Yeah, exactly, what *about* him? My God, if Vanny *ever* found out . . ." Ariel shivered. "C'mon, we're getting you out of here ASAP."

"But I don't want to go! I didn't do anything! We were just dancing!"

Ariel drove me home in Jocelyn's Jeep, screaming at every intersection: "I'm risking an MIP *and* a DWI for you—I hope you're happy, you little brat!"

She was too pissed off even to drop me off outside our house. Instead, she pulled up outside our neighbor's place, and—before I had even closed the passenger door—gunned the engine, then sped off into the night. I couldn't believe it. I felt humiliated and depressed—and I hadn't even done anything! The worst thing was, Ariel had left Rachel at the Marquis without me, huffing, "*Some* people are responsible enough to be left with grownups!"

I stormed into the living room furious and smelly and exhausted. The last twenty-four hours had royally blown, and now all I wanted to do was sleep for the remainder of my visit. If I had to stay four more days in Texas, I could at least spend them in a coma.

Creeping through the kitchen, I collided with a two-foot-tall seatless rocking chair that Maurice had tried to weave out of firewood. "Ouch!" I screamed. I probably would've burst into tears if my mother hadn't called out my name just then.

I found her crouched over the coffee table in the den, doing a crossword puzzle and drinking tea from her favorite DON'T ASK ME—I JUST KNOW EVERYTHING mug. Everything except her awful haircut and humongous bathrobe were straight out of some bad Doris Day family-values movie. I had no idea why she was awake—the woman lives on this extremely insane schedule, bedtime at ten, coffee and paper at six, power walk around Rice at six-forty-five, and so forth.

"Mims," she said, her voice slurred with fatigue. "I've been waiting for you for *hours*. What time is it? I wanted to have a little H-to-H with you before the big meal."

I edged back toward the kitchen. "What? Are you talking about hemorrhoids or something? I think that's definitely a boundary, if you don't mind."

"Mims, don't be snide with me, please. This is *serious,*" she sighed, a note of desperation rising in her voice. I was starting to feel sorry for her but then I looked up at the mantel above the living room fireplace and noticed a photograph of herself and Maurice in the black leather picture frame—the same frame that once housed a photo taken at a pizzeria in Rome of me, Ariel, Mom and Dad. "Look," she went on before I could, "I don't want to put you in an uncomfortable position here, honey."

"Then don't," I said, and turned on my heel. "And don't call me 'honey,' either," I added under my breath as I skulked down the hallway and into my room—or what *used* to be my room, before Maurice hung posters of The Great Gardens of the World on the walls.

I had just crawled under the covers when the door creaked

open to reveal my mom peeking in. She started speaking right away in that muffled, exhausted voice: "Listen, I have to ask you, because I don't know anybody else who I can turn to. Is Roger doing all right? Whenever we talk, he sounds so"—she paused to let off a great horselike sound—"*distant*, you know? Is there something going on I don't know about?"

What incredible nerve. She wanted me to rat on my dad but didn't care one bit about how her own flesh and blood was holding up. I couldn't believe that this same woman had once lullabied me, picked me up at Jungle Gym Jamboree and handwashed my leotards, kissed my scrapes and cuts, and held me when I cried. I felt exactly zero connection to her. She was some random midlife-crisising stranger with the fashion sense of a substitute science teacher.

"Mom," I said, "I think I'm going to go home early."

"Home?" she repeated. "Home? But what do you mean, Mimi? This *is* your home!"

But right then, I knew that it wasn't, and never would be again.

Back in the Saddle

"DID YOU BRING US BACK ANY LASSOES?" Pia demanded.

"Or cowboys?" said Jess. She grimaced—she had heard from Preston only once in the past week—then sighed. "Do they make preppy cowboys down in Texas?"

The girls and I were celebrating my premature return with a shopping trip in the East Village. It had been my idea. After seeing all those color-coordinated pantsuits in Houston, I was in major need of retail therapy. The rest of my stay had been an unqualified catastrophe, especially our Thanksgiving meal. Maurice, who had overnight decided that becoming a vegan might alleviate his intestinal problems, made "nut loaf" instead of turkey, and for dessert Ariel served unripe cantaloupe: one slice each. My mother seemed distant and fake, and Myrtle had attempted to snort Maurice's vegan dressing out her nose.

I succeeded in leaving a day early only by concocting a complicated lie about a group marine biology project that was taking place on the shores of the East River the Saturday afternoon before school started again. My mother—still hoping that at least one of her daughters had inherited her academic passions—reluctantly agreed that school was more important than family. I headed for the airport, visions of Quinn and the takeout menu drawer dancing in my head.

But Quinn was still in Ohio, and my dad was so happy to have me home a day early that he didn't even mind when I made plans to take off again while still in the cab from the airport.

"But Mimi, don't you want to take a father-daughter walk, how 'bout it?" That tradition had never materialized, and I wasn't about to initiate it now. I could tell by my father's crinkled brow that my mother had called him that morning.

"Not really, Daddy. Nothing personal, but I've had enough family time for one holiday season. I'll be back for dinner, I swear!"

He seemed satisfied, then allowed me to hijack his cell phone and call the girls. I was in the mood to shop. Jess had suggested Bloomingdale's. Lily demurred—"I *refuse* to enter any store that sells my mother's linens"—and Viv suggested East Seventh Street instead, home of the coolest (and most expensive) vintage shops in Manhattan. This time it was Pia who objected—"The last time I went to the East Village, I never got rid of the stench"—until Vivian described the size-four Balenciaga zip-up dress that she had just seen in one of the windows.

Luckily, the dress was still there, and it was perfect for Pia. She paid, I am proud to say, with her dad's platinum card.

The only good thing about my trip to Hell—I mean, Houston—was the euphoria of coming home. Until that point, I had treated New York like one crazy extended vacation: I was loving it, but I still didn't quite feel as if I belonged there. Thanksgiving changed all that. Because I no longer belonged in

Texas, by process of elimination, New York took the place of home.

Our spree began at a store called Fab Purple 109, a tiny space run by a tiny Japanese woman wearing awesome metallic yellow eye shadow. The store was hardly big enough for two racks of clothing. The remaining wares were stapled to the wall like animal hides.

"I would have brought you guys something," I said, flicking through a rack of cardigans, "but the hot accessory in Texas these days is a huge gold ring in the shape of a saddle. And it's not meant ironically."

I stopped at a small red sweater and examined it carefully. It had a Peter Pan collar and a band of fuchsia lace across the chest. It was a perfect companion to messy hair and my new pleated miniskirt. Throw in a pair of fishnets and I'd be totally seventies glam rock.

"Don't even *think* of getting that," Lily warned under her breath, pointing out a nasty coffee stain near one of the armpits that I hadn't noticed.

"Saddle-shaped rings," Vivian whistled. "That sounds cool. Like a horse saddle, right?"

"Exactly." I nodded. "One guy I saw in the airport was wearing one with four holes, so the saddle took up four fingers."

"Hot," Vivian said, "very, very hot. I think you could rock that look, Mimi. If only your accent were noticeable, you could be our pet cowgirl."

"This is amazing—check it out!" Lily held up an itty-bitty blue hooded sweatshirt that looked like it had been stashed in a gym locker since around the Franco-Prussian War. "Isn't it?" Amazingly, no matter where you took her, Lily always dug out clothing identical to everything she already owned. Even at a Chanel sample sale, she'd unearth the one item featuring terry-cloth and drawstrings in seconds.

"Truth?" Pia arched an eyebrow. "Not amazing."

Lily's face fell.

"Not even close to amazing. This, on the other hand, is. *Totally.*" Vivian reached up to pull out the price of a lilac Valentino butterfly top that hung on the wall. "And better yet, going for a mere two hundred dollars." Vivian thrust the shirt toward Lily. "You're getting it, and no buts!"

"It was made for you," the beautiful lady at the register agreed, looking up from her Italian fashion magazine.

"I can't—" Lily started.

"My treat," said Vivian. "Don't even think about putting up a fight. Daddy just won another humongous case and he's going through one of his manic postvictory stages. He'll never blink an eye."

For herself Viv scored a blue wraparound dress that called attention to her fragile collarbone, and she was so pleased with the way it made her look, she insisted on buying me a vintage white suede belt and a pair of black silk parachute pants with slits running up the sides. Usually I dress more conservatively than that, but after Houston I would've worn a black vampire suit: anything to prove that I was back in New York for good this time. And, after all, when you have friends rich enough to buy you designer castoffs, you have no choice but to accept them.

"What time is it?" said Jess. "I'm freaking famished."

Vivian looked at her watch. "Almost two."

"Two?" Pia asked, looking up suddenly from the store's other rack. We all nodded. "Shit, I'm supposed to be in Astoria in fifteen minutes. I'm going to have to reschedule or something."

"What on earth are you doing in Astoria?" I asked. "Isn't that in Queens?" The girls exchanged awkward glances, but no one said anything. Then I remembered the truth about Pia: bitchy hottie by day, compassionate tutor by night.

While Pia called her student to cancel, Viv cajoled us to visit "Rotate This."

"Rotate what?" Jess looked almost as confused as I felt.

"It's the coolest-ever music shop, right across the street," Viv explained. "It specializes in old school vinyl records and only ever has, like, three CDs. Even eight-tracks are too newfangled for this place."

It sounded awful, like one of the places Sam was always trying to drag me to, full of undernourished dudes and their bossy overly made-up girlfriends. I even hated the way those places smelled, with all that dust and incense.

One by one we all squeezed outside the tiny shop, making every effort not to knock over the high-fashion mannequin tilted over the doorway. Once on the street, Pia retreated onto a stoop with her cell phone.

"C'mon, Rotate This is right here, let's go," Viv said, leading the rest of us across the street.

As we walked single-file inside Rotate This, another absurdly narrow store, Lily curled up her lip and said to Viv, "No offense, but do you even own a record player?"

"No, but I'm getting one soon. It's a major purchase, so Sam's helping me pick one out at some point in the near future," Vivian answered, strutting toward the register.

Before I had a chance to ask Vivian exactly when she and Sam had made their electronic shopping plans, I noticed a familiar head of hair hunched over the "Neo-Punk Fembot" section near the back. Of all the spin joints—

"Speak of the devil!" I exclaimed.

Looking up, Sam dropped one of the gazillion records that were gathered near his chest. Vivian scurried over and picked it up.

"I have the EP of this," she said in a nervous voice an octave higher than usual. "It's got a remix with David Bowie beats and it's awesome." After handing Sam the record, Vivian started fiddling with the sparkly cherry barrettes holding back her short black hair. I prayed to God that Sam would exercise the right to remain silent.

Her barrettes resnapped, Vivian mumbled, "I'm going to check out the 'Indie-Outie' section." She walked quickly to the other side of the store, leaving me alone with Sam.

"Why aren't you in Houston?" Sam asked me. "Did you miss your flight or something?"

"Unfortunately, no. One more minute alone with Maurice, and I might be locked up in juvie by now."

"That annoying, huh?"

"It's going to be some time before I appoint him my personal sex god."

Yuck-o. I regretted using the word *sex* in front of him, given the circumstances, but Sam seemed unscarred and laughed.

"No dirty talk," the skinny, possibly cross-eyed employee yelled from behind the register. "This is a family institution!"

"Ignore Bart," Sam said. "He just likes fucking around with the customers. Anyway . . ." Sam coughed and shifted from one foot to the other. He seemed mega-nervous again, which made me feel pretty mega-nervous myself. I tried to keep my cool, but flashbacks of his naked shoulders in the dark of my bedroom kept popping into my head. I took a step back, fearing the girls might be able to sense that something was up between the two of us.

After a quick lap around the store, Vivian called out to us haughtily, "Everyone's ready to go, Mimi. We're waiting outside, so whenever you're ready." The Rotate This door slammed behind her.

"What's with her?" Sam asked.

"Beats me," I shrugged, backing toward the door.

"She's so weird sometimes," he said.

"Right." I rolled my eyes. "*Weird*'s the first word that comes to mind." I had no desire to define the Completely Obvious fact I had just that instant figured out: Viv liked Sam. "Anyway, looks like duty calls. So, I guess I'll be seeing you around."

"Yeah? When?"

In response I only waved.

"Sam is so weird," Vivian observed on the cab ride to China-town.

"Funny you should use that word."

"No, I mean, he has, like, zero social skills," Viv persisted.

"Sounds like Preston," Jess said.

Somewhere around Essex Street on the Lower East Side, Lily switched her Knicks T-shirt for the shirt that Vivian had bought her. I could see the cab driver readjusting the angle of the rearview mirror to get a glimpse of a half-naked fifteen-year-old. Her belly definitely had a few rolls, and I wanted to tease her and grab a handful of them (in Texas we used to call this "Roll Call"), but I held back, seeing no need to intensify Lily's self-consciousness about her perfectly normal body.

"It looks fierce," I said.

We ended up in a dim sum joint, where Lily, Jess, Pia, and I pigged out, and Vivian drank a shitload of green tea. I kept shooting sly glances at Vivian, wondering why she wasn't eating. Could she be mad at me—suspect something, perhaps? I thought about my little insight in the record store: Could Viv possibly like Sam? Of all the guys in school, *my* Sam? I shook my head and tossed back another steamed dumpling, dismissing the thought. I was just paranoid, that was all. Vivian and Sam inhabited completely different social universes: She was more out of his league than Quinn or Max Roth—or any hot guy, for that matter—was out of mine.

On our way out, Vivian perked up rather abruptly. "Let's go check out this jewelry shop on Canal Street," she said. "It's right around the corner."

"All the models get their nameplate necklaces here," she said, scanning the displays. "This place has *everything*." That was true. There were fake gold Pumas, fake gold palm trees, fake gold Cadillacs.

"Over here," Lily called from the back of the store. "Come here! Look!"

Pinned into the velvet case, positioned between a pendant that said "I Want You" in cursive and another shaped like a hot dog, was a glistening golden saddle.

"We'll take five!" Pia said, and brandished the Am Ex. "It feels so good to buy stuff sometimes," she said with a wink.

Have You Ever Been Experienced?

Eₙ ʀᴏᴜᴛᴇ ʜᴏᴍᴇ, ɪ ꜰɪɴɢᴇʀᴇᴅ ᴍʏ ɴᴇᴡ ɴᴇᴄᴋʟᴀᴄᴇ. Strangely, though major areas of my life were falling to pieces, I felt insanely happy, almost as if it were summer vacation. When I reached my house, I was still swelling with love for my new friends—and that was when I saw Sam sitting on my stoop. My stomach hit the sidewalk and kept going.

Double shit. I walked the remaining steps slower than a caterpillar, trying to figure out what to do. Scared to invite him inside, I sat down next to him on the step. We sat there in silence, shoulder to shoulder, as a man waited for his black Lab to pee on the tree directly outside my house. Everything seemed odd and off-kilter. When I first spotted Sam, I felt only dread and anxiety, but for some reason I couldn't come within ten feet of him without flashbacks of his naked shoulders swirling in my head. I wasn't attracted to him—never in a million years. Still, something had definitely changed between us, and our friendship no longer made any sense.

Sam spoke only after the relieved dog and its owner had walked on. "Mimi," he began, "I'm not here to hook up with you."

I sighed, relieved that Sam was experiencing similar feelings of confusion and remorse. "Oh, thank God. I was *so* freaked out about everything, weren't you?"

Instead of answering, Sam put his finger over my lips. "Let me talk here, all right? I've been thinking about things, and, er, us. And, well, I need to tell you . . ."

"Sam, can this wait a little bit? I've hardly even unpacked."

"Mimi, I really like you," he said. Then, just like that, he lunged forward and aimed his face at mine. So much for not wanting to hook up with me! I couldn't believe Sam's obtuseness—he was actually expecting a make-out session on my stoop! And in broad daylight!

It was clearly time to take action.

"Whoa." I popped to my feet, leaving Sam's face pressing into my knees. "Let's hold our horses here. Sam, look," I tried to think of the diplomatic way to put it, and couldn't. "The other night, that was about experience. Something we *both* needed to get out of the way. Just think of the whole stupid event as . . . a random hookup."

All color drained from Sam's face, which was otherwise as young and innocent as in my family photo album. "How can a hookup be random if it's with somebody you've known your entire life?" he said very quietly.

"If it's with somebody you've known you didn't feel that way about your entire life. And still don't."

You should have seen his face. I'd say it fell, because it did, but before settling into an expression of emptiness and sorrow it contorted into about sixty-seven depressed permutations.

"OK," he said. "I see."

"You do?"

"Yeah. I understand. And you know what I also understand?"

I waited, wishing I could hit Fast-Forward on my life and escape this situation.

"I understand that I hate you," he said very slowly. "I hate how insecure and fake you are, and I hate the way you use everybody. And for what, I haven't the foggiest."

There was a long silence, and then he rose, pushed me aside, and dragged his body down the steps, all without looking at me. Before reaching the sidewalk, he spun on his heels: "You're lucky you have that stupid Coolie Diary. You know that? You're really freaking lucky. Because if *I* were to get my hands on it again, just think of the things I could do with it."

And then he walked off.

I just sat there, speechless, crushed. Dumping Sam felt like more than just another growth experience. It felt like having my whole heart scraped out.

Two images flashed through my mind: Sam's shoulders, and that snapshot of us as kids, me in my Superwoman costume and Sam as Spiderman, racing across the Brooklyn Bridge with our arms extended behind us, like wings. My arms had been in that same position more recently, when I was trying to help Sam unhook my bra. This was borderline sick.

I wanted to go inside and stare at the television, but I was too rattled to face my dad. So I began walking, aimlessly turning corners and crossing streets. By dark I was all the way down in

Battery Park City, my fingers freezing. It was almost eight when I got back to the Village, but even then I wasn't up for going back, so I stopped at the Magnolia Bakery for some mental medicine in the form of chocolate cupcakes.

As if that afternoon weren't weird enough already, right after I'd paid, I heard a familiar voice behind me: "Mimi? Mimi Schulman? Is that you?"

My jaw dropped when I twirled around and almost collided with Max Roth, the heart-melting artist from World Civ. Max Roth with his arm around a miniature old lady. Max Roth, who had completely slipped my mind over the last week of self-absorbed sorrows.

"Oh, hey—hey! Hey, Max. Funny running into you here!" *I thought you lived uptown* I (thank God) didn't add. *On Eighty-fourth and Amsterdam?*

"Long time, no see." He nodded. "How was your break?"

"My break? Oh, all right, I guess." I paused, distracted by his long black eyelashes. "I was in Texas."

Max nodded, then pressed his palm into the shoulder of his fashionable companion. "Oh, I'm sorry, I'm so rude! Mimi, meet my grandmother, Bubbie."

"Allo," the woman said. She removed her sunglasses to reveal gorgeous liquid gray eyes surrounded by massive sunburst eyelashes: Max's eyes. Max's eyelashes. While I was still gawking, Bubbie offered me her hand, which was as delicate as a child's.

Taking it, I felt as huge and loud as a whole team of five-foot-eleven oxen.

"Bubbie and I always spend Saturdays at the museums, then stop by for cupcakes right before I drop her home," Max said. "Today we hit a bunch of galleries in Chelsea."

"Tradition," Bubbie said, turning her neck to give her adorable grandson an adoring smile.

"We saw the Bruce Nauman installation at the Dia Center," Max said. "It was pretty intense. There was this one room with a water faucet that squirts out green Jell-O. It nearly hit Bubbie in the eye. It happens every time"

"Tradition!"

Max was so cool, and Bubbie so rocking, that I felt embarrassed, buying lard-cakes by my lonesome lard-ass self. "That's so neat," I managed to get out. "I live around the corner from here, so my tradition is coming here and eating as many cupcakes as possible every day!" A stupid comment, and my shrill giggle did nothing to conceal it. Had I really used the word 'neat'? Unable to deal, I clasped my cupcake armor to my chest and backed out of the tiny bakery before he and Bubbie had reached the front of the line. "I've gotta go, actually—it was great to see you, Max, and you, too, Bubbie! Or to meet you, I mean, I . . ."

I hurried down the street, trying hard to forget Max and the fact that I'd addressed his beyond elegant, foreign grandmother as "Bubbie." Why was Max so cute and nice? Why had I made such a mess of my life?

Home at last, I still wasn't quite ready to face my dad—my own depression was enough to juggle that day—so I lingered in the hallway, sorting through Judy and Judy's South American crockery catalogs. I was studying Ecuadorian tile designs when Sam's parting words about the Coolie Diary ballooned in my head: "If *I* were to get my hands on it again, just think of the things I could do with it."

Those words had been a threat, definitely, a bona fide evil threat. I tried to recall the last time I'd seen the diary and drew a blank. I was pretty sure it was on my bedroom floor, but I wanted to be more than pretty sure. For peace of mind, I had to find it and hide it, if not burn it.

I raced past Dad without even acknowledging his hello. Once in my room, I ransacked all my drawers and crawled under my bed, turning the whole room inside out, but the spiral notebook was nowhere. Fifteen minutes later, when the diary still hadn't surfaced, a sensation of nausea began to tickle my collarbone.

I was rummaging the medicine cabinet in my bathroom when my dad, all smiles, walked in. "*Qué pasa,* Mims? You zoomed by so fast I don't know if you heard me. Sam swung by earlier this afternoon to pick up some video he lent you. Hope it wasn't R rated, ha."

Oh. My. God.

I caught a glimpse of myself in the grimy, toothpaste-streaked mirror. My skin was the color of aspirin. *Mimi Schulman,* I told myself, *you are one screwed cowgirl.*

Out with It

WITH SAM HOLDING THE DIARY HOSTAGE, that Monday I returned to Baldwin crazy with anxiety. Our weeklong vacation from school had done exactly nothing to relax me. True, Sam was usually the world's mildest guy, but he sure hadn't looked mild on the stoop that day. There was, I figured, about a fifty-fifty chance that he'd go public with the diary, a fifty-fifty chance that life as I knew it would terminate. The girls gave no indication that anything was amiss, so I spent that whole day pretending that everything was hunky-dory with me, too. By three o'clock, I was completely exhausted from smiling so much.

By Tuesday morning, I almost wished Sam *would* follow through on his threat, just to end my agony. Saturday, Sunday, Monday—the days since that awful moment on the stoop had numbered among the longest of my life. Instead of getting into my bed and falling asleep, I would lie there replaying versions of my social funeral. I spent Tuesday night tossing and turning, looking at my beautiful golden saddle necklace with deep despair. Bright and early on Wednesday morning, I ran into Amanda on the way out of the subway. "Anything new, Mimi?" she asked me as we rounded the corner to school.

"Not much." I shrugged.

"Nothing at all?" she pressed, so insistent that I became suspicious.

I shot a sideways glance at her, but Amanda continued to grin as if posing on top of a yacht. I shuddered a little: I couldn't even *remember* all the nasty comments I had made about her in that cursed book. Poor Amanda. She was only trying to recruit another friend to her fat-free team. Little did she know that her early efforts to befriend me had indirectly led me to strike that catastrophic deal with Sam.

In the front hall of Baldwin, I said goodbye to Amanda with extra cheeriness. It was only when she suggested that the two of us "grab some coffee" later that week that I remembered the dire warning Sam had issued at Nona's party—Social Suicide—with a shiver. It occurred to me that I might have even recorded this in my diary. Had I really? Why couldn't I even remember anymore? It's amazing how deep the graves you dig for yourself can get.

Every hour contained another such torment. The icing on the cake was my friends: They had never been nicer to me, acting like we'd all been BFF since first grade. Vivian had borrowed my new parachute pants and returned them with an awesome mix tape stashed in one of the pockets.

That Friday morning, Jess rang my doorbell. I was shaking in my slippers, certain that she'd come to beat me up, but when I opened the door she was grinning at me, chipper as a virgin. The circles under her eyes were bigger than usual, but they didn't compare to mine: I had stayed up until three that morning, worrying about nothing.

"I couldn't sleep last night," she said, "so this morning I got up super early and rode the subway all the way to Times Square with my mom. She loves having an escort to her office. I had another half-hour to kill, so I decided to pay some social calls on the West Side." Jess made a little curtsy. "You are my first and only callee," she said with a little laugh. "Ready to come back to Brooklyn with me? C'mon, we'll flirt with businessmen on the train. You'll love it."

"I couldn't sleep that well, either," I confessed as we headed toward West Fourth Street Station arm in arm. For a second I was tempted to tell Jess why, but I resisted. "What's your excuse?" I asked.

"I don't know," Jess said with a shrug. "The usual, I guess. My mom took me out to dinner last night, and it was really nice. She's not the coolest mom you'll ever meet—but I love her. Sometimes I feel guilty I don't spend that much time with her. Because she's one of my best friends, she really is, and I'm just as close to her as I am to you guys. The problem is Preston. My mom's not sophisticated or Ivy League enough for him, and last night at dinner, I just couldn't stop thinking—what is Preston's *problem*? Why is he such a total snob? I swear, he's spent a total of five minutes conversing with my mom throughout our whole relationship even though he knows how much she means to me. I guess she's too outer borough for him. It's ridiculous."

"It *is*," I agreed. Jess was so heartbreakingly sweet I couldn't take it. "At least you have a cool relationship with your mom. I wish *I* could say as much." But Jess was worked up and wasn't listening.

"Also, like, the second we walked in from dinner last night, my dad called. He's having *another* kid, which—take my word—is completely unbelievable. Omigod, is that Arthur Gray?" she asked, pointing at a guy a few steps ahead of us. He looked a little bit like Arthur Gray and was holding hands with what appeared to be a drag queen. This was definitely not Arthur Gray from World Civ.

"Must be his older brother," I said.

The train was crowded, and the subject of Jess's new stepsibling never came up again, but when we emerged from the subway in Brooklyn, Jess beamed a radiant, grateful smile at me. "Thanks for listening to me earlier, Mimi," she said. "I know I'm such a total bore, but I really do appreciate it. It helps so much, having friends like you. It's nice talking to you because you're from here, but you're not exactly *from* here, either. I'm not making any sense. I love the rest of our friends, but sometimes I get the sense they're bored stiff of hearing me talk about Preston and my mom. But what am I supposed to talk about? My stock portfolio? My weekend trips to Monaco?" She laughed bitterly, then added, "Life can be really difficult, you know?"

Did I ever. I was a total monster. Jess and the other girls' kindness made me feel, if possible, even more rotten about myself. The tension soon became so overwhelming that I resolved to tell the truth. Every last detail: the fat-free muffin, the bet, the journal, the deception, my unexpected attachment to the girls. I would humiliate myself before Sam had the chance. Coming clean, of course, was easier said than done. Every time one of the girls approached, I wimped out.

After assembly that morning, Jess and I entertained Lily, Pia, and Vivian by describing our A train adventures. "You should have seen the expression on this investment banker's face when Jess put her head on his shoulder. He had been ogling her like crazy out of the corner of his eye, but soon as she cozied up to him, he made this really angry expression and shot up."

"It was classic," Jess said. "Such a hypocrite."

"You're a very bad schoolgirl," chided Vivian. "Naughty, naughty."

We were still cracking up when Ulla Lipmann, the senior editor of the school paper, approached the circle and began clawing at my elbow. Ulla, Baldwin's greatest all-protein diet devotee, also happened to be the only child of Jim Lipmann, the deposed CEO of Toy Boy, who was now serving time for tax evasion. Given how often embarrassing stories about her father made front-page headlines, you'd think Ulla would shun modern media, but in fact the opposite was true. Ulla was always scurrying through Baldwin with a ratty copy of the *Wall Street Journal* clutched to her chest. Journalism was her obsession, topped only by the Dr. Atkins diet in her affections. She talked to people only with a tape recorder in her hand, for quotes.

"Mimi," Ulla said, flashing the metal scaffolding on her upper teeth. (Ulla was known for her elaborate orthodontia, among other charms: The inside of her mouth resembled an aluminum train track.) "I *need* you!"

"Sorry?"

"We're putting out a special supplement on college applications, and I have only a week to do it and my deputy went on a last-minute vacation to Aspen and, and . . ." Ulla looked in danger of hyperventilating, but after several wet nasal exhales, she seemed to recover. "I just need help with photo-editing stuff mostly, and I'll take care of your dinners the nights you stay late! Anything you want. Free sashimi? T-bone?"

My friends had all stopped talking to stare at Ulla, who was making bizarre barnyard wheezing sounds. From across the hall, Amanda waved a racket at me.

"Oh! Let *me* do it," said Pia. "Sushi is *soooo* expensive. I didn't think I was going to taste it until I was an adult."

Ulla, who had no sense of humor whatsoever, shook her head. "I'm sorry, but I need Mimi. Her dad's a photographer and she has skills I need. She's also semiliterate."

"Ouch," Pia glowered. "Hittin' where it hurts."

"Pia got a 1580 on her SAT, thank you very much," Viv boasted. "As a freshman."

"What about Lily?" I asked. "Isn't she way higher-ranked than me?"

"Yes, well, duh," Ulla returned. "That's precisely why she has her own pages to manage this week—she doesn't have time to help—do you, Lily?"

"No," Lily said, "definitely not."

I saw no other exit. Q.T. with Ulla didn't strike me as particularly heavenly, to say the least—or not until a vision of Quinn and I flipping through potential cover art possibilities flickered through my head. A full-time distraction could seriously save me right about now.

"Mimi?" Ulla squinted. "Hello?"

"Oh, sorry," I said, snapping back to reality. "Sure. I'll do it. When do we start?" I asked my boss.

I soon figured out that Ulla had recruited me not for my photo skills but out of sheer desperation, after the rest of the newspaper staff, Lily included, had flat-out dissed her. Because there were only two pictures running in the entire supplement, I mostly just copyedited, and while spell-checking my classmates' names wasn't exactly fun, the busywork *did* reduce my paranoia.

Ulla and I worked in the newspaper office until nine or ten every night that week, writing headlines for SAT horror stories and reformatting graph comparisons of Ivy League cafeterias (Brown's wasabi mashed potatoes won hands down, but Princeton had the only decent espresso bar). Whenever I was in a room alone with her, Ulla would babble about her up-and-down relationship with Dr. Atkins while snapping the rubber bands on her braces. I didn't mind this habit until an aquamarine rubber band landed on #4 of the "Top 10 Reasons You Know You're Too Old For Baldwin" list that I was proofing.

"Oops," Ulla said. "Can you pass that back to me? I need it." My stare must have been mega-bitchy, because Ulla jumped up to retrieve the spit-soaked rubber band herself. "I'm so sorry. It's for my overbite. See?" She stretched her mouth wide open for my viewing pleasure.

Ulla was inescapable, but I was in no position to complain. Whenever I left Rubber Band Land, even if it was just to go to the bathroom or the cafeteria, I seemed to run smack into Sam. He was everywhere I turned, leaning against lockers, splayed across U-Croft's carpeted floor, just waiting for the perfect opportunity to ruin my life. Call me paranoid, but mere coincidence doesn't explain the number of times we crossed paths that week. We never spoke: Sam preferred to glare every time I hurried past.

Late one night, about a week into my ultimate Ulla experience, I found Quinn in Dad's darkroom, pouring chemicals from a white jug into a basin. "Hi there, lady," he said. "Just in time to watch me readjust the fixer solution."

I crept in, holding on to the publicity photo of the Great Walkway at U Penn that I needed him to enlarge. I thought of Max Roth suddenly: just as cute as Quinn, and a million times more age appropriate, and yet somehow less compelling. Or perhaps all those developing solutions were just going to my head.

"Listen," I said. "I'm working on this photo project at school and I wanted to get your advice about a photograph."

"Hold on one second." Quinn turned from me to dilute the toxic liquid with water from a pitcher. "We're almost done. OK. Where were we?"

"Yeah"—I took a deep breath—"I have this project where I have to pick a picture for the cover and I have this one, but I'm just not sure about the composition," I said, thrusting the photo out at him. I was nervous, and my hands were unsteady, and so instead of gently handing Quinn the picture I whacked him on the stomach with it, sending him reeling backward, colliding into the chemical trays on the counter behind us.

"Oh my God!" Quinn shrieked, giving a little jump as one of the toxic mixtures splashed all over him. With a dismayed expression, he pulled his raincoat away from his belly button. "I spilled some fixer, damn it, and it's bleaching my Burberry!"

Within seconds Quinn had vanished, off to bang down the door of the local luxury dry cleaner, while I remained alone and depressed in the darkroom. What was he doing wearing an expensive raincoat in the darkroom in the first place? Oh, well. So much for love under the red safety light.

That night, the girls rescued me from Ulla's clutches and took me to a house party at Bridgid Krone's. Brigid was a junior who lived in a brownstone on the Promenade in Brooklyn Heights. The place wasn't that big, but the Manhattan panorama was thoroughly awesome. Her parents had gone to Argentina for some reason and left her in the care of her twenty-year-old brother, who apparently had been locked away in his bedroom with his girlfriend for the past thirty-six hours.

I was having a decent time chez Bridgid. More than a week had passed since Sam's threat, and I was beginning to relax, to believe in his essential harmlessness again. He was way too dorky to ruin my life. I had wandered into the master bathroom with my third alcoholic lemonade and was thumbing Bridgid's stepmother's copy of *InStyle*. Suddenly there was a loud pounding on the door.

"Chill out!" I screamed. I flipped the pages faster, searching for the cover story on celebrity abdominal workouts. "I'll be out of here in a hot sec."

The banging continued, so I flushed the toilet for dramatic effect. I opened the door to find Lily in hysterical tears. She lunged at me, hugging me so hard I thought I might choke.

A gross senior guy in a beanie hat standing nearby entered the bathroom, grunting, "Don't piss me off or you'll get pissed on," as he pushed us out of the way.

"Classy!" I shouted through the door at him. "Very nice!"

"I just got a call on my cell phone," Lily sobbed. "They've been trying to—my mother—Utrecht—airport—" and she kept talking. The words were impossible to make out. I understood only that something had gone terribly wrong. I hugged her, rubbing the back of her hooded cashmere sweater with the palm of my hand.

Vivian glided over with my coat and, without saying anything, packed Lily and me into a cab. I had no idea what was going on until we were halfway across the Manhattan Bridge and Lily started to make a little sense. Her mother was scheduled to fly to Amsterdam that night to produce a Valentine's Day special about old world flower arrangements, but en route to La Guardia she suffered a nervous breakdown. Instead of Dutch tulip fields, Margaret Morton ended up in St. Vincent's psychiatric unit. Once Lily started talking, she seemed unable to stop.

Apparently, Margaret Morton—the world-famous home entertainer I still hadn't ever met in person—had been more nervous than usual over the past few months. As always in these circumstances, she calmed her nerves by drinking—tons. I found it almost funny that the queen of mint yogurt smoothies and ginger honey peach-ade drank gin and vodka in her off-hours, but Lily sure wasn't laughing right then. The other night, she told me, she and her father had to block the apartment door after Margaret Morton downed a pitcher of Hanoi martinis and tried to walk out of their Park Avenue building in her bathrobe and furry slippers.

"Lils, I had no idea," was all I could say. I kept stroking her head and hugging her.

"If the gossip columns find out about any of this," Lily said, "her career is toast. She'd lose her show, her magazine, her home products—I can't think of what else."

"It's going to be OK," I promised her. "I'm here for you."

Once at the hospital, we had trouble finding Lily's mother—the staff was protecting her like a state secret. Then, after keeping us waiting for eons, the burly receptionist, Tyrone, announced that he didn't believe that Lily was really related to her mother. "You just don't look like her," he said again and again, a real Sherlock Holmes. "Where's your hedge clippers? He-he."

"Are you also her daughter?" he asked me after Lily's identity was finally confirmed.

"No. I'm a friend."

"Her *son?*" he said. I realized he had earphones on. "What's that, a joke? What kind of ride you kids trying to take me on?"

"Why don't you just go ahead?" I hissed to Lily.

"No. I need you to be here with me. I can't—"

Her voice cracked, and that was when it hit me. Out of all her friends, Lily had chosen me to help her through this. I shivered, simultaneously moved by the compliment and nauseated by my dishonesty.

After about an hour of trying to be heard over rap music, Lily and I were allowed onto the sixth floor, into the psychiatric unit where Lily's mom was resting. Tim Something-or-Other, a bald doctor, greeted us in the lounge, where he described Ms. Morton as being in a "sensitive state" and then advised us to wait a few more hours before trying to see her.

Lily's father sat on the other side of the room from us, reading the Goings on About Town listings in *The New Yorker* as calmly as if he were on the subway. Lily and I huddled together in silence on the other side of the room. There wasn't much to say, and besides, we were tired. We must have fallen asleep at some point because all of a sudden Pia, Jess, and Vivian were standing over us, shaking us awake.

"Hi." I smiled up at them sleepily. "This is like Fort Knox in here. We *still* haven't managed to—"

My voice broke off when I saw how Pia's lip was curled. Something was up.

"Excuse us, Lily," she said, staring at me the whole time. "We thought we'd bring our *friend* Lily something," she snarled, and tossed a ream of sheets at Lily. "Lily, the timing may be inconvenient for you, but we printed this out from the Web."

Holy shit. I didn't need to look over and see what the pages said. It was the Coolie Diary. On the Web, of all places.

My day had come. All my fears multiplied by about a million: Sam had posted the diary on his link from the Baldwin Web site. He had actually scanned the diary page for page, so that the printout was in my handwriting. There was no way I could deny ownership. Nothing, nothing, *nothing* could be worse.

"You guys," I croaked. "I can explain."

"I'm sure you can," Jess growled. "But you couldn't *pay* me to listen."

"And speaking of money, my dad could make seven figures for a lawsuit of this caliber." Vivian wasn't looking much nicer. "You've libeled us on every possible level."

"I have two favorite examples," said Pia. "There's your October tenth entry, where you describe the 'interesting Jackson Pollock–like arrangement of moles on Pia's back.' That's very poetic, Mimi—you really do have a flair. And I also liked the one from November twenty-seventh, most of all the part about quote-unquote Pia's willingness to go to second base with anybody so long as his name rhymes with 'Draino.' "

"Of course, *I* would never stoop to suing my friend. I doubt even my *dad* would," Viv said.

"So-called." Jess could hardly even glance in my direction. Her voice was wobbly when at last she started to speak. "How dare you say such obnoxious things about me and Preston? Just because he said 'I love you' in a public place does *not* mean it was for public record! And I'm sorry you think he's a 'total boob' with a 'subpar IQ.' I'm sure your taste in men is *much* more sophisticated!"

To the left of me, Lily was frantically flipping through the pages. Her chin was tilted so far down, I couldn't make out the expression on her face. Maybe she would hear me out. Or at least that's what I thought until I heard her, in a flat, dead voice, read out: "The Mortons' kitchen is as sparkly as on *House into Home*, but that's because the only thing the counter's ever been used for is takeout cartons. Who ever heard of a domestic goddess incapable of boiling water? Margaret Morton's housekeeping habits make even Dad look good!"

Mr. Morton glanced up from his magazine to shoot me a deadly glare.

"Can I please—can I please tell—?" If only I could speak—if only I could say anything worth hearing. But what defense did I have? How could I possibly excuse my action—or even my existence? I was mute, my throat clogged with cotton balls. I wanted to breathe. I wanted to gag. "It's not what it looks like," I managed finally. "You guys are my real friends—I swear you are! I never meant to—"

Lily met my eyes at last, and when she spoke her voice was sweet, steady, lucid. "Mimi," she began, and I just *knew* she was ready to hear me out, to compare my little mistake to all the far worse problems in the world, to forgive and forget and wipe the slate—or the Web—clean of my betrayal. "Can I ask you a favor, Mimi?"

"Yes?" I said, relieved beyond belief: Lily had intuition. A heart. She knew that I'd committed all my mistakes—the bet, the diary—long before I'd come to care about her.

"You can ridicule my sweatshirts and sex life all you want—believe me, I'm used to it. All I ask is that you keep my mother out of future publications, all right? Thanks a lot—I'd really appreciate it." As she turned away, her puffy, tear-striped face displayed the most horrible hurt imaginable. "I think"—she paused to collect her composure, then continued—"I think I'd like to be alone now."

"Yeah, could you leave, please?" Jess snarled at me.

"There are enough psychopaths on this floor as it is!" Pia couldn't resist throwing in.

Vivian only narrowed her eyes at me, and that, as they say, was that.

A Tale of Two Mr. Cheeses

THE PREVIOUS WEEK, I'D BEEN SO HUNG UP with worrying about whether my friends would catch wind of the Coolie Diary that I hadn't even thought about how utterly devastating it would feel when they did.

Now that everything was out in the open, and my dirty parachute pants were hanging out in front of all of Baldwin to dry, I descended into total abject misery. Whatever security I had in life had deflated like a defective air bra.

On Sunday afternoon, twenty-four hours after the confrontation in the hospital, I was sitting at the kitchen table, waiting for Dad to come back from the supermarket with the frozen pizzas I had requested. I didn't feel brave enough to face even the Ray's delivery guy. I had tried calling all the girls approximately a gazillion times each, but only once did anybody pick up my call. It had been Pia, who said in a faux-electronic voice, "We're sorry, but this phone does not accept calls from losers, bitches, or fakes. And you are all of these." Click. My eyes brimmed with tears, and I gazed despairingly at my saddle necklace, which was gathering dust next to my laptop.

When I heard the front door open and close, I got up and ran down the hall, and—I am embarrassed to admit—screamed, "Mr. Extra Cheese saves the day."

"I've been called Mr. Cheese before, but not in a long time," somebody replied.

It was Quinn, in a mysterious pair of sunglasses, yummier than ever. And there I was, in baggy jeans and a T-shirt, disheveled and disgusting. My Mr. Cheese witticism hadn't exactly improved matters.

"Um, how's your raincoat?" I asked him.

"My raincoat?" Quinn didn't seem to know what I was talking about. "Oh, *that* old thing! Fine, fine, good as new, really."

"That's a relief," I said idiotically.

"Isn't it, though?"

This was my cue to run upstairs and brush some glossing drops through my hair in preparation for the world's most gratifying consolation scene, but I was too transfixed by Quinn to budge. So, idiotically, I just stood there and watched him as he shucked his radioactive orange messenger bag off his shoulder and examined his delicious reflection in our hallway mirror. My mother would call my fixation on Quinn a sort of "transference" from the various other agonies afflicting my life.

I just stood there, watching Quinn watch himself, both of us slack-jawed as we stared.

"Mimi," he said, turning to me and pulling his aviator sunglasses up until they rested on the top of his head. "Can you tell me something?"

Sure, I could tell him quite a few things. How about the fun fact that I had ruined my life in order to fine-tune my kissing skills?

"Uh, sure." I tried not to look too long at him.

"Do you see something different about me?" Quinn leaned in nose-to-nose close to me. "My eyes? Do they look different?" I don't know how this was possible, but he brought his face even closer to mine. So close that it would be safe to say that the airspace between us was no thicker than a grain of rice. "I took these drops," he said. "I think I'm getting an infection from the darkroom, and I'm afraid I look drugged out and freaky."

"You," I said, my tongue tripping over the simplest words in the English language. "Look. Perfect."

I was so worked up, I didn't even bother to pull away far enough to see Quinn's expression. I felt like I was going to fall over. Come to think of it, I hadn't eaten since Friday night. Which is my excuse for my next, unplanned move: lurching forward convulsively and planting my lips directly onto Quinn's rosy mouth.

But Quinn didn't kiss me back. No, instead of the passionate response I deserved, he squealed, "Mimi!" He drew away. "You're barking up the wrong tree there, girl."

I took a step back, mortified and astonished.

"You don't dig me? Am I too young or—" You know everything they say about desperation bringing out the utter, inner fool in you? It's true. Trust me. I have evidence.

"I totally dig you," he grinned. "But, well, not as much as I dig boys."

Boys! I knew he was arty and fashionable, but who in New York isn't?

"But I," I started. "I . . ."

And then it all came back to me: The two-hundred-dollar jeans. The obsession with back-up bands. The resolution to hit the gym after every slice of pizza. Pia's repeated avowals. My stubborn refusal to listen. My absolute heinous incomparable idiocy.

"It's OK," Quinn said. "It's not the first time it's happened. Hardly. I'm *flattered*, Mimi—you're such a hottie! You're the queen of pubescence!"

He gave me a quick, not particularly comforting hug, squeezed me, and let me go. Then, checking me off his list, he resumed squinting in the mirror. "You're such a little diva," he said, pulling down his lower lids with his pinkies, so as not to damage the delicate eye tissue. "What you need is a nice straight boy who can do all those things nice straight boys are supposed to do for their girlfriends. You know, like take you to the drugstore for sodas and to the drive-in for heavy petting. What about that Sam kid?"

"Now there's a thought," I said just as the door popped open to reveal Dad and three overflowing grocery bags.

"Anybody order pizza?" Dad said, looking happier than I'd seen him since the breakup, which irritated me somehow. It didn't seem right, that Dad should get a new lease on life just as I lost mine.

"Mr. Cheese," said Quinn. And, with a sly wink, he added, "Mr. Cheese saves the day."

Prozac, Anyone?

THERE'S ONLY SO FAR A BOX OF MAGNOLIA cupcakes and a stack of back issues of beauty magazines can do for a ruined existence. If you're a pathetic, lonely pimple of a tenth-grader, taking the "What's *Your* Kissing Style?" multiple choice quiz on some random Web site can only depress you more. I spent both days after the sudden termination of my entire life staggering around the apartment, alternating between numbness and sobs. Sunday night Dad knocked on my door. "I just invited Quinn, Judy, and Judy over for Indian takeout," he said in a gentle voice. "How many samosas do you want?"

"I'm so not hungry," I said from under my covers. Dining with a pair of overweight lesbians in homespun wools was bad enough, but Quinn—I couldn't take it. If I had set out to ruin my life, I couldn't have covered more bases.

"We can invite your friends, too, if you want!"

Wrong again: now I'd *really* covered them all.

"No, thanks."

"You have to eat, Mims," my dad insisted. "I refuse to let you get all Karen Carpenter on me."

"Not to worry," I pushed myself up and pointed across the

floor to an empty box of cupcakes, then whimpered: "Can't you just bring me a plate? I'm feeling antisocial."

"I guess. You sure?"

"Sure."

Once he was gone, I felt even lonelier and wished he would at least try to make me sit at the table with them.

You would think that with time, Dad's single-parenting style would have hardened, grown a little more parental, but his extreme wishy-washiness remained the framework of our domestic constitution. I kind of wished he'd be slightly more normal, but I doubted he would ever develop a taste for discipline, at least not before my semester-end reports arrived. Still, right now I wouldn't mind if he proposed a father-daughter walk again. This time, I'd definitely take him up on it.

Back from a long weekend in Guatemala, Judy and Judy were exceptionally garrulous—and loud. Because the laughter from the dining room upstairs was making me sick, I cranked up my MP3 player really loud and listened to Massive Attack with appreciation. But not even music helped, or not music that Sam had introduced me to. I rolled off the bed to turn the speaker's volume knob all the way to the left. Off.

Off.

Why couldn't I do that to my life, too? Without actually, you know, doing that to my life?

I looked at my electric alarm clock, hoping it would be late enough to disappear into sleep, but it was still only 9:18, exactly four minutes later than it was at 9:14, the last time I checked. But 9:18 was at least late enough to bury myself under my covers and fake sleep. Mom had told me once that pretending to sleep often led to the real thing. Wrong again. It took only about ten fake snores to remember that faking sleep is one of the least relaxing activities short of a root canal.

I shot out of bed and grabbed the cordless. It was 9:19, time to get things off my chest.

I started with Rachel. We hadn't spoken since Thanksgiving.

"Mimi?" She couldn't have sounded more taken aback if I'd been calling from the Afterlife. "What's up, girlie?"

I wasn't strong enough to confess that I'd turned into a monster, so I just said, "Just chillin'."

Long silence.

"Oh. Can I call you back?"

"Why?"

"It's lame, I know, but I taped the news this week and I didn't get a chance to see it all weekend. I've been getting really into world affairs."

"But Rachel, I—"

"What's up? Is everything OK?"

"Yeah, I guess. Sure. Sorry to interrupt with my personal affairs. Later."

Next up on my list was Amanda, who was apparently as forgiving as she was persistent. Since the broadcast of my shame, she never changed her behavior toward me, and maybe even became a little nicer when she saw how alone I was. When I called, she invited me to go ice-skating at Rockefeller Center, and I accepted eagerly. Friendship with the Squash Girls wasn't sounding so terrible these days.

As a large object, like a mattress or boulder, settled in my solar plexus, I knew whom I had to call next: Sam. I actually sort of missed him, or at least I missed the pre–Hannibal Lecter/Benedict Arnold Sam. Over the last few days of utter isolation, rather than get angry at Sam for betraying me, I felt sorry for him instead, thinking about how much getting dumped must hurt. More important, if Sam had gotten me into this mess, maybe he could be a rocket scientist and get me out of it. Or, at least, be somebody to hang out with now that I wasn't sure there was anybody else around to do that.

Sam, unlike me, was not pining away in bed, daydreaming about his funeral. No, he was with his friend Dave at CBGBs, that rock-and-roll club featured in all those nostalgic TV specials about seventies bands. Sam must have been standing inside a speaker, it was so loud. Background noise on the phone usually annoys me, but that night it cut out all those awful throat-clearing, heavy-breathing pauses.

"What are you guys doing there?" I shouted.

"WHAT?!"

"WHAT ARE YOU DOING THERE?"

"I'm at a trunk show!"

"A trunk show?"

"Hold on, Mimi." The sounds were changing and Sam kept saying "Excuse me."

"OK, I'm all ears," he said, audibly at last. "I'm outside. Dave and I are at a punk show. This band we're sorta into, the Suckoffs, are going on in a couple of minutes, but, uh, that doesn't really matter. Sorry."

I was startled by how clear his voice sounded. It was almost as if he was sitting there with me, stretched across my pinstriped sheets, his shoulders—Ack! Why did my mind have to keep returning to That Incident?

"Mimi, I . . . I—" Sam's voice quavered. I could tell this was difficult for him, and I was glad. "I've been wanting to call you so much, but every time I pick up the phone, I chicken out."

"Why's that?" I said, trying to keep the anger level in my voice high. "To get more secrets for the sequel?"

"Come on, Mimi, you know why. To apologize. I can't say I didn't mean to do what I did, because, well, I did it and all, but when I, you know . . ."

"When you what?" No reason to make it easy on him.

"When I posted the diary on the Web, I thought it would only be a temporary thing, that nobody could get access to it without a password. It didn't occur to me that Tilda and the hacker crew could crack it so quickly. I'm sorry. I never thought anything like this would *ever* happen, I swear. Please believe me, Mimi."

"If you're so sorry, Sam, why didn't you tell me that before?"

"Because I know how you are. I knew you'd eat me alive."

I took in a breath. "Yeah, and you'd deserve it, too. Do you realize what this has meant for me and my life? My nonlife?"

"Of course. And I wasn't trying to sabotage anything, I swear. I just wanted to give you a scare, but putting it up on the Web was a lapse in judgment."

"A lapse in judgment? That's like saying Baldwin's *kind of* weird."

"OK. More than that. A five-alarm, double-whammy, triple-decker lapse in judgment. Look, I'll be the first to admit it: I'm a jerk. A fool. A human mistake. I'm, I'm so sorry. I mi—" He stopped short. "I miss you, Mimi."

I didn't say a word.

"And there's more," Sam said. "You know how I was giving you a hard time for having poor taste in girls to hang out with?"

"Yes. You called them phony bitches. Godless lushes, too, if I remember correctly."

"Right. That. Well . . ."

"Well? Well, what?"

"I take it back."

This was not anything close to what I expected.

"Huh?"

"You should see them. I didn't realize how much you mean to them. They swung by a party at Don Hill's last night, and they seemed so sort of lost without you—seriously. I know they put on a front, huffing and puffing in front of you, probably giving you nasty looks, but when you're not around they look all beaten and depressed, worse than after Nona left. It's like without you they don't even know how to have fun."

"What*ever*." Sam had a tendency to go too far.

"No, Mims, I'm not joking. Pia was so bummed that she probably only had like three sips of her whiskey sour last night."

It was the first time that he had called me Mims since—since the shoulders and the night I refused to think about. "Well, that's just great! Thanks to this disaster, Pia's given up drinking and I've started doing it alone. Awesome. You've really dug yourself a hole, Sam, and groveling on the phone isn't going to fix it."

A sound pierced the background, a male voice screaming, "Go home, will you! My curfew's not till eleven!"

"Oh my God," Sam said. "I'm sitting outside the club and there's this kid whose parents followed him down here in their Lincoln Town Car."

There was a knock on my door, and my father's voice called out, "Mimi? You sure you don't want to eat with us? There are a couple of mighty fine samosas bearing your name!"

"Leave me alone, Dad," I answered without opening the door. "I'm never eating again." I then returned my attention to the phone. "Don't try changing the subject on me, Sam," I warned him. "It won't work."

"Look, Mimi, I know this whole thing was partly my fault. I was talking to Vivian the other day and—"

"*Partly?* You're the one who came up with the bet!"

"I know, I know, but I think I can help you out, OK? Will you let me? Just leave it up to me."

Leaving things up to Sam was never the best idea, but at that point I saw no alternative. It boiled down to leaving things up to Sam or leaving New York.

"You'd better not mess up this time," I said. "And this does not mean you're forgiven."

"I can stay focused. So long as you don't even *think* about kissing me, baring your stomach, anything. You hear me, missy? No distractions allowed, you understand?"

"I'll wear a burka. And pick my nose a lot. But you'd *better* get me out of this."

"It's a deal," he said.

"Leave me alone! I already did my homework!" the kid in the background cried.

And I couldn't hold it in: I let out a little giggle. This kid was *killing* me. Maybe I *could* handle some saag paneer and the Judys' tales of Guatemalan macramé conventions. Just as I was thinking this, there was a knock on my door.

"Dad, I *told* you—" I began, but when the door opened it was Judy #2 who appeared bearing a tray of scrumptious samosas.

"Mimi, will *this* persuade you?" she asked, coming across the room with a tray of food.

I nodded and smiled at her. "You're right," I said, and followed her up to the kitchen. Food was the only friend I had left, so I'd better not abandon it.

Confessions of a Tenth-Grade Social Climber

THE NEXT MONDAY, I DECIDED TO ACT. I was in the Undercroft bathroom, in the same handicapped stall where the Coolies and I had once toasted, when I heard Vivian's smoker's voice. A chorus of three more voices, all achingly familiar, followed. Did they know I was in there? I couldn't help wondering—I was wearing my red cowgirl boots, which poked out of even that supersize stall. As soon as I heard what they were saying, I stopped caring: I was too hurt, too hurt and numb.

Vivian spoke first. "How psyched are you for the trip? It's going to be *amazing*."

"But isn't it kind of weird," Jess asked, "to give our credit card numbers to Leila like that? I mean, we hardly know her. What if she goes on the Internet or something?"

"Oh, Jess, chill—what's she going to do, subscribe us to some kiddie porn service?" Pia, who else?

"Yeah," Vivian said. "How else is she going to book our tickets and keep it a surprise? If it makes you feel uncomfortable, Jess, we can charge the whole trip to my dad's platinum card. He'll *never* notice."

"Neither would mine," Pia said. "Now that I'm paying for my

own clothes, I realize that he has never looked at a single statement—I should've gone the honest route *years* ago!"

Next I heard Lily sigh. "Too bad," she said. "It's usually five girls, but Nona's not going to get out of Misty Acres soon enough," she said after a moment.

"Not as if she'd be allowed to go anyway," Pia said. "I hear they eat their breakfast cereal with the local rum down there. Not exactly the doctor's orders."

"Too bad. Do you have any idea where it could be?"

"My sister's never breathed a word," Vivian said, "but I have this feeling that it's not a tropical island like we all seem to assume. We could be going to some small town in Nevada or New Jersey, for all we know."

"Then how come they always come back with major tans, year after year?" This from Jess, the perpetually tan.

"They do have tanning booths in Jersey, you know," said Pia. "Could be some big hoax."

"It'd better not be," Lily said. "I did not spend three hours on the Internet shopping for a flattering one-piece for nothing."

Silence. Was it possible they suspected I was there? But how? Still—their conversation was so scripted and stilted and fake. It made sense only as a ploy to get me to feel even worse about myself. And, I admit, it worked.

I was trying to figure out ways to sneak out the building through the toilet pipes when Jess spoke again. "It's *totally* going to rock."

"Yeah," Pia said, "unless undesirables appear. Then the whole thing could turn into a *night*mare."

And on it went, bikini this and beach umbrella that and flip-flop this and snorkel that. Thanks, guys. I got the point. Why not send me a postcard from your blissful getaway, just to ram the point home a little harder? My former friends were off on the most glamorous vacation of all time, and I, Mimi Schulman, was cordially not invited.

I went straight from school to the Yemenite café, hoping to track down Sam. He was there, at the same grimy table, drinking the same tea, only instead of the Arabic newspaper he was leafing through *Word Smart*: *Help Boost Your SAT Verbal Score*. Underneath his gray hoodie sweatshirt he was wearing a Suckoffs T-shirt that depicted a poodle fending off a rapacious boa constrictor.

I stood half an arm's length from his table and watched him memorize *genuflect* by lowering himself to his knees and chanting the word ten times. He was so absorbed in the ritual that he never looked up and noticed me.

"Hey," I said. Things were still shaky between us, and I didn't trust him, but I had no choice. I needed his help, and I needed it badly. "Nice threads."

Sam looked down at his chest to remind himself what he was wearing. "Oh, hey," he said, evidently confused by my sudden appearance.

Then, before I could change my mind, I told him how miserable I was, sparing no detail of my long lonely nights and predawn ice cream pig-out sessions. When I was done talking, I paused to catch my breath, then gripped the sides of the rickety table. "So," I said, "what do you think I should do about it?"

And right then I had it—a plan. The greatest plan ever. The only conceivable way I could undo my social demise. It was humiliating, but necessary. "Sam, you said you would do anything for me, right, to make it up to me?"

"I did?"

"Yes, dammit, you did. And so I know what I need you to do. I am going to write a letter, a letter of apology, and you're going to post it on the Web for me, on the same page that you posted that awful diary. You will help, won't you? You owe it to me, Sam."

Sam could tell I was serious. "Fine," he said. "I think you're crazy to do it, but I said I'd help, and I will." Without even finishing his tea, he got up, and the two of us hopped on the subway to his apartment on Riverside Drive. Nodding hello at the thousand-year-old doorman, I realized that I hadn't visited Sam once since the fourth grade—bizarre considering that, these last few months, he was practically receiving mail at the Judys. "Is that the same guy?" I whispered in amazement as we got into the old-fashioned elevator. "Yep," Sam confirmed. "Mr. O'Gorman's been working that desk since 1962, and shows no interest in retiring anytime soon."

The Geckmans, who were both serious workaholics, wouldn't be back for another few hours, which was lucky because I was in no mood to deal with any reunion festivities. Sam and I went straight to his room. I sat in front of his computer and started to type while he reclined on his bed and pretended to study the Metropolitan Opera newsletter. Every few seconds, he would look up from one of the glossy graphics and beetle his brow in my direction. Twenty minutes passed. Sam hadn't flipped a single page, but I was finished—in more ways than one.

Dear Friends (and Nosy Readers),

I hope I'm still allowed to call you that, because that's how I still think of you, even if you can't claim to feel the same. I'm not asking for your sympathy here, or even your kindness. And, trust me, I don't expect to be invited to another party for as long as I live. All I need from you now is an ear (or pair of eyes, whatever).

I have spent the last four months lying, cheating, stealing—doing whatever it took to shimmy up Baldwin's very slippery social ladder. Four months of mooching and misrepresenting myself. Four months of being a loser and an impostor. But over the course of those months, something amazing happened: I became friends with four of the funniest, cleverest, and kindest people I have ever encountered in my entire life. Seriously.

I know that they have a reputation for being too hot to handle—Pia with her European fashions, Jess with her perfect face and body, Lily with her down-to-earth indifference to her mother's fame, and Vivian with her cutting-edge taste in just about everything—but trust me, I've gotten to know them. And underneath it all, their hearts couldn't be any more golden. They are the most generous people I've ever had the privilege to know.

I know that I've blown all future chances with the gang, and in no way am I trying to get in their good graces again. But for whatever it's worth, I'd like to state that I was a complete and total jerk. My new (and now ex-) friends took me in with such open arms and *warmth that I'm almost embarrassed to think about my betrayal. If I've embarrassed any of them in any way, and I'm sure I have, I just want that shame to evaporate from their shoulders and settle onto mine, if that makes any sense.*

I'll never forget my first semester of tenth grade. Most of all, I'll never forget my friends who made it the happiest few months of my life.

Never.

With love, humility, and cupcake frosting,
Mimi Schulman
Grade 10

"You sure?" Sam whistled after his thirteenth read-through. "You don't think it's a little—"

"Cheesy?"

He nodded and cringed simultaneously.

"No way. Not cheesy enough."

I didn't need to say another word. Sam understood the severity of the situation and pressed Send. It soon appeared on the special address he had created for me, www.baldwin.edu/studentwebpages/~mimischEXCLUSIVE. I was still scanning the awful online confession when I felt Sam's hands on my shoulders. "So," he murmured in an alarmingly low voice, "does this mean we're letting bygones be bygones?"

Something brushed against my hair, and it took me all of .01 seconds to realize it was Sam's hand. I shot up. "Ugh, give me a break, Sam, no way! I can't *believe* after all you've done to me, you're actually trying to cop a feel again. You've really outdone yourself!"

I ran out of the house, leaving my soul posted on the Web for the entire world to behold. Or all of Baldwin, at least. Then again, was there any difference between the entire world and Baldwin?

I for one couldn't name it.

An Amazing Season

Over the next week, I tried distracting myself from the disaster of my life by plunging deep into the Christmas spirit, which was a first since my family tended to ignore the holidays. (Mom was Protestant, Dad was a Jew, Ariel and I were everything and nothing in between, and none of us was religious.)

This year was different, though. Dad and I loaded up on corny tinsel decorations from the drugstore and threw them around the house. We even got a tree and put a blown-up picture of "Simon the Angel" on top. Dad was beyond psyched by my enthusiasm. It was pretty clear he'd been dreading going through the holiday season without Mom, so he had no objections to my sudden interest in home life. He rented *The Bells of St. Mary's*, which had nothing to do with Christmas except that Ingrid Bergman played a nun and presumably believed in Jesus.

My father indisputably believed in Ingrid Bergman. "Even in that habit," he'd sigh every few scenes, "she's marvelous, just marvelous."

Because my Dad was gallant and kind, he addressed this observation to Amanda, who had eagerly shown up at movie night at the Schulmans' with a massive bag of fat-free popcorn and a quart of marshmallow fluff-flavored Tasti-D-Lite. Old habits die hard, I guess. I'm sure deep-down she was devastated by my comments in the diary, but she had chosen not to get pissy about it, and instead seize this opportunity to force me to hang out with her. People were all so interesting and mysterious, even Amanda.

"I've never heard of her," Amanda replied. "And aren't her cheeks sort of round? It's so sad when skinny women have fat faces. There's like nothing they can do." She heaved a great sigh. "What's this movie called again?"

"*The Bells of St. Mary's*," I told her. "One of our favorites."

"Nineteen-forty-five, Leo McCarey, a classic," Dad seconded.

This information seemed to perk up Amanda, who'd seemed a little mopey since Dad had rejected her "party food" suggestion. "I don't eat things with the words 'fat' and 'free' on the same label," he had said. "And I've got no issues with carbs, so what say we order in some pizzas, huh, Mimi?"

Five days had passed since Sam posted that fateful Web apology letter. And nothing had happened—absolutely zilch, unless you count even more whispers in the halls and sidelong glances from upperclassmen. Most of the time, I ignored the nasty stares and looked forward to burrowing in my room at home. When the weekend rolled around again, I had no choice but to accept Amanda's twelve-thousandth "hang out" invitation. Not, I should say, because Sam was making me. No, the bet had reached a stalemate, and not because I had lost, but because Sam had cheated. Now everything between us was invalid, void.

"Omigod, speaking of Mary, you know which movie I *love*?"

Amanda exclaimed. "*Mary Poppins*—have you seen it?" She addressed us both excitedly. "Julie Andrews is really great, don't you think? You know she started out as a model, and like—"

"Black olives?" Dad was not listening.

"It's not just that she can sing and dance. I think she's a really serious actress, you know?" Amanda went on. "Like she'd be famous anyway, just because she's *sooo* pretty—don't you think—but she's also really talented, you—"

I was brainstorming excuses to ditch Amanda and retreat into the silence of my bedroom when the phone rang. My dad and I both rocketed off the couch, saying, "I'll get it!" in unison. But I, being younger and faster, reached the kitchen first.

"Hello?"

"Mimi! Sweet pea!"

"Hey, Mom." Amanda's passion for the chimney sweeper dance interested me more already.

"How are you, honey? It's been weeks since we talked. Not since—oh, I can't even remember how long!"

Not since Thanksgiving, I didn't fill in. It was totally typical and infuriating of my mom to gloss over my dramatic early departure, or rather not to see any drama in it at all, since drama didn't suit her purposes. She was into communication and transference. Drama was way too lowbrow for her.

Not that I was thinking about this stuff as she talked. No, during the actual conversation I was way too busy stomaching her latest bombshell and thinking about that old Morton salt commercial, "When it rains, it pours." Which of course reminded me

of Margaret Morton and Lily and my social ostracism and unend-
ing miserable future—

"—on sabbatical together next year," my mom was saying.
"With Myrtle starting college and both of us up for a semester
off, we were thinking of going to Berlin together—Maurice is
giving a seminar at the American Academy next fall, and we figured, why not stay?"

"What?"

"Berlin! Maurice and I on a romantic little waltz down the
Kudamm—doesn't that sound dreamy?"

"Dreamy? Mom, are you possessed by an alien or what?"

"—I mean, I *never* got to do these kinds of things with your
father, who seems all freewheeling and spontaneous but is really
this paralyzed stick-in-the-mud afraid of *ever* leaving his comfort
zone—"

I hung up.

Before I could return to the couch, however, where my dad
was nodding all glaze-eyed at Amanda, the phone rang again. I
hated my mother. Why couldn't she ever just give it up? Why
did she have to embroil me in her every single petty decision and
resentment and issue? I knew I had to pick it up, too, or my dad
would come to the phone and learn about his ex's intended
romantic getaway at Zoo Station, and then it would *all* be over.
If there was one thing I needed right now, it was my dad's
strength.

"Hello?"

"Hello? Oh, darling, Mimi, is that you?"

"Uh, yeah?" I was confused: definitely not my mom, but a throaty, smoky, indeterminately European simper. In other words, definitely not Myrtle, either.

"Fenella von Dix, darling, remember, from the Pazzolinis'? Well, as I'm sure your daddums told you—we had an absolutely *smashing* night at the BAM over Thanksgiving, and I was just calling to say that tonight only they're showing *The Jazz Singer* at the Screening Room. It's a special benefit, and, well, I happen to have an extra ticket that I'd—I'd . . ."

I felt like such an idiot. I had no idea that Dad—Daddums—had struck it up with Miss Jingle-Jangle-Bracelet Society Doyenne. Was I troubled or amused?

"Hi there," I said. "Why don't you tell him that yourself? He's right here."

"Oh, darling, yes, yes, of course. Yes. I don't know why I assumed—"

"Dad?" I called out. "It's for you."

I plodded back to the sofa. Had my dad mentioned his Thanksgiving at the BAM to me—I tried to remember—even once? Had I ever thought of it once myself since my dinner in Bridgehampton about twelve lifetimes ago? When I returned from Texas, I'd been way too preoccupied with my own worries even to ask about how my fabulous setup had turned out. I felt incredibly self-centered, not to mention dumb.

"Have you ever seen *The Sound of Music*?" Amanda asked me. "With Julie and Christopher Plummer? It's *so* wild! I would *never* wear a nun's habit on TV, they're so not form-flattering."

"Oh, great, great, great," my dad was saying, pacing back and forth from the kitchen to the TV room. "Yeah, of course—no, we're not doing anything, just watching the old boob tube."

The "old boob tube"? It was so depressing, how even the hippest forty-five-year-olds talked like bad fifties sitcoms when thrown in the same room.

"Oh, you're coming over here? No, no, why don't I just—? Yes, yes, *that's* true—I could meet you there? . . . Oh, all right. Yes—no! That's perfect . . . See you in forty."

As soon as he hung up he went into a tailspin that, if nothing else, proved just how much I'd missed these past few weeks. "Quick, let's get rid of the pizza boxes, on the double! Fenella's coming *here*, to pick me up—in only forty minutes! This place is a total disaster zone!"

"God, Dad, Quinn and I've only been begging you for *months* to get a cleaner," I said. The only thing I moved was my index finger, to press Pause on Ingrid. Amanda was staring at my dad as if he'd just taken flight with his umbrella.

Forty minutes later, the apartment was looking a little more decent, though still nothing Lily's mom would feature. It wasn't as if we had actually swept or vacuumed or anything, but we *had* cleared the old napkins and plastic forks off the coffee table, replacing them with artfully composed ziggurats of good-looking photography books. Rather than find a place for the miscellany on a shelf or in a closet, we had simply stacked everything on all available surfaces. And, of course, we made sure to put *American Revelations,* the book with Dad's portrait of John Waters, on top of the heap.

Dad was getting really nervous, not actually tidying up as

much as he was rearranging, pushing chairs from one side of the room to the other and back again. Amanda had found a project: She was plumping up all the cushions and throw pillows, working slowly and caressing each individual feather.

We weren't ready when the doorbell rang, but that didn't keep it from ringing.

"Can you get that, hon?" Dad called from the bathroom, which smelled disgustingly of aftershave.

"You got it, Romeo," I said, and bounded toward the door. "Nice to see you, Fenella," I began as I opened it, then gasped when I saw Lily standing there instead.

My first reaction was fear; I thought Lily had come to have her final words with me, or to kidnap me so that one of Pia's Mafia cousins could beat me to a pulp. But there was something peaceful about her expression. It was kind of confusing.

"Hi," I managed.

"Hi. We've all paid a little visit to the Internet," she said, motioning behind her. Panic shot through my spine as I faced not just Lily but the entire gang in military formation across my stoop: Pia, Jess, and Vivian, all my executioners in tow. I looked into Viv's eyes to try to get a better read on the situation. She was clearly pretty pissed. Looked as though Santa was bringing me coals this holiday season.

We all stood there silently, like bullfighters staring down the predator before the action begins.

Finally, Jess fired the first salvo: "We wanted to ask you something."

"Yup?" I said meekly.

"Everything OK?" Amanda interrupted from behind me.

"It's fine. I'll be there in a minute." I shooed her away.

"Well," Pia cleared her throat, "we realize it's a little late to be asking you this." She turned to Vivian, giving her the floor-is-all-yours nod. Vivian grimaced and passed the virtual baton back to Lily.

"Do you think you can lay off the tell-all diaries?" asked Lily. "They're kind of played out."

I nodded stupidly and whispered, "Of course."

"And Web entries, too?" Lily asked. "Can you lay off those?"

"Yup." I sniffled.

"Sweet. So do you already have plans for New Year's?" Pia asked.

And that was when I noticed the golden saddle hanging from Jess's neck. I looked from one collarbone to the next: They all had their pendants on—with the exception of Viv, whose collarbone was noticeably powder white and unaccessorized. What did that mean? That she wasn't willing to forgive me? I suspected she was mad for reasons other than the diary. But, I decided, three out of four—not so bad. My vision blurred, but right then I *knew* that everything was going to be all right.

"Plans?"

"It's just, we decided even the slimiest and weaseliest of friends deserve second chances," said Lily. "If they're worth it."

"Does this mean I have plans now?"

"Our flight leaves in less than four hours," Lily said. "That's your flight, too."

I couldn't believe Sam's assistance on the Web page had actually worked. They must have read it and taken it seriously. I wanted to uncork a hundred bottles of Moët.

Perhaps it wasn't the most appropriate thing to do, but I reached out my arms and initiated a group hug. Viv made a scowl and stepped back. "Come on, Viv, stop pouting," Pia said, and she was the first to reach forward and hug me. Lily and Jess followed suit, and our timid huddle soon gave way to a group hug, all of us smooshed together like commuters on the Q train at rush hour. I felt tears mist my eyes and I squeezed my friends a little tighter. So this was what it felt like to exit the gates of hell. I felt fantastically, ecstatically relieved and I squeezed even tighter.

"Watch it, girl," said Pia. "I don't need claw marks."

"How about another kind of mark instead?" I asked, and immediately planted a fat pink lip print on her left cheek. "Who's next up?"

So sue me. We're all entitled to our Velveeta moments.